"You're under arrest, lady," Matt said.

Her eyes widened, she turned, bewildered, saw the shield first, then his face.

And gaped.

Recognition.

Unmistakable.

Matt smiled, to let her know it was all a joke.

"Hey, Fancy. Congratulations."

She faltered before her voice came. "I'm—I'm sorry, you have me confused with someone else." That said, she began pushing through the crowd with the force of a small tank. "Excuse me, excuse me," she said, the words tinged by desperation, and then she broke free of the crowd, off and running, past Cathy who looked after her with an expression akin to sorrow. Or pity.

Alien Nation Titles

#1: The Day of Descent
#2: Dark Horizon
#3: Body and Soul
#4: The Change
#5: Slag Like Me
#6: Passing Fancy

Published by POCKET BOOKS

For orders other than by individual consumers, Pocket Books grants a discount on the purchase of **10 or more** copies of single titles for special markets or premium use. For further details, please write to the Vice-President of Special Markets, Pocket Books, 1230 Avenue of the Americas, New York, NY 10020.

For information on how individual consumers can place orders, please write to Mail Order Department, Paramount Publishing, 200 Old Tappan Road, Old Tappan, NJ 07675.

PASSING FANCY

A NOVEL BY DAVID SPENCER

POCKET BOOKS
New York London Toronto Sydney Tokyo Singapore

This book is a work of fiction. Names, characters, places and incidents are products of the author's imagination or are used fictitiously. Any resemblance to actual events or locales or persons, living or dead, is entirely coincidental.

An *Original* Publication of POCKET BOOKS

POCKET BOOKS, a division of Simon & Schuster Inc.
1230 Avenue of the Americas, New York, NY 10020

ISBN: 0-671-79517-1

First Pocket Books printing December 1994

10 9 8 7 6 5 4 3 2 1

Printed in the U.S.A.

WITH LOVE AND THANKS, THIS BOOK IS DEDICATED TO . . .

. . . my family: William, Florence, Steven, Roxanne, Molly, and the memory of Lee . . .

. . . the inner circle's longtime charter members: Daniel & Laura, Greg & Agnes, Golladay & Congdon, Jeff & Janet; Patrick, Robert, Denis and Joe; Walter, Steve, and Alan B.; Kay, Ann Marie, Janie, Sarah, Stephanie, Maureen, Zina, and Melodie; of course Scott, which implies Pat—and especially Joan . . .

. . . the wondrous new friends who have meant so much in the two years since: Wendy B., Elise, Doug, Danny, Adele, Lou, Julia (who might have inspired Fancy and, in a just world, would have played her)—and especially Luane . . .

. . . and the memory of Bruce Peyton (You were one Christmas shy, bub. I wish you might have held the finished goods in your hands) . . .

. . . because while it's all well and good to keep the faith in tough times . . . it's nicer if you don't have to do it alone.

ACKNOWLEDGMENTS

To Kate Loague, fellow former inmate at Citibank, for providing the spark; to Peggy Kerrigan for research and friendship, both with a smile; to friend and collaborator Skip Kennon for the lovely tune that prompted the lyric; and especially to Nancy Golladay, for block-breaking, plot pointers, wry wisdom, deft counsel, and various other benefits that she will merrily take out of my hide in lieu of (and possibly in preference to) payment.

AUTHOR'S NOTE

Sometimes you write for television, not because the money is good (and the money is great) but because the medium has actually produced something of value, something that you want to be part of.

I vigorously pursued writing for *Alien Nation* while it was on the air, and was rewarded for my efforts by being allowed to pitch stories to the staff of the series and their stalwart, passionate leader, Kenneth Johnson. The openness with which I was greeted is, I think, typical of the show's unusual generosity of spirit and humanism. I am based in New York, where I do most of my writing for the musical theatre; at the time I was in no position to travel to L.A.; and Johnson & Company allowed me to pitch *over the phone.* I won't say that's an unheard of circumstance, but—the logistics and politics of television being what they are—it sure is rare.

The staff liked the way I thought for the show, seemed to think I "got it," in terms of format, character, and philosophical subtext, and, from a number of storylines discussed (developed in tandem with my sometime collaborator and full-time great friend, the late Bruce Peyton), one survived two pitch sessions and was set for a third. Traditionally, and according to Writers Guild regulations, if a story makes it to a third meeting, the writer has an assignment.

A day or two before my third scheduled pitch session, I was told that the Fox Broadcasting Network had put a freeze on all outside pitches to *Alien Nation.* And shortly thereafter the series was canceled.

But I was genuinely passionate about the work I'd done, terribly fond of the fictional universe I'd been allowed to borrow, so I kept my notes, and, at least in my heart, the stories survived.

This novel is based on the one I cared about most.

HISTORIAN'S NOTE

Shared universes inevitably yield discrepancies. To riff on a popular colloquialism: split happens.

While staff writers for a television series strive to keep a *gestalt* going, the authors of the *Alien Nation* books worked independently of each other. Thus, while I have done my dogged best to stay true to the lore, tone, diction, and texture of the TV show proper, I am not always "humming" in harmony with my splendid fellow novelists. (Occasionally this even applies to novels based on scripts. For example—while I was using the original fifty-six-page teleplay of *The Change* as a backstory reference, I had no way of knowing how extensively [and entertainingly] Barry Longyear would reconceive it as the basis for his 309-page novel of the same title.) Since it was impossible—and, in the end, impractical—to coordinate my work with that of the other tellers of Tenctonese tales, I have deferred *only* to the primary source material I had to guide me when I wrote the bulk of this novel in late summer of 1992: the several extant unfilmed second-season teleplays; one unscripted story treatment; the occasionally contradictory *Alien Nation* Writers Guide; and, of course, the complete library of filmed episodes . . . plus, needless to say, the feature film scripted by Rockne S. O'Bannon that inspired it all, along with Alan Dean Foster's invaluable novelization of that film.

So saying: I have retained George's Tenctonese name as Stangya (rather than Nicto), Captain Grazer's first name as Bryon (rather than Bryan or Milton), I have referred to George's menopausal condition as *Gahsec* (rather than *riana*)—and Buck remains a rebellious high school senior, using his family's RV (recreational vehicle) as a home away from home (a premise established in "Runaway," the unscripted treatment by Diane Frolov and Andrew Schneider mentioned above).

In my interpretation of the continuity stream, the sequence is *Body and Soul;* a month later, the teleplay version of *The Change;* and three months later . . . *Passing Fancy* . . .

FIVE YEARS FROM TO-DAY;

TWO MONTHS BEFORE DAY ONE . . .

PROLOGUE

ON THE MORNING of the last day of auditions—a Friday it was, with rehearsals scheduled to begin Monday—director Dallas Pemberton was holding fast to his conviction that you didn't have to settle for mere competence. He had learned through long experience that if you didn't panic, that if you remained patient, there was always *someone* who'd walk through the door, *someone* who'd fulfill the vision—or, at least, make you rethink the vision in a new and exciting way.

Never lose faith, that was the trick.

By midafternoon he was losing faith.

He felt his mind would be next if the producer kept chafing at him.

"Dallas," came the whiskey-voiced rumble of Iris McGreevey, "I'd like you to take another look at that Callaway girl. I believe she can be worked with and she does come highly recommended."

Dallas, a small, wiry man of fifty, closed his eyes, craned his skinny neck back, opened his eyes, stared at the ceiling of the theatre. Nice job of renovation, he thought. Felt like a theatre but hadn't lost the comforting feel of the synagogue it used to be.

"*Highly* recommended," Iris pushed.

Just at this moment Dallas was finding it ironic that Iris had chosen to call her new theatre The Healthy Workplace. It was to be the home of a new rep company, intended, eventually, to be a prestigious retreat for young L.A.-based actors—a place to keep their theatre muscles in tune and, just as importantly, a place to escape from the madness of Hollywood. But it wouldn't make an enormous weekly "nut"; (the theatre sat only 299, what in New York would be called a mid-size house); it was located in an out-of-the-way part of the city (so with a small publicity budget, it would depend almost exclusively on reviews for audiences to know it was there, much less care); and as a new outfit with no reputation as yet, it had to depend on finding gifted unknowns. Pay for any cast member was bargain-basement scale. Favored nations: big role, small role, all the same; barely enough to keep you in Big Macs and rent.

"Dallas?"

Dallas closed his eyes again, leaned forward, forearms on the back of a chair in the next row, chin upon an arm.

"I'm certain she comes highly recommended, Iris. But I can't have her as Nora in *A Doll's House* just because she's an attractive trouper."

"Oh, she's more than that. She's very skilled."

Dallas scratched his mop of prematurely gray hair, faced Iris. Her whiskey voice was deceptive; she was a sober, square-jawed woman in her late fifties. You'd describe her, because of her bearing, as handsome. He wondered if even in her youth she was ever something *other* than handsome. Say, for example, pretty . . . ? He had no idea if she was married. Or had ever been. She wore no ring, and she was not the kind of lady you got personal with.

"I know, Iris," he said, "but as I warned you at the top, it's not a question of skill, it's a question of persona. The audience has to believe in the depth of Nora's dilemma. And since so much of what she feels is kept under the surface, we require an actress who's *lived* a little, who can communicate that kind of repression and still let us know she's a roiling cauldron. Your Miss Callaway is far too lightweight for that."

"I thought she read those angry passages quite well."

"Any good actress can work herself into a state of agitation. But this isn't a play about anger. It's a play about rage. There's a difference."

Iris, the managing producer of the theatre, was an independently wealthy woman who'd used her contacts to raise the money needed to run this operation, and who, Dallas suspected, had finally primed the pump mostly with her own money. Like a lot of patrons in the grand tradition, she was a fervent theatregoer and a passionate believer in the art, but ultimately, for all her sophistication, still an amateur. She'd never actually *worked* at the process from *within*. She'd only observed. An honest lady, if bull-in-a-china-shop blunt, and not remotely stupid—but Dallas found he had to guide her through everything like a child.

It was wearying.

And there were abstract intellectual concepts that eluded her no matter how well explained. Dallas had told her at the beginning: *A Doll's House* was a classic, but it had not aged well and needed total verisimilitude to succeed. Plus, it would be the flagship production of a fledgling company—this in a town so suffused with movie deals that it actually viewed theatre (and *classic* theatre at that) as uncool. The production had to get attention and press, but it had to be the *right* kind of attention and the *right* kind of press. It was a long shot if done *well*. Therefore, if the actress in the role of Nora was laughable—or, perhaps worse, simply nondescript—the entire enterprise would lose its momentum. With no chance of recovery.

He'd seen it happen before.

He'd also tried debating large issues of artistic sense with money people before, and it was a losing proposition. So he responded to Iris only in simple, declarative sentences and monosyllabic words wherever possible. But he kept his tone respectful. In the end she was still the boss, and despite his significant East Coast track record, he could still be fired.

Getting fired. He'd done that before too.

"All right," Iris was saying, "Claudia Callaway is too 'lightweight,' as you put it, to communicate 'rage,' whatever that means."

Whatever that means. Her inability to "get it" combined with the barely veiled condescension echoed dully in Dallas's mind. *Oy,* he thought.

"But I want you to tell me," Iris continued, "who have we seen who was *better?"*

"No one, which is why I urge you again to let me call Danielle Burstein in New York. She's holding off another offer as a personal favor to me, waiting for the word. It's no shame to have a ringer do the central role in a first production. In fact, guest stars in rep companies are something of a tradi—"

"No! This is for the young men and women in the area! I want them to feel they have a home here."

Dallas lifted his eyebrows, raised his hands, as if to say, *Have it your way,* and gestured at the stage. "Then we keep auditioning. If we haven't found anyone by the end of the day, I'll give serious consideration to Miss Callaway. Fair enough?"

Iris allowed herself a curt, almost military, nod.

Dallas called up to the stage manager. "Buddy, who's next?"

Buddy, a young apprentice, had been waiting onstage in dutiful silence. This was his get-ready signal to call and read with the next actress. He consulted his clipboard.

"A Miss Pauline Emperild."

"As in the Perils of Pauline? Are you *serious?* What the hell kind of stage name is *that?"*

"No kind. She's Tenctonese."

"Oh. Right."

The Tenctonese. Newcomers, they were called. The beings from another world. Originally bred to be slaves and supervised by sadistic Overseers—who were creatures of the exact same species, with but a wrist marking and an attitude to distinguish them from their "inferiors." A quarter million of these beings had arrived in a ship—an actual, honest-to-God spaceship—that had crash-landed in the Mojave desert half a decade ago. Granted a boon of sudden, and sometimes disorienting, freedom, they had adopted the language and customs of modern American society with alarming rapidity, though their assimilation was by no means always total, complete, or graceful. And they were an everyday sight out here in L.A.

There was still a relatively low concentration of Newcomers on the East Coast, however, and Dallas, New York-based for the better part of his life, had forgotten momentarily about the joke names that had frequently been inflicted upon the poor creatures by an insensitive California-based bureaucracy. Skip Tracer. Serge Suit. Ann Arbor. Not that New York would have been much kinder. Though the jokes might've been subtler.

"A Newcomer Nora," Dallas mused. "Bring her on."

Pauline Emperild was ushered onstage and introductions were made by Buddy. She was poised and attractive, and when she began to read the indicated passages from the script, some of the tension in Dallas's face drained away. Her voice was well-modulated, her delivery assured, her intelligence unquestionable. She wasn't great, but there was potential . . .

And as she finished reading, and Dallas thanked her, and she was escorted out, the thought continued . . .

. . . there was potential if *only* it weren't for the smooth, bald head . . . the spots in lieu of hair forming a design as unique to her as a fingerprint, which narrowed and continued down the small of her back . . . the merest suggestion of small ears, gentle swells around the kind of apertures you'd find on a lizard's head.

"I don't think I can get around the appearance," Dallas said, finally, thoughtfully. "Shame."

Meaning it. Altogether unfair for the young artist to be penalized by an accident of birth . . . but art could equal life for unfairness, since the one reflected the other anyway. So that was that. If Miss Emperild had been an ethnic type—even black—it would have been a stretch, but, perhaps, workable. At least a black woman would be the right *species.* You might conceivably seduce an audience into suspending its disbelief *just enough* to accept the notion that a woman of color had a place in the Sweden of 1879 . . . at the very least, to make the leap of faith on the basis of pure humanism.

But Miss Emperild wasn't human.

She'd be an anomaly in the play's setting, a glaring anachronism, a constant reminder that a *play* was in progress—fighting the goal, which was to make the audience *forget* the artifice. If the illusion was shot, there'd be little else that mattered.

He turned to Iris.

She looked as if she wanted to say something.

"If you disagree, persuade me," he said gently.

"I *do* believe in nontraditional casting," she ventured, somewhat lamely. "But . . ."

But. One syllable. Confirmation enough.

"Buddy," Dallas called up, "how many left?"

"Just one," came the answer.

"That 'serious consideration' you promised to give the Callaway girl seems to be in order," Iris nudged.

"Maybe so, but let's go through the *motions* and at least *pretend* to give this last girl a fair shake."

"Certainly, certainly," she replied, and Dallas felt as if he were being humored.

Buddy announced the actress's name, but it didn't register in the wake of the young lady's entrance . . . for instantly, the air in the room changed. There was a *something,* a what, a *frisson,* and Dallas tried in vain to analyze it. The face was compact, almost girlish, but it suggested a dark beauty that came from within (precisely what you'd dream for in a Nora), and more, there was—he didn't know how else to phrase it—an *agony* behind the beauty, or perhaps just a depth of soul, because this girl brought a quality with her that you couldn't teach, couldn't buy, couldn't even (God help him) *direct,* though you might be lucky enough to subtly *guide* it; it was just goddamn *there.*

He felt his heart pounding. Heard it.

And so far, she hadn't said a word.

Dallas prayed now, prayed with all his might that when she *did* speak, the poise and allure would be matched by the voice, that when she opened her mouth, she wouldn't issue forth a screech or a whine or a twang or a rumble or a whisper or a bellow or a limit he couldn't defeat, that she wouldn't dash his fondest wish and bweak his widdwe heart in twain.

Buddy was making introductions. Dallas missed the name again, but he heard his own and remembered to follow through with the amenities as Buddy said, ". . . our guest director, and this is Iris McGreevey, producer," at which Iris nodded, smiled.

Dallas, finding his voice somehow, said, "Hi, how are you?"

And the vision said, "I'm honored to meet you both, thank you so much for seeing me," and oh, yes, the voice was like honey, sweetness itself. Also richly inflected, capable of all sorts of complexity—yet, paradoxically, simple, direct. And, in the manner of truly great speaking voices, even musical. Ten words she'd uttered, that was all, but Dallas knew. Now he knew. Sometimes it happened that way.

Asking her to read now was but a formality, still, ask he did, and she clicked on every possible cylinder, the face able to convey violent emotions the words could not, *connecting* to the rage and what suppressed it; and she read with such understanding, such passion, such wisdom, that he knew *he* was the one truly honored, that God had *blessed* him with the discovery, that he must've been a good little boy indeed;

and he turned to Iris, to make sure he wasn't crazy, and there was something odd about the expression on Iris's face that Dallas couldn't place, not right away, and then it occurred to him, *Iris had stopped breathing!* Dallas turned to face the stage again as the rounded tones of this fine young artist, this eleventh-hour savior, completed her final speech, and he was dimly aware of his voice asking her to wait outside and Buddy escorting her, pausing to raise an eyebrow at Dallas as if to say, "Holy cow!" When she was gone, out of earshot, Dallas spun to face Iris again, saw that she was finally pulling breath, clocked the tears of revelation just starting to form in her eyes and he *clapped his hands on her shoulders,* something no sane person should do, not to this particular woman, and shook her, vigorously, enthusiastically, which was even more preposterous, and he exulted as if to the very heavens.

"You see?" he cried joyously. "You see?"

In the four-week rehearsal period that followed (which would lead to the kind of opening night that sneaks in on little cat's paws and suddenly garners the kind of reviews and attention careers are built upon), Dallas Pemberton kept a very tight lid on his new discovery, wanting the brilliant young actress to be a surprise. To the press *and* the public. Wanting not to tempt fate. He had long ago learned the folly of braggadocio.

Inevitably, though, some word leaked out on the street; rehearsals were so "hot" she was a tough secret to keep. So when Dallas was cornered by anyone, he chose to demur, merely allowing that, "You'll have to see for yourself, but . . . Yes, she *is* something else."

Never knowing how right he was.

DAY ONE

CHAPTER 1

MATT SIKES WAS not precisely in his element, but he was doing his damndest to be a good sport about it. Given his tolerance for matters artistic, there were easier things to be.

The theatre lobby of The Healthy Workplace was too small to contain all the bodies, so the pre-show crowd spilled out onto the sidewalk, an area of which had been cordoned off for ticket holders, a smaller area of which penned in those desperate few awaiting cancellations, looking pathetic and anxious.

Alone among the crunch of culture mavens, Matt would have preferred being anywhere else. In a ball park, in a hamburger joint, in a gym, in his living room with his train set. Maybe especially in his living room with his train set.

Alas for him, Cathy Frankel was on an Earth literature kick—devouring everything she could about the classics, no doubt to compensate for the lack of such material on the slave ship—and he felt he had little choice in the matter.

But, of course, he really did have a choice. He had *plenty* of choice, he could "just say no," as the popular phrase went, but Cathy was . . .

Well, what *was* Cathy exactly? To him? She was hard to compartmentalize. A neighbor. And a friend. A very *good* friend. Good and stunningly attractive. All of which had led, in time, to her being his lover as well. (And *that* had taken some serious preparation, even formal study. Matt still occasionally winced at the concept. But, as he'd discovered the hard way, intimate relations with a Newcomer were not something embarked upon casually.) Yet, though Cathy lived in Matt's building, just down the hall from his apartment, there had not yet been any serious mention of consolidation, of *moving in together.*

So he wasn't sure exactly what Cathy was. To him. He only knew that he was prepared to be monogamous for the duration; and that, in general, he was happier at the thought of spending time with her than the thought of spending time without her.

Therefore, when she'd knocked on his door and said she had "connections"—said she could get herself, Matt, and the Franciscos into this sold-out *play* everyone was talking about—he'd bitten off the impulse to ask "Who?" ('cuz they sure weren't gabbin' about no plays in *his* crowd, lemme tell ya), adopted his best no-strain smile and said, "Sure. Absolutely. You bet."

Matt felt a hand on his shoulder.

"It was good of you to be here," said his partner, Detective Two George Francisco. (George's wife Susan was several paces away, studying the display of enlarged rave reviews bolted to the wall. Cathy was up ahead in the throng somewhere, waiting in line to pick up their tickets at the box office.)

Matt's expression offered up a pinched smile, his voice an unconvincing grumble. "Yah. Well. Culture. You know."

George looked at his shoes and stifled a chuckle. "Oh, Matthew," he chided.

Caught, Matt grumbled in earnest. "All right, fine, so I'm here for Cathy. I admit it. Happy now?"

"Cathy's happy. That's what matters."

The notion secretly pleased Matt, but he sidestepped it gruffly. "Women are always happy when they get to educate men. I'm sure Cathy thinks the experience'll be good for me. She says this play by that Ibsen character is seminal or something."

George's brows created a furrow on his Tenctonese forehead, he assumed his pontificator's expression, and Matt regretted his words instantly. "Well, strictly speaking," George corrected, "it is more the playwright than the play, as he was the progenitor of the modern well-made drama."

"Well made." In dead tones, so George couldn't miss his disinterest.

Didn't help.

"Yes," George continued, "so-called because of the way in which plot elements and themes are introduced, developed, resolved."

"Uh huh." Starting to feel intimidated now.

"However, the play *is,* in fact, notable as the first serious dramatic treatment of the subject of women's rights. Although, ironically, Ibsen himself would never have claimed to be a feminist."

Matt rolled his eyes. "Jesus, does *everybody* know this play except me?"

George shrugged apologetically. "Pretty famous drama, Matthew."

"Isn't it enough I'm stupid about *your* culture? I have to be a boob about *my* culture too?"

George pursed his lips. "You do not *have* to be, Matthew. It's just that you are so *good* at it." And then he grinned mischievously.

Matt threatened to deliver a mock slap, growled in his best Moe-the-Stooge voice, "Why, you, I oughtta—"

—and Cathy shouted, "I've *got* them!"

Turning to see her, Matt had to admit (strictly to himself) that it was sorta kinda worth everything if only for this moment. Cathy was almost skipping back from the box office, holding the two pairs of tickets aloft like some cherished prize, the soft, small features of her delicately boned face so radiant that—the thought leapt to his brain unbidden, and it was all he could do not to give it voice, lest George misunderstand—she looked like a beautiful light bulb.

She and Susan huddled over the tickets, cooing over the excellent location. In a trice, each had her respective man by the arm, George strolling forthrightly with Susan, Matt allowing himself to be pulled into the theatre. As they merged with the crowd, squeezing together the better to funnel past the ticket taker, George cautioned Matt, "Remember, this is a legitimate theatre, not a movie house, there is no *popcorn* to be had here." Matt groped for an appropriately cutting reply, it didn't come to him fast enough, and then they were inside.

As they took their seats, Matt picked up on the buzz in the auditorium, the excited chatter of the patrons, the sound of program pages being riffled, and people reading tidbits from artists' bios.

He noted too, with apprehension, how close he was to the stage. Third row center, too close for comfort. It threatened his space.

"Matt?" said Cathy.

"Yeah?"

"Are you okay?"

"Just thinking. They're really going to be on our noses, aren't they?"

"I know. Isn't it exciting?"

The houselights started to dim.

"No popcorn, huh?" Matt muttered to himself.

The play began.

She entered as hundreds, perhaps thousands, of Noras had entered before her, a flurry of excitement, atwitter with Christmas packages to present to her finicky, judgmental husband, Torvald . . . but the yearning for approval she brought with her was as palpable, as substantial, a thing as any of the gift-wrapped packages. And because of it, you wanted to hold her. Tell her everything would be all right. Protect her.

At first, Matt had to admit that, like everyone else in that theatre, he was experiencing the thrill of discovery.

The thrill faded quickly, though, and was quickly, unnervingly, *supplanted by a stronger emotion. Like many a star—and though she wasn't a star yet, she was clearly on the come—Fran Delaney had a strong, welcome personality that would wear well with familiarity. At first, Matt chalked up his reaction to the spontaneous comfort he felt watching her, even slight infatuation, and a subsequent, entirely natural, sense of* déjà vu. *But his reaction persisted. It persisted so strongly that he discounted* déjà vu *and went to the next logical question—where have I seen her before? On television? The movies? No, couldn't be, she was supposed to be some kind of "find," previously altogether unknown, knocking around in obscurity until this, her first break . . .*

And that left one possibility.

I've more than seen her. I *know* her.

But from where? Dammit *where?*

The familiarity was not so comfortable now. Now it assailed him, irritated him, like a word on the tip of the tongue, like a crucial thought inexplicably lost, like that where-the-hell-did-I-misplace-my-car-keys? kind of feeling. He had lost touch with a part of himself—*the machinery. And he was a* cop *for God's sake, an officer of the—*

Click. Into cop mode.

Did I meet her in my capacity as a cop?

Perpetrator? Suspect? Vic, maybe? Put her in different clothes, his mind commanded, and his imagination complied, running through possibilities. Give her a different hair style, came command number two, and in his mind's eye he took the full-bodied, shoulder-length, enticing brown hair and brutally cut it, cut it, first to a shag, then to a pageboy, no, no, still not it, then to a crewcut, then to . . .

Nothing. Then to nothing.

And now he had it. Thought *he had it, heart pounding, because if he had it, it was too fantastic. His program had slipped off his thighs to the floor, where it was too dark to root around for it, so he rudely plucked Cathy's, whispering a cursory "sorry" and flipped through the pages, flipped, flipped, flipped to the cast list, and there it was.*

Nora Helmer ....FRAN DELANEY

The name was too close, like a bad alias. And, of course, it was, a bad alias for an even worse name, but it was the name by which he had known her, and now that he had the name to go with the face—

—he had the memory.

And it played in the back of his mind, every bit as live and real as the play in front of him.

She had the gun aimed between his eyes and her hysteria was bone-chilling.

"Stay away! Just stay the hell away from me and stay away from the bedroom!"

Matt Sikes, newly turned detective, his best copside manner at work, had his arms out straight, palms down, pushing gently at the air, trying to calm her.

"Ms. Delancey . . . we just want to see are your children all right, that's all. After that . . . we can talk. It's all negotiable."

"Sure. Right. Placate the dumb slag. I put this gun down and negotiation's over."

"Not if nobody's hurt."

"You don't touch my children!" The words lashed out as sharply and suddenly as a slap, causing Matt's partner, Bill Tuggle, to cock his department-issue revolver.

"Tug, no!" Matt implored the muscular black man, and Tuggle's eyes shifted uneasily in his direction.

"Matt, you sure?"

"Yeah, yeah, I'm sure, put it down."

"Down!?"

"Down! On the floor!"

"Matt . . ."

"Just *do* it."

Releasing a deep, apprehensive breath through his nose, Tuggle shifted his wrist to hold the gun flat, parallel with the floor and slowly, reluctantly, bent at the knees, down, down—

Matt never took his eyes off the woman, but he heard the sound of metal clicking against tile, sensed Tuggle rising again, knew the gun was down, and said, "There. Negotiations have just opened." His words measured, soothing, like honey. "What do you say?"

The gun never moved, but her gaze seemed to go elsewhere, mere *degrees* elsewhere, it could snap focus back to him at any time, and her voice became something distant, abstracted.

"My children are in Celine's cradle, watched over by Andarko. Nothing can hurt them now."

Matt struggled to keep his anger down. This was a twist he hadn't expected. Celine and Andarko were the female and male Tenctonese gods. Saying her children were with them was like an Earthwoman saying her children were with Jesus. Gone home to the Lord. Freed of their mortal coil. Oh, man . . .

Matt said nothing. Getting his bearings.

Just as abstractedly, the Delancey woman asked, "Don't you want to know if I sent them there?"

"Let's jump over 'if,'" Matt chanced, voice husky and low. "What'll help is 'why?' . . ."

"Help . . . ?"

"All negotiable. Like I said." A beat. Eyes frozen on her, he gestured almost imperceptibly with his chin toward one of the kitchen chairs. "Mind if I sit?" Hoping to get in close. Get in, get under. Grab the gun. That was permissible, if you could manage it. All the while talking like a friend.

"Sure." Small, remote.

He moved the chair out from under the table with his fingertips, hardly scraping the scuffed tile beneath, lowered himself into it but was dismayed to find that she was ready for him, moving the gun inwards, crooking her elbows, maintaining her potential target.

"Talk to me," he entreated.

"Right. 'Why.' I think you wanted to know why. I believe you said it would help."

"Couldn't hurt." Wondering if the old vaudeville response would elicit a slight smile; wondering if she'd even get it, if her slag sense of humor extended to Earth idioms.

"Because they were becoming aliens to *me!* Because I couldn't *see* them anymore for all of Earth's corruption. The slave ship was awful, but at least we had our place, knew who we were, knew what Andarko and Celine expected us to be. Here we know nothing. Nothing. And no one wants to teach us. It's worse than the ship. On the ship we were at least slaves. Here we're non-people. No culture. No purpose."

"And your children . . . ?"

". . . they were growing ears . . ."

Oh, God, thought Sikes. "Ears," he repeated.

"Hair, too, I think. I couldn't see them anymore."

Tuggle spoke quietly from behind. "They were assimilating."

It was as if she didn't hear. Not that it mattered. The comment had been for Sikes, who took in its import.

"Neither Celine nor Andarko would want them in that state," the Delancey woman said. "I had to keep them . . . from being damned."

"Ms. Delancey—"

"My name is Zho'pah. And in saving my children, I have damned myself."

So casually and smoothly she might have been lifting a spoon, the Newcomer lifted the gun to the underside of her chin. It happened in a blink, once again leaving Matt totally unprepared.

"Don't," he croaked, and then, regaining slightly fuller use of his vocal chords, added, "Don't. Wait."

She pressed the barrel deep into the soft flesh beneath her jaw.

"Now *you* talk to *me* . . . Why?"

The voice no longer abstracted. Purposeful as hell now.

"Uhh . . . Because . . ."

"Yes?"

"Because . . . the gods . . . will forgive you."

For a moment she stopped breathing. Then with the hopefulness of a child . . . "You think?" The gun lowering but still pointed at its target, Matt aware of the pink ring it left in her flesh.

"Oh, yeah," he assured her. "Absolutely."

The tension drained out of her body.

Matt relaxed.

Tuggle relaxed.

"Nice to know," she breathed.

Then she pulled the trigger.

The hammer hit the chamber with a soft click. And that was all. But the sound, because of what it represented, was just as profound as a gunshot. More devastating still, though, were her next words.

"That's it. I'm dead."

Matt slapped the table, rocketed up, knocking his chair back. *"Goddammit, that's not fair!"*

She was utterly unperturbed, maddeningly unimpressed. "You had the case histories to study. I was right on point."

"Aw, bull*shit*, you were makin' up the rules as you went along!"

Bill Tuggle's hand fell on Matt's shoulder. "Easy, Matt," his partner said, but easy was not in Matt's repertoire, not right at this moment, and he shrugged the hand off in favor of drilling the Newcomer woman more viciously still.

"Pleased with yourself? Put on a nice little performance, did you?"

And now Delancey was on her feet as well, just as

pluperfectly pissed as Matt, drilling back with full force. "You arrogant *kakstu,* don't you blame *me* because *you* didn't do your homework—!"

"—I don't need to be told what my homework is by some, some—"

"—some *what,* some *what*—"

"—just never you mind what—"

"—*'slag broad,'* is *that* what you were going to say?—"

"—if the spots fit, lady—"

And now a new voice spoke out, hands clapping for silence: "All right, children, that's it! Break it up, or no more sour milk and graham crackers!"

It relieved some of the tension in the classroom and the twenty-odd officers at the desks, as well as the three other performers grouped in a corner, chuckled. A bit.

Paul Winograd, fortyish, with dark, kinky hair and a bold mustache, strode to the head of the classroom. "Good, Bill, thanks," he nodded perfunctorily to Tuggle, who shrugged "Ain't nothing," and meandered back to his seat. In referee position, Winograd put his hands on the shoulders of both Fancy Delancey, the Newcomer actress, and Matt Sikes, and squeezed each reassuringly. To Fancy: "You did good, kid. A little heavy on the dramatic irony, but good. Back to your corner." Turning to Sikes: "As for you, remember, the motto here is *no shame.* You're *supposed* to fail in here so you don't fail out there. Back to your desk."

Matt obeyed, grumbling all the way.

The class was a seminar on dealing with crisis personalities, a requirement for rookies but, with the introduction of Newcomers into L.A. society, required *again* for experienced cops as well. Most of them were surly and resented it ("Logging Slag-time," they called it), despite the assurances that this was not a *refresher* course so much as a follow-up—to disseminate new, previously uncodified information. Recently the course had begun to integrate the services of an organization known as P.A.C.T.—Performing Artists for Crisis Training. Contributing actors would study case histories of crisis personalities under the guidance of a so-called director, who was, in truth, a psychiatric expert in such matters. Then in classroom situations the actors would improvise crisis scenarios along with cops who might face similar—but dangerously real—situations on the street.

Paul Winograd was the director for this unit.

"Now remember, boys and girls," he cautioned the class at large, "by the book for humans is *not* by the book for Newcomers. The differences are mind-bogglingly subtle, but they are, literally, killers. Matt, you back in control?"

"Yeah, yeah." Grudgingly, impatiently, not happy about it.

"You know what you did wrong?"

"Forgot to call in sick."

A bigger general laugh erupted from the group. Winograd shook his head, didn't reprimand, but deliberately chose not to join in the merriment. The point was lost on some, but Matt caught it. Winograd turned to the Newcomer actress.

"Fancy, tell him."

Looking at her director, she began, "He said that the gods—"

Which was as far as she got before Winograd's hand went up, the voice as flat and forceful as the palm that silenced her. "—Fancy, I *know* the drill. Tell *him.*"

Fancy Delancey, dutifully and clearly under protest, spun on her heels to face Matt Sikes. Sikes forced himself to return the gaze.

Not fun, not pleasant, not easy.

"You said that the gods would forgive. To a Tenctonese in that state, their *forgiveness* is yet a *further* loss of self-esteem because it implies that the victim is to be *pitied.* It is perceived as a *negative.* What the crisis personality wants to hear is that the gods would *approve—"*

"Approve?" Matt thundered. "She killed her goddamn *kids,* for chrissake—"

"Enough!" Winograd snapped. Burning his eyes into Sikes. "Matt, get with the program. The woman is *already* irrational. The trick is to key into *her* logic, not bring her around to *yours.* Or, for that matter, to your *human* notion of a forgiving God. Save lives first and save practical philosophy for later."

"Ahh," Matt muttered under his breath. Winograd, who'd seen the reaction before, and knew it to be cop-natural, turned back to the class.

"Ain't we got fun, people? Who's next?"

The memory of the classroom performance played over and over in his head, like a loop, all through Act One, all through intermission (during which his companions took his sullen preoccupation for interest in the drama, and just as well; he was happy not to have to explain himself before he was sure there was anything to explain), and continued through Act Two.

He kept imposing the classroom performance—in the role of the psychotic killer mom—over the onstage performance—in the role of Ibsen's repressed housewife, Nora; they were different in detail, each a different creation, yet there was something fundamentally the *same* at the core: tics, nuances, and inflections that beggared coincidence into impossibility. It was *definitely* the same woman.

The final scene, in which Nora finally tells off her husband, rang bells too. It was less a performance than an echo of real life. He'd been on the receiving end of that temper; he'd done his time as her Torvald—

—and at the famous door slam that ends the play (though hardly famous to Matt, who'd never seen the play before and thought it, frankly, hokey and quaint), he was up on his feet with the rest of the audience for Fran Delaney's standing ovation. But the applause and whistles he contributed were not really for art.

They were for Auld Lang Syne.

And when the houselights bumped up again, he turned to Cathy and said, "Can you wait for me. I gotta get backstage," and, not pausing for an answer, dashed off.

Leaving the Franciscos and Cathy to marvel that, wonder

of wonders, Matthew Sikes had been the most affected by the play of them all . . .

Cathy caught up with Matt in a narrow corridor leading to the dressing rooms, jammed with well-wishers. She was pleased to see him craning his neck over their heads for a glimpse of Fran Delaney, shifting from foot to foot like a star-struck kid. She wondered idly if she should be jealous.

"Hey," she said, touching his shoulder lightly.

He flashed her a cursory, preoccupied smile.

"Hi."

"George and Susan had to get back. For the kids, they said. But I don't know, I think they're just shy about waiting around backstage. For that matter"—she laughed—"I didn't know you had it in you."

That seemed to have an effect on him. He blinked, smiled at her sheepishly, scratched the back of his head, and said—

"Uhh—look, I hate to disappoint you, but—it's not what you think."

A beat followed. Then she asked, "You didn't like the play?"

"No, no. Hell, I liked it fine, but . . ." He gestured vaguely past the milling, buzzing throng . . . "What if I told you I know her?"

"Who?"

"Nora."

"Fran Delaney? You *know* Fran Delaney?"

"Yeah, but see . . ." He ran a hand through his hair. "This is nuts. But—bear with me, okay?"

"Sure . . ."

"All right. You're an actress. I mean, *suppose* you're an actress. A Newcomer actress. Playing a human. What kind of makeup would that require?"

"Same as when Earthers do it in science fiction movies, I guess. Prosthetics, that kind of . . ." It dawned on Cathy in midsentence where Matt was headed. "Awfully expensive process, Matt."

"Yeah, especially for a low-budget outfit like this. That's what I was thinkin'."

"Meaning what?"

"Meaning that when I knew *Fran Delaney,* she was *Fancy Delancey,* Tenctonese, and a huge pain in the ass." He gave a short shrug. "Okay, tell me it's impossible."

A terrible sadness and apprehension gripped Cathy.

"Let's go, Matt."

"I wish I could tell you I was joking, Cathy. I *know* it sounds impossible but—"

"It's *not* impossible, Matt, but you don't understand. If it's *true,* it's—"

The babbling of the crowd suddenly rose to an appreciative roar as Fran Delaney stepped out of her dressing room in civilian rags, sweater and jeans, makeup so removed her face was pale, but still indecently pretty. She began to make her way through the well-wishers in the front, and Matt broke away from Cathy to bull his way through the crowd from the rear.

"Matt—" Cathy called, but he was out of reach or hearing, sucked into the mass of babbling bodies.

Whatever damage he did, she hoped it would be minimal.

They met in the middle. She didn't see him at first; she was almost past him, chatting with others—

—and so he flipped his shield right where her peripheral vision would be distracted by it.

"You're under arrest, lady," Matt said.

Her eyes widened, she turned, bewildered, saw the shield first, then his face.

And gaped.

Recognition.

Unmistakable.

Matt smiled, to let her know it was all a joke.

"Hey, Fancy. Congratulations."

She faltered before her voice came. "I'm—I'm sorry, you have me confused with someone else." That said, she began pushing through the crowd with the force of a small tank. "Excuse me, excuse me." The words were tinged by desperation, and then she broke free of the crowd, off and running, past Cathy who looked after her with an expression akin to sorrow. Or pity.

Matt ignored the hostile glares from those close enough to have witnessed, now deprived of the star's good graces, and made his dazed way back to Cathy.

"She recognized me."

"I know."

"What the hell happened? *She recognized me!*"

Cathy took him firmly by the shoulders. "I *know.*" A beat. "I saw." A beat. "Come to the car. We'll talk."

They started to move out when, from the street beyond the stage door, they heard a collective cry of dismay.

Matt exchanged a look with Cathy and they hustled out, Matt in the lead, reaching for his police special.

Outside, a group of ten, maybe twelve, people were huddled in a circle. Matt broke through. "Police. Move aside, people, move aside."

The voice commanded authority, but the gun commanded speed, and they parted very fast to reveal Fran Delaney, collapsed on the sidewalk.

"All I did was ask for her autograph," said a young man, "—and she just twitched—and fell . . ."

Cathy, just catching up, was pushing onlookers aside. "I have some medical training. Let me through . . ."

Matt reholstered his gun, observing with uncomprehending fascination as Cathy knelt by the comatose actress, gently lifted the head, brushed the hair back, peered at details Matt could not begin to discern . . . and then touched the ears lightly. Stroked them. Made them bend.

Then she looked up and said, "Matt, you were right. Call an ambulance."

CHAPTER 2

GENTLY, A BEROBED George lowered Vessna into Susan's grasp. The baby's eyes were closed, but with unerring baby instinct, it knew: body warmth, mother skin, feeding shape —that last being Susan's left breast, freed from her slip and waiting. Vessna greedily encircled Susan's nipple with her mouth and worked her gums vigorously against it, squeezing out *Yespian,* the milk.

"Ow," sighed Susan affectionately. "Ow, ow, ow, ow . . ."

She looked up at George from the bed, on which she leaned her back against a pillow propped against the headboard, suffering the needs of her youngest. Her expression was both blissful and helpless.

"I know," George said soothingly. "I know."

Susan's breasts were especially sensitive, rare in Tenctonese women, and for her the sensual pleasure of breastfeeding was an elusive myth. It had less to do with the baby's vigorous gumming than the sensation of *Yespian* squirting, which was unsettling and, when she was very full, even painful.

There'd been a day not long ago, George remembered, when Susan had read in a magazine that some human women experienced similar pain upon breast-feeding. He remembered, too, her touchingly triumphant realization that she was not alone in the universe. The profound difference was that *human* females could opt to feed their babies with cow's milk or specially prepared formula, easily obtainable in any drug store. Not so for a Tenctonese mother. A Newcomer baby's very survival depended upon a steady infusion of mother's milk.

And so Susan bore the feedings stoically, with love and kindness, but always behind the eyes, that little tension flashing the message: This is torture. I can handle it. But torture.

George empathized as best he could—which was, in fact, pretty thoroughly. He had taken into his body each of their three children as unborn pods and carried them to term. He remembered vividly the exquisite yet excruciating pain of birth all three times.

The consolation Susan held to was that after Vessna was weaned, she would never again have to endure the loving agony. She and George had decided to stop at three children.

There were pragmatic reasons: Their income was already stretched to its limit. George had gone through an early *Gahsec,* making more children unlikely. But these reasons paled before the fact that they felt fulfilled. Their house and their lives had long been full with children, and at long last, three were enough.

"George," Susan said, stroking Vessna's soft, smooth head, "would you bring me my portfolio?"

"Of course," George replied, and padded to her dresser, against which the portfolio leaned.

"I want to check out the sketches for the new ad campaign again."

"Are you nervous?"

"Uhm. Apprehensive. The product is a very tricky one to advertise tastefully. I have to remind myself that my proposal is really as good as I think it is."

Probably that was true, thought George as he placed the portfolio beside her on the mattress and dutifully unzipped it. Just as likely, though, she was looking for any excuse to distract herself from the tiny agonies of Vessna's feeding.

He pushed the portfolio open and it fell forward, revealing the sketches. Susan reached for them and—with admirable dexterity, considering how fully occupied she already was—spread them out.

"What do you think?" Susan asked.

"Ah," George hemmed.

Looking at them.

"Em," he hawed.

Susan looked at him.

"You hate them."

"No," he said quickly, "not at all."

A pause.

"But—" she prompted.

"It means much to me that you wish to ask," he said carefully, "but . . . it has been brought to my attention that I have no talent for appraising art."

She blinked. "Who told you that?"

Embarrassed, he paused a bit before answering. "Uhm . . . Matthew, actually."

"Is this the same Matthew who never heard of Ibsen?"

"There was a . . . contextual application."

"Context or not. What a mean thing to say."

"No, no, he wasn't being mean. In fact, he didn't exactly put it that way."

"What way did he *put* it?"

"Well, we were on our way to question a witness on Sepulveda Boulevard when we passed a street vendor who had a row of paintings for sale."

"And?"

"And I paused to admire them." George smiled in recollection. "Oh, they were really quite something. Children and cats with big, round eyes. Colorful circus clowns. One especially striking canvas showed a man in a white spangled outfit, with full lips set in a rather pouty sneer . . ." George tried to assume the expression he was describing. ". . . hair in a kind of pompadour . . ."—he gestured vaguely at the top of his bald forehead, then touched his cheek—". . . and long sideburns. He was speaking into a microphone."

"Sounds almost . . . regal."

"Interesting you should say that. Apparently it was a picture of a . . . a *king* of some sort." His expression became wistful. "But my favorite was this very amusing canvas. It featured a group of canines in a smoky room, seated around a table, playing a card game. Poker, I think."

George looked down at Susan's face. She was smiling broadly, the discomfort of Vessna's feeding almost forgotten. Encouraged, he continued.

"The pictures weren't terribly expensive, not by the standards of fine art, anyway, and I thought to buy the dog piece for the living room."

"Why *didn't* you?"

"Because Matthew said that people would regard us less seriously if we hung it in the living room. He claimed, in fact, it had kitchenesque connotations."

"Kitchenesque?"

"Yes, I recall quite clearly. He said that the canvases were just a lot of kitchen."

"Oh." She mulled that over for a while. Then said, "You know what I think, Stangya . . ."

He brushed her cheek with the back of his hand, pleased that she had used his Tenctonese name.

"What?"

"I think I want your opinion anyway."

Touched, he turned his full concentration toward the sketches. And as he did so, Susan extracted Vessna from her left breast and repositioned both slip and baby to give the child access to the right. "Come on, Neemu," she purred, "that's right. Come on . . ."

And they were both immediately distracted by a rhythmic pounding from another room.

Thump-thump-de-thump.

A short pause and then . . .

Ka-flump.

Thump-thump-de-thump.

Ka-flump.

"What in the world . . ." muttered George. The sound seemed to be coming from Emily's room, and the repeating pattern made it seem purposeful. He exchanged a glance with Susan, whose expression read, *I don't know any more about this than you.*

"No doubt Emily is engaged in some sort of physical activity," George surmised.

"Think you should stick your head in and see?" Susan asked.

Thump-thump-de-thump.

Ka-flump.

George briefly considered Emily's right to privacy; briefly considered too how hard it had been to talk to Emily about the necessity of staying up late, as it was not good for Tenctonese youngsters to get too much sleep. If she was happy and occupied, he didn't want to disrupt her . . .

Thump-thump-de-thump.

. . . rhythm . . .

Ka-flump.

. . . and it might be just as effective to speak to her in the morning.

But then the decision was taken out of parental hands—the thumping suddenly stopped and an argument ensued. Buck, their eldest, was shouting at Emily and Emily was shouting back, the words unclear and muffled through the walls, but the emotions obviously high.

George nodded at Susan's sketches. "To be continued," he sighed, and strode out of the room, knowing, as he entered the hallway, that Vessna had once again attached herself to mommy.

"Ow," he heard, softly behind him, "ow, ow, ow, ow, ow . . ."

And heard Buck, much more loudly, just ahead of him, shouting, "You have *no* sense of proportion, *no* sense of time, *no* consideration for anyone else, I'm down there trying to *concentrate* and *you—*"

"And I *what?*" Emily fired back. "You moved into your precious RV, you *have* your 'space,' if you need quiet, why don't you—"

"Buck! Emily!" George snapped, in his best martinet fashion. They went abruptly, gratifyingly silent. George shifted immediately to solicitous politesse.

"Can I be of some help?"

"She's just making this noise, Dad!" Buck complained.

"And it was disturbing you."

"Yeah, sure, it would disturb *anybody—*"

"Sure," mimicked Emily, "anybody who didn't have a place of their *own.* He can't move out and also expect to control things in the house any time he—"

"Emily," George reprimanded gently, "I was talking to Buck."

He held the gaze of his teenage eldest, studied the fierce eyes in the boyish, almost beautiful face.

"However," George added, "Emily has a point, of sorts. You are always welcome in the house at any time, you know that, but we arranged to let you establish residence in the RV so that you could have your independence and solitude there."

"See?" said Emily.

"On the other hand," George continued, shifting his gaze to Emily now, "the noise *was* a trifle excessive for this time of night."

"Oh, I get it," said Buck, "I know this game. Nobody's right, nobody's wrong, you're off the hook, we go back to our corners."

George kept himself calm. It was so easy sometimes to get

sucked into the vortex of Buck's rebelliousness. To forget, with a loved one, that anger is not met best with anger.

"It is entirely possible, Buck, and in this instance especially, that there *is* no right or wrong. I don't see where Emily's intentions meant to hurt you directly or indirectly. Do you?"

Buck remained silent. George continued:

"What were you doing when you felt disturbed?"

"Thinking," Buck replied. Cryptically.

". . . Dare I ask?"

"I don't think you—"

Would understand, George finished in his mind, with a father's intuition, but Buck pulled back, leaving the thought unresolved.

"—uhh, kind of personal."

"I see. Well, it does rather seem as if the RV would be useful for that kind of introspection. In fact, I always thought you meant to use it as a retreat for just such occasions."

"You chasing me out?"

"Never."

And then something, some sixth sense or *something* popped an odd question into George's mind. After all, Buck *did* usually spend his nights, and his thinking time, in the RV. The Recreational Vehicle had originally been purchased for the family's use, but as Buck's need for independence had become fiercer and fiercer, it became apparent that its greatest use would be as a place for Buck to call his own: outside of the household but close enough to the family to afford him the emotional support a teenage boy would need.

"But I do wonder, and understand I am *just* wondering. Was there any particular reason you needed to do your thinking here in the house? Anything you needed our presence to—"

And George knew he'd hit a nerve because Buck utterly circumvented the question. "You *are* chasing me out, I knew it," he announced, and then whirled on his heel and made a show of pounding down the stairs.

"Buck," George called.

"Just forget it!" Buck shouted from the foyer, and then he was out of the house, the front door slamming behind him.

George turned his bewildered gaze on Emily.

"Don't look at *me,"* she said expansively, with an exaggerated shrug. *"I* didn't do anything."

George allowed himself a small smile. "Well, actually you did do *something.* What was all that jumping about?"

Emily's expression lit up. "It's my turn to come up with a dance exercise for the gym club in school." And that was the moment George registered the fact that Emily was in her gymnastics outfit. "I was putting the finishing touches on it. Wanna see?"

First Susan's sketches, now Emily's choreography. Both his big girls, it seemed, wanted his appraisal of their creations tonight.

"Certainly," George smiled.

She invited him into her room with a toss of her head. The floor had been cleared to give her as open a space as possible.

"You have to imagine the running start. There's not enough room in here to do it full out."

"I'll do my best," George assured her.

Starting flat against the wall, Emily took a single hop, bounded up several feet, landed,

Thump,

deep bending at the knees, arms up, uncoiling like a spring, arms at the side now, pirouetting full in midair, landing,

Thump,

kick starting a forward tumble,

de,

landing on her hands,

thump,

bending at the elbows, uncoiling again, pushing herself into the air, somersaulting backward until she was again erect and landing,

Ka-flump!

with a flourish.

Her face was beaming, radiant, flush with the enthusiasm of accomplishment, her eyes had turned from blue to brown with the exertion.

What, George wondered, was he to say?

That the coordination was lovely, but that the style lacked cohesion? That in his eyes it was less a dance routine than a youthful, slightly self-conscious, slightly self-aggrandizing display of dexterity?

His daughter's extraordinarily pretty face was a study in twelve-year-old vulnerability.

Tell her what I truly think? The night before her presentation?

Nope, he thought. Not me.

"It's just wonderful, Emily," he said. And he did not lie.

"Really?"

"Oh, yes."

"Thanks, Dad!" And he was rewarded with a bear hug, which put all the hardship of fatherhood in perspective.

He then bade her good night, advising that *some* sleep was necessary, and exited her room into the hallway, reflexively belting his robe tighter for the walk he was about to take outside.

It was a cool Los Angeles night in late September, cool even for George as he padded barefoot over the front lawn to the door of the RV. He knocked.

"Buck? Are you in there?"

There was no immediate response.

It was possible he wasn't. It was possible he'd gone for a walk, but George hoped not. He didn't like the idea of Buck walking around the streets this late. In a mood.

"Buck?"

Then, at length, through the door:

"Go away, Dad."

Ah. Well. Some relief, anyway.

"I just wondered, son, if you wanted to talk. In private."

"Not necessary, Dad."

Father and son shared a leaden silence. George opened his

mouth to break it when, from inside the RV, in a softer tone, Buck said:

"I'm okay, *okay?* I mean, I appreciate it, but I'm fine."

George wanted something more than that, but it was clear that more would not be forthcoming, nor could he reasonably expect more without forcing the issue. And he wouldn't force. Not without good reason. It was important these days that Buck find his own way. George only wished he knew what the hell his son was trying to find his way *through.*

"All right, son," he conceded. "Good night."

He said the last with a little emphasis, hoping to elicit a response. But there was silence from within the RV—and from without: crickets and birds, birds and crickets. The odd sounds of cars approaching and fading in the distance. The cold, burning indifference of the stars above.

He went back into the house, suddenly very tired, wiping the soles of his feet on the inside mat, and climbing the stairs to return to his bedroom. He found Vessna asleep in her crib, Susan likewise asleep on her side of the bed. He popped quickly into the adjoining bathroom, quietly attended to that which needed attending, emerged again into the bedroom, slid between the sheets, thinking of Vessna's voracious appetite, Susan's tender breasts, Emily's need to impress, Buck's enigmatic crisis, and everybody's desire for his approval.

He then wondered if he should bother nudging Susan gently awake to tell her how much he admired her sketches. But as he rolled over, his hand touched her side and, rather than rocking, nestled comfortably in the warm valley of her hip, and he half thought he'd remember to tell her in the morning—which, of course, he would not, it being only a half thought—and then his eyes closed and there was no clear thought anymore, half, whole, or otherwise, only the abstraction of dreams . . .

CHAPTER 3

SOMETIMES THE SHIELD worked wonders. Sikes flashed it at the paramedics and circumvented all the crap when Cathy insisted that the case of a normal-looking white woman had to be rerouted to the nearest hospital with a Newcomer trauma center.

He and Cathy rode with the ambulance, and Cathy oversaw Fancy's treatment until the hospital. (*Fran's* treatment, Matt corrected himself, but he couldn't quite wrap his mind around the new name.)

The trauma team was there at the ready when the ambulance arrived and Fancy was whisked away, Cathy following, as Matt stood at the threshold of the big hospital doors, feeling alone, useless, and stupid.

At length, he wandered into the waiting area, sat, flipped through magazines. And eventually looked up to see Cathy consulting with a human intern—there, no doubt, to train for emergency service in centers where Newcomers were rarer—and then an older Tenctonese doctor. She disappeared again for something like a half hour.

Flip through the magazines. Flip. Flip.

He was half dozing when he sensed Cathy's warmth next

to him on the couch. She touched his arm and he roused himself.

"Hi," she said.

"Hi. You were a long time."

"Fortunate we were there, actually. Some of the medical research I've been doing at work came in handy. She's out of immediate danger, anyway."

"Good. That's good." He paused. "Hey, I didn't—"

She touched his lips. "Set her off? No. What happened was building up all by itself. Coming for a long time."

"What *did* happen?"

Cathy shifted her position, knees no longer in toward Matt, but facing the opposite wall. She leaned her head against the couch and sighed.

"There's a . . . procedure. That some of our people have undergone on Earth. Very underground, very low key, usually only discussed in hushed whispers. It allows Tenctonese men and women to take on human appearance. It involves very specialized plastic surgery, plus a combination of skin grafts and skin dyes, in addition to an infusion of certain genetically engineered hormones. It's very difficult, sometimes painful, but it produces credible human ears, hair, removes 'telltale' markings . . ."

"Sounds dangerous."

"It can be. Incredibly dangerous. Primarily because the Tenctonese physiology is delicate and complicated—somewhat more so than yours."

"You don't have to tell me. I'm the one delivered George's kid when he went into labor on the job."

"Then you'll appreciate what I mean when I tell you that a Tenctonese body receives cosmetic medical alteration as a kind of mutilation. The body's natural predilection is to regenerate the unaltered form of fleshy appendages and renew its original appearance. Not a pleasant process, though. It's like kicking heroin cold chicken . . ."

"Turkey. Cold turkey."

"Oh. Right. Like that, yes. But worse. The only thing that

keeps withdrawal at bay and maintains the cosmetic alterations is a drug called Klees'zhoparaprophine."

"Quite a mouthful."

"Quite. Which is why no one much uses the chemical name. The street name is Stabilite. Tells everybody what it is, what it does . . ."

Matt sat in silence for a moment.

"How come I've never heard of this?" he asked eventually.

"Two reasons. Among my people, the willful alteration of appearance mocks the gifts of our gods, Celine and Andarko. It's considered an act of shame. Secondly, Stabilite is hideously, even prohibitively, expensive. I don't know what Ms. Delaney can be earning doing the play, but it can't be much. I'm astonished she can afford the drug at all."

"But she *has* been affording it. So what happened?"

"I can answer that," said a male voice.

Matt turned to see the human intern with whom Cathy had consulted earlier. The man was young, sporting curly blond hair worn in a near shag.

"I'm Dr. Steinbach. I'm working with Dr. Casey on this case. He'd be talking to you right now, but he's breaking the news to two more friends of the patient. Or colleagues, I guess." He extended his hand and Matt glanced around him to see the older Tenctonese doctor speaking to a wiry, prematurely gray man and a matronly, strong-jawed woman.

Matt looked back into the intern's eyes, said, "Matt Sikes," took the proffered hand, and smiled lopsidedly. "Let me guess. Dr. *Ben* Casey?"

Steinbach returned the smile. "Courtesy of Ellis Island West."

Matt *tsked* in understanding. Just like bureaucratic Earth humor to find out that a Newcomer had medical training and name him for a fictional 1960s TV neurosurgeon.

Matt released Steinbach's hand and said: "How about that answer?"

"Sure." Steinbach unceremoniously lowered himself onto a corner of the magazine table, pushing aside some periodicals. "Your friend Ms. Delaney is a very sick gal. She was taking Stabilite, all right, but not in its pure, FDA-approved form."

"It's FDA *approved?*"

"No reason not to be. Manufactured by an otherwise pretty stand-up company, Richler Pharmaceuticals." He pronounced the name with a soft "ch," as in chuckle.

"Richler," Matt repeated, filing the name away.

"Uh-huh. But because it's so pricey, there's an illegal knockoff that's been showing up on the streets. It's cheaper, but it's slow poison. The buildup of impurities can cause any number of illnesses. Including the big one you don't get to cure. In your friend's case . . . too soon to tell. I'm sorry."

Matt leaned forward, dry washed his face. "Aw, Jesus . . ." he whispered. "Is it worth all that just to blend in?"

Cathy put a hand on Matt's back.

"For a serious actress who can only do what she can do? What if blending in were the only way you could be an effective cop?"

"The truth? I'd find another profession."

"Then I envy your pragmatism. For some people there's simply no choice."

"I don't buy that. What she's done to herself is—I have to say it, forgive me—inhuman."

"Actually," Steinbach interjected, "no, it's not."

Matt just looked at him.

"I don't know about you," Steinbach continued, "but in high school they made me read a book by John Howard Griffin, *Black Like Me.* Remember it?"

Matt shrugged, guiltily. "I was one of your Cliffs Notes personalities. And I didn't retain much of that."

"Oh, you'd remember this one. It's an autobiographical account of something that happened in the late fifties. A white reporter took drugs and underwent ultraviolet skin treatments to make himself appear black. And then he went into the Deep South."

"Kind of like putting a loaded gun to your head, isn't it?"

"Well, that's sort of the point. His firsthand experience with racial prejudice was . . . pretty grim. And he was just a visitor. Now imagine yourself living on the inside as a permanent resident. Looking out. Wanting out. Or if not out, wanting to be 'in' somewhere else. Where your kind isn't appreciated. I always think about that book when I treat these Newcomers pumped up with bad Stabilite."

Matt looked at Cathy. He tried to imagine her *altered,* humanized. He couldn't. And realized it was because he didn't want to.

Cathy returned the look.

"What?" she said.

In lieu of answering, he turned his gaze back to Steinbach. "How long's this phony Stabilite been on the market?"

"Not real long."

"Lot of variations in the formula? Like from different suppliers?"

"So far it seems to be pretty much from the same batch. Why?"

"Sooner we start looking, sooner we can zap it at the source."

"We?" asked Cathy.

"Me and George." Adding, for the intern's benefit, "I'm a cop, George is my partner—and a Newcomer."

"I have to warn you," Steinbach cautioned, "Dr. Casey and I have reported other cases to the police. This problem is not first on your colleagues' list of priorities. I think some of them even want to bury it. You know, the fewer slags they have to deal with . . ."

"Let me worry about that. Can I see Franc—I mean, Fran?"

"She's pretty heavily sedated."

"Is that a 'no'?"

"It's an 'I can't imagine what good it'll do.' But I don't suppose it'll do any harm." The doctor rose from his perch and gestured. "Come on."

They entered Fran Delaney's room as Dr. Steinbach opened the door for them—and immediately Matt was struck by how pale and fragile she looked. What a contrast to the woman onstage . . . the woman in his memory . . .

He was walking down a corridor in the station house. It was the same one she was walking up, and there was no way to duck out of sight or avoid her gaze. Their eyes had met and contact was irrefutable. Shit.

"Hi," he nodded perfunctorily and shouldered past her, a lame but efficient getaway, or so he thought, until she called, "Hey, Sikes."

He turned. Waited.

"I'm sorry I had to give it to you with both barrels in class the other week."

He nodded. Her gesture was half-assed, but it was something.

"Apology accepted."

"That's not quite what I meant."

"No?"

"I meant to say I realize it wasn't a real good time for you up there, and it was not intended personally. But I *had* to. It's the job."

Just looking at her standing there, so self-assured, so unshakable in her righteousness . . . it was punching all his buttons.

"Oh, I think it was personal," he said. "It was sure as hell personal for *me*. I was giving you my best, and you never stopped twisting."

"I told you, we're *required* to throw you curves."

"And I'm trained to catch them. But 'the gods forgive, the

gods approve'? What the hell kind of margin for error does *that* leave me? You were grandstanding."

"I was going by the numbers!"

"You could've left me room to maneuver, thrown me a bone, something. Even your director said you were, what was it, 'a little heavy on the dramatic irony,' so it's not like I'm the only one in the room who noticed."

She stared at him for a long moment. Then the words came. And though he wouldn't admit it even to himself, not until much later, each one was like a knife in his soul because each had the ring of truth.

"You're right. It was a judgment call. I'm supposed to make two in each improvisation. The first is to determine how far I should play out the event. I can stretch it, I can cut it short. That's the show biz part. But my second decision is what predicates life or death for the next suicidal Tenctonese you deal with in the *real* world. And that's to determine what kind of cop I've got on my chain. You're trustworthy, Sikes, I'll give you that, and you're good as far as what you know. But you revel in your ignorance about what you *don't* know. I can't tell if it's because you're afraid or lazy or both, but I do know when you first entered that room you were cocky. When you told your partner to put down his gun, that was showing off. You'd never have done that on the job, and I saw it was *my* job to knock you down to size. To do it *hard* and *fast*. Apparently it worked."

"What the hell are you talking about?"

"You can't be that thick. Didn't you hear yourself? You *remembered!* You *remembered the difference!* The gods forgive, the gods approve, you said it yourself. I gave you an associative memory. In your case, the association is a brief humiliation, but the details are sharp and clear in your mind. That's how I know I've done my job and how I know that, when the time comes, you'll do yours. Because. Now. You. Will. Never . . . Forget."

The defensive rage rose from the pit of his stomach and

felt, literally *felt,* as if it was exploding out the top of his head.

"You know, if you were *any* kind of actress at all, you wouldn't have to be doing this kind of crap, you'd be out there in a real production entertaining the masses instead of manipulating humans for fun and profit!"

She recoiled slightly as if slapped. *Good one,* thought Matt. *He shoots, he* scores! The satisfaction lasted about two seconds.

Because tears leapt to her eyes and he hadn't meant for that to happen (had he?), nor was he prepared for what came next, in trembling, controlled fury, through the awful pain.

"First of all, Mister, there's not much fun in it and damned little profit. My job is a valuable public service and it's *hard,* and the money hasn't been *printed* that would make the workload and stress worthwhile if I didn't know I was doing some good. And second of all, if this society of yours was as enlightened as it claims, I wouldn't have to subsist solely on my public service work. I'm good at my craft, but they're only hiring Newcomers to play little green men from outer space, and that's where I draw the line, because that does no good at all. It just *hurts,* it just goes in front of an audience and creates more crisis personalities for you to deal with, more downtrodden jerks stripped of self-esteem." She started to move off, had another thought, pivoted, fired it at him. "And if you were any kind of *cop,* you'd've figured that out." She half turned again, but still wasn't finished, came up for air again and—"P.S., asshole, if I'm able to manipulate a hard case like you, then I'm the best actress in the world." This time she stalked off for good.

Matt stood there, feeling guilty, furious, wounded, and—most agonizingly—put in his place. If he'd had it in him to cry, he would have. But he didn't. So instead he held the tension like a pressure cooker and obsessed about the incident for the rest of the week.

And stayed away from mirrors whenever possible . . .

* * *

The young human-looking woman in the hospital bed had in her face none of the anger he remembered, none of the rage. But in repose, her expression still held the same deeply profound sadness. She was absolutely right about associative memories, he thought. He was feeling ashamed of himself all over again.

Eyes on Fancy, he said to the doctor, "She have any Stabilite pills on her?"

Steinbach nodded.

"Purse, in fact. We found it when we went searching for information, insurance, who to contact, that kind of thing. That's why we were able to medicate her so quickly without waiting for extensive test results."

"Can I see the bottle?"

Steinbach led him and Cathy to a desk where a nurse produced a large plastic bag with Fancy's personal effects. Matt reached into the bag and withdrew the bottle to examine the label, which was suspiciously generic, without the imprint of a specific pharmacy. The prescribing doctor's name was typed on the label, though:

C. LeBeque

Matt didn't know why, but the name seemed creepy, like something out of a Hammer horror film. Like something . . . appropriate.

"Can I take this?" he asked the intern.

Steinbach shrugged. "You're the cop, you know the law. It won't do *her* any good to keep it, that's for sure. And we've got enough for analysis, if that means anything."

Matt pocketed the small vial. "Thanks."

"Doctor," a nurse called urgently from down the hall, and Steinbach flipped a wave before sprinting to his next calamity.

Matt caught Cathy's gaze and held it.

* * *

She didn't know exactly what lay behind his eyes, but she sensed it was very dark, very private.

"You said the withdrawal is bad?" he asked.

"It's awful, according to everything I've heard," Cathy replied. "According to the doctors, what I've heard doesn't begin to describe it. And with the impurities in her system, there's the risk of other complications."

Matt put his hands on her forearms. His touch felt . . . good. Warm.

Trusting.

He looked as if he wanted to trust her, trust her with something very important. Very important and immensely difficult to articulate. The words would not come out of him easily. She'd been intimate with him, and he was still sometimes so hard to know.

"I realize it'll be an inconvenience," he said, finally, "but I want . . . I'd appreciate it . . . if you'd stay with her, guide her through. Whatever time you have to take off work, I'll make good on your salary. I just . . ."

He bit his lower lip.

She tried to make it easier for him.

"What, Matt?" Softly. "Tell me."

". . . I don't want her with strangers now, Cathy."

Strangers to him, she realized he meant. Because certainly she was a stranger to that girl. But she understood and didn't correct him.

Besides, if she stayed to do this thing Matt was asking of her, she would not be a stranger to Fran Delaney for long. Not in any sense of the word. She wondered if Matt had any notion . . . No. For if he did, he'd rescind his request. The question was whether or not to tell him.

He took one of his hands, closed his fingers lightly into a fist and pressed it gently to the side of her head. It was the first Tenctonese gesture she had taught him, one of great affection and respect. Not so intimate as humming prior to the act of love, but more profound than an embrace or even, in these circumstances, a kiss. She reached for the hand, cupped it in her much smaller one.

"Why does this mean so much to you, Matt?"

And of course, he was evasive. "I can't . . . it's complicated. I owe her, okay? I just . . . I owe her. And if I'm gonna nail the bastards who sold her that stuff, I need what little sleep I can still get tonight. So . . . will you do this for me?"

It was not what she had hoped to hear. But it was no more than she had expected. And he had managed to say . . . enough.

"You know I will," Cathy replied.

"Light bulb," he whispered absently—she had no idea what he meant—and then he opened his palm against her cheek, his mouth was upon hers as if both to draw and give strength, and then he was bolting off, down the corridor, out the doors, and into the cold, cruel world.

To do battle against the forces of evil.

Or something.

DAY TWO

CHAPTER 4

George Francisco had often seen his hot-tempered partner impassioned. But rarely so monolithically determined as he was this morning at the precinct house. Barely had George said hello when Matthew began telling the fantastic tale of how Fran Delaney had been rushed to the hospital and why. George had been too surprised by the tale to respond or think clear-mindedly, nor had Matthew given him much time. For he finished his narrative by saying, "So . . . are you with me on this?" Matt's ardor was so overwhelming that George could only nod a bit dumbly and follow his partner to Captain Bryon Grazer's office, where Matthew quite literally barged in, requesting—no, *demanding*—the assignment, claiming he had a good enough lead to wrap it up clean and quick.

At first Grazer seemed a tad put out that they hadn't noticed his stylish, new shoes.

"I'm trying a softer, hipper look," Grazer said, to which Matthew replied, cursorily, "Nice, Bry, now about my request—"

At which point Grazer began to hem and haw. He

somewhat superciliously reminded the two detectives how heavy their caseload was already, and how designer drugs catering to a limited clientele was not all that important in the grand scheme of things.

And then—quite amazingly, considering Grazer's stubbornness—Matthew was able to (as he might have put it) "cut through the garbage" with just four words.

"Remember your sister's kid?"

Grazer froze for a moment and looked at Matthew as if to gauge the measure of the man—or hit him.

But he merely picked his cigar off its ashtray and pointed with it.

"Clean and quick," he said. "Every minute over forty-eight hours is worth ten in weekend volunteer service. And I mean park duty—trash pickup and horsie patrol."

"Understood, Cap'n," Matt acknowledged.

"Francisco, keep 'im honest," Grazer adjured—threateningly, it had seemed to George.

"Yes, Captain," George replied.

Matt didn't need or wait to hear anything else. Almost that quickly he hustled them both into their unmarked patrol car, and they were cruising toward the office of high society plastic surgeon, Dr. Christian LeBeque.

George had not yet confided to Matthew his ambivalence about the case, about being *drafted* into its service—ambivalence that had only grown with the passage of minutes. Obviously this actress was somebody his partner cared about deeply. But George did not like the idea of what she'd done to herself. A part of him didn't even like the idea of helping her out. He kept that part in abeyance, though, adopting a wait-and-see posture. Maybe he didn't know enough about the particulars yet. Maybe his emotions were premature. He looked over at Matthew behind the wheel and chose another topic to discuss.

"What did you mean, Matthew, when you reminded the captain of his sister's child?"

"Couple of years ago his nephew Joel was hangin' with a

bad bunch. He had his own problems anyway, but the company he kept didn't help."

"Because . . . ?"

"Usual. They were into drugs, they got *him* on drugs, and one fine day at the ripe old age of fourteen, he took a shot of impure heroin and nearly kacked. Grazer practically ripped the city apart to find the gang, the pusher and the supplier. Against the odds and, at the start, against orders."

"Grazer, renegade? Impolitic? It's hard to fathom."

"I still have a hard time with it and I was there to *see* it. But he was one angry puppy and wouldn't let go. His determination led to one of the biggest drug busts in the history of the department. That's why they bumped him up to captain at such an early age."

"I had no idea. He's usually such a publicity hound. I'm surprised he doesn't flaunt it more."

"I've never quite figured that out either, George. But I'm not about to look a gift horse in the mouth."

"Assuming you were given such an animal, why would you do such a thing? And what has that to do with Captain Grazer?"

Matthew laughed. "It's an *expression,* George."

George nodded, feigning understanding. This happened to him rather a lot. "Oh," he said. Then, after a bit of thought, *"Oh!* Yes, I see. Gift horses. Very intriguing." A beat. "You would not happen to know the derivation of that expression, would you, Matthew?"

Matthew seemed momentarily uncomfortable and then, rather too enthusiastically announced: *"Ah! Here we are!"*

The car glided into a parking space in a lot that flanked a medical building whose facade bore more resemblance to a Four Star hotel than a place of healing. But then, one would expect no less on Bedford Drive in Beverly Hills.

George and Matthew rode the elevator to the floor numbered 14 that was (secretly) 13 and found their way through the lushly carpeted hall to the offices of Christian LeBeque.

They were greeted by the strains of generic Muzak as they entered into a soft, blue waiting room with hanging plants, plush chairs, peaceful watercolors of boats floating idly on clear blue lakes, and the ambience of a parlor, broken only by the sliding window built into the far wall, which looked into the nurse's cubicle.

George exchanged a few words with her as Matt passively adopted an "I'm with him" stance. They'd opted not to identify themselves as cops, not right away, the better to check out the doctor's practice unobtrusively. The strategy had some merit, as the nurse directed them to *another* waiting room, quite separate from the one they were in now.

This one was more clinical.

The walls consisted of plain wood paneling, the chairs were wood-framed and functional. A window looked out onto the parking lot, and the sunlight streaming in did nothing to beautify the decor; it simply made appearances harsher.

The pictures on the wall, though, were what gave the room its *particular* identity.

No soothing watercolors these.

These were schematic diagrams and sketches.

Clinical befores and afters.

The "before" pictures were Tenctonese faces.

The "after" pictures were the same faces. Humanized.

Two other Newcomers, both women, occupied seats. They sat apart from each other, seeming intent upon not making contact.

The room was scrubbed clean, yet it felt squalid to George. And as he studied the pictures, his mind flashed to another place, another time.

Chorboke is coming.

And he told himself, Stop it, stop it, different issue, different context, this is not at all the same thing, you can't honestly equate this with—

Chorboke is coming

—and he was picturing the lab at Dual Pharmaceuticals,

the lab run by Newcomer Dr. Hadrian Tivoli, in all respects a force for good, until you discovered, as had George and Matthew, that the altruism was a cover, that on the slave ship, Hadrian Tivoli had been

Chorboke

the scientist who had performed biological "experiments" using the slaves as his subjects, the better, in his sick and twisted mind, to advance the species, to create a purely mental being. What he'd created instead was any manner of atrocity, causing the deaths of thousands and

Chorboke

was dead, of course.

Dead and gone in the fire that destroyed his lab. George had been there to see it happen. He was dead.

Chorboke was dead.

But in these pictures—

Chorboke is coming.

—his spirit lived on

Chorboke is here.

George snapped then, his gorge rising, and it was all he could do not to shriek his outrage. He turned on his heel and left the room before his disgust and unsolicited judgment became apparent to the waiting women. He strode out of the doctor's office, Matt at his heels.

The nurse saw them leaving, called out *"Sirs?"* and Matt said, "We'll be right back," over his shoulder before following George out the door.

George found a wall in the hallway to lean against, took in deep breaths in an effort to calm himself. He bent over slightly, his palms on his thighs. So the first things he noticed were Matt's feet. George's gaze traveled up the body to Matt's face from there. The face seemed puzzled.

"What's wrong, George?"

"Really," George snapped. *"How can you ask such an inane—"* He caught himself, bit off the sentence. Struggled for some control. Found it. Some. "I am sorry, Matthew."

"Look, I know why you bit off my head just now: We went

from a living room into a slag chamber. I'm not asking why you're pissed off. I'm asking what gives? I thought we were gonna play it out in there."

George nodded tightly. "I thought we were too," he conceded, quietly. "And when you told me this morning what that young actress was doing to herself—it was an abstraction. Not to mention that I was trying, for your sake, to be sympathetic."

"I appreciate the effort. Cathy told me how most Newcomers feel about that stuff."

"I thought I was willing to be open-minded. But those *pictures*—they were an *abomination.* I could not stay in that room a moment longer."

A rueful grin from Matt. "Yeah, I noticed. So what now?"

George shrugged a bit helplessly. "I suppose we—"

His thought was interrupted as the doctor's door opened and a voice boomed out, *"Gentlemen!"*

George and Matt looked back toward the office, to see a porcine, well-appointed man with thinning hair and beady eyes approaching. He wore a lab coat.

"Check it out," announced Matt with some amusement, under his breath: "the mountain's coming to Mohammed."

Before George could question this new idiom, the mountain (aptly identified, in George's view) was upon them, smiling obsequiously.

"Is anything wrong?"

"Kind of a startling display you have in there," Matt offered. "You know, if you're not prepared for it, I mean."

"I understand," said the mountain, and without waiting for George to extend his hand, grabbed it. "I am Dr. Chris*tian* LeBeque," he proclaimed, his otherwise unaccented voice going inexplicably nasal at the pronunciation of his first name, "and I've seen your reaction before. The shock of the new, that's all. Believe me, there's nothing of which to be affrighted."

Matt flicked a gaze at George. *Affrighted???*

Not releasing George's hand, LeBeque inspected it. Then looked at George's face, not as if he were a person, but as if he were a specimen. LeBeque raised a hand, touched fingertips to the outline of George's jaw, gently angling his head into better light.

"Oh, yes indeed, we can do wonderful things for you."

George nearly slapped the hand away—with his strength, he might have broken the doctor's arm in the process, for good measure—but out of the corner of an eye, he caught a shift in his partner's expression. *Let this clown ramble a bit,* it tacitly urged. And so George bore the man's stare, endured his unwelcome touch.

"I must say," George commented, gingerly trying to extricate himself and at length succeeding, "you do go out of your way to . . . *woo* your potential clientele."

LeBeque tut-tutted. "Let's not refer to *clients,* please. *Patients.* And, yes, my zealousness can appear to be, oh, why not say the ugly word, *aggression*—but it's misleading, truly. I just get concerned when it seems a patient may not be fully informed as to what we do here. You should have all the facts before coming to a decision."

"I told you this guy didn't have to drum up business, George," Matt said, playing the part broadly but, as it happened, convincingly.

"Of course not," LeBeque laughed self-deprecatingly. "Look around you. What need? No, my interest is in doing what's best for *you.* Mister—?"

"Francisco."

"*Mister* Francisco!" Grandiloquent. "Please. Come back in. I promise not to keep you waiting long. And the first consultation is free," he added pointedly.

"Fine," George said, having decided to play along. "In truth I do not know quite why I was so apprehensive. I had been told your rates were equitable and your service—top drawer."

"I'm so pleased," beamed LeBeque, gesturing toward his

office, beckoning them to follow. And as they walked: "Who recommended me to you?"

"A Miss Fancy Delancey."

LeBeque froze in his tracks, hand on the doorknob. He turned about slowly, scowling and growling.

"What is this?"

"I don't know what you mean," George responded innocently.

"I *mean* I never treated any such patient."

"Ah," smiled George, "I believe I can help you there. She has, of late, been using the name Fran Delaney. Perhaps when you treated her—"

"I tell you I treated no such woman!"

Matt pulled the bottle of Stabilite from his pocket, held it between middle finger and thumb, rocked it back and forth on the balls of the digits. "I got a label here tellin' a different story."

"That's it!" LeBeque exploded, jowls aquiver. "Leave this building or I'm calling the—" He cut himself short. Paused. Nodded to himself. Grimaced ironically. "How absurd of me. You *are* the police."

"Man's a quick study, George."

"Let's can the banter, gentlemen. I'd like to see some ID. Just to be on the safe side."

"The man is also cautious, Matthew."

"Maybe he's got reason."

They both flipped their shields. LeBeque inspected them for a long time. "All right," he said finally, "fine," and the shields disappeared. "What is this charade all about?"

"The charade, sir, would seem to be yours," George accused.

"Excuse me?"

"You just pretended not to know one of your most notable clients," Matt pointed out. "Oops. Sorry. *Patients.*"

"Part of my service involves strict confidentiality. Ms. Delancey went through great lengths to keep her treatment private. She would not have *spoken* of it to anyone, much less made a recommendation."

Appraising LeBeque, George asked slowly, "And would you say your work on Ms. Delancey was successful?"

"Exemplary. As you must know from her recent triumph."

"You must be very proud of yourself."

"It is *always* good to know that one's labors have helped another achieve a lifelong dream," he responded defensively.

"Yeah, well, the celebration's a bit premature, Chris*tian,*" Matt asserted, mocking the affected pronunciation. "The lady's down from bad Stabilite."

"When?"

"Last night."

"Pity."

"'Pity,'" echoed George. "Is that all you have to say?"

"What would you *have* me say?"

"You might try assuming some responsibility."

"Me? For what?"

"For seeing that she was fully prepared for the consequences of her . . ." the word caught in George's throat; he managed to extricate it, ". . . treatment."

"Consequences such as . . . ?"

"Such as the high price of the habit," Matt contributed. "Such as the existence of bum product and the dangers of ingesting it."

LeBeque pulled himself up, huffily. "No, gentlemen, I'm sorry, my responsibility *ended* when I asked Ms. Delancey if she could afford treatment and medication. It was she who sought *me* out, remember. And when her answer was yes, I proceeded accordingly."

"With no regard for the state of her finances after she paid you off?"

"She's an adult, making an adult decision. It's not my job to be a detective. That's your department."

"Yes . . . Of course . . . You are correct," George nodded.

His tone was so overpolite that Matt backed up a step, saying, "Oh my."

"Indeed," George continued, "we are detectives, and a very minor bit of detecting led to the discovery that when you wrote Ms. Delancey's prescription for Stabilite, you did not make it out to any of the pharmacies specializing in its handling and dispensation—such as the one *right here in this building*—but instead you gave her an *open* prescription. Good anywhere."

"Standard practice," LeBeque countered. "A courtesy. Ms. Delancey did not, obviously, live in the immediate area and I thought—"

George grabbed the fat man's tie and jerked him forward so that they were almost nose to nose. "Standard perhaps," he said in soft, lethal tones, "but of questionable ethics where expensive and controversial drugs are concerned and there is a known threat of inferior merchandise. Especially since *'obviously'* the young lady did not live in the area because she *'obviously'* had no access to the financial resources. Which might have led a reasonable mind to the conclusion that *'obviously,'* and by extension, she would find it difficult if not impossible to afford the required medication."

George tightened his grip on the tie.

"Gack," said LeBeque.

"The unconcerned but *diligent* mind," George continued, "might, at the very least, have filled out a *restricted* prescription to insure that if Ms. Delancey could indeed lay hands on the drug, she could get it from nowhere but a qualified apothecary. Since, in the case of Stabilite, an open prescription is generally regarded as an invitation to charlatans."

"Let go of me!" LeBeque gasped.

"An *open prescription to Stabilite,*" George concluded, "says 'Look at me, I'm poor, can you get me a deal?' "

"I'm not responsible for that, now let me go, you're choking me!"

Interesting word, choke, George thought. *How it sounds so much like Chorboke.*

Casually, Matt said, "What a world, huh? Nobody's responsible for nothin'." And, then, touching George's shoulder lightly, he said, "Let 'im go, George."

George snapped open his fist, releasing LeBeque so suddenly that he reeled against the door.

"That was very good, partner, I'm *impressed,"* said Matt. He smiled jauntily at LeBeque. "Usually *I* get to play 'Bad Cop.' "

LeBeque wagged an admonishing finger at them both, adrenaline rush giving him a new head of steam. "I gave that young lady the best treatment possible, and need I remind you, it was *elective surgery* and *no one twisted her arm!"*

George cocked a hairless eyebrow. "You mean as you tried to do with me just a while ago?"

"Pah! Salesmanship hardly qualifies as coercion. And you gentlemen have taken my patience to its limit."

Matt sighed theatrically. "Man's right, George, we don't have anything on him. There's been no crime committed, at least none on the books, none we can make stick." He patted LeBeque on his beefy arm, smiled.

Smiled like a shark.

"But wouldn't it be fun to try?"

LeBeque sputtered. Noises, all ending in question marks.

"Well, I mean," Matt explained, "you could try this case in the news media and never have to bother with arrests, paperwork, the expense of a trial. Let the *public* decide what constitutes negligence. Just present 'em with the facts—that you *knowingly* performed elective surgery on a patient who couldn't afford to maintain proper treatment. What do you think, George?"

"Oh, I think the release of such a story would put a strain on his . . . patients . . . just as he said."

"An old pun, but a gem."

"All *right,"* LeBeque spluttered, exasperated. Then, more subdued, trying to recover some dignity, "All right. Clearly you—officers of the law are after something." He pulled clumsily on his lapels. "How can I—*as a law abiding citizen*—be of service?"

The detectives exchanged a look. George took a step toward LeBeque. LeBeque leaned back into the door. Crooking an elbow, George pointed lightly across his chest at Matt. And spoke with exaggerated civility.

"Write out an open prescription for Stabilite. Make it out to my partner, Matthew Sikes."

"That's Sikes with an *i,* not a *y,*" Matt added helpfully.

LeBeque appraised the features on the human detective's face with a clinical eye—also evident distaste.

"And let people think I worked on *you?*" he asked unpleasantly.

"Isn't that cute," cooed Matt. "A professional scruple . . ."

CHAPTER 5

Grazer was trying to dust off his shoes. Or, more appropriately, he was trying, with intense concentration, to lift particles of dust out of them. Piece by piece.

He had Scotch tape wrapped around his fist, sticky side out, and continually applied the tape to the shoe he was working on

—crinkle—

and lifted

—thwop.

Applied and lifted.

Crinkle, thwop. Crinkle, thwop. Crinkle, thwop.

Every forty-five seconds or so, when the strip of tape had outlived its usefulness, he pulled it off, damning the accretion of stickum on his skin, and wrapped his hand in a fresh strip from an ever-decreasing roll. Whereupon he began knuckling the shoe again.

Crinkle, thwop.

Crinkle, thwop.

He was muttering over the task like one possessed when Sikes and Francisco knocked and entered his office.

Matt exchanged a look with his partner and spoke very tentatively.

"Uhh . . . Cap'n?"

"Suede."

"What?"

"Suede, dammit." Grazer held up one of the shoes and shook it angrily in front of his face. "White suede at that, can you be*lieve* it?" He brushed at the top of the shoe with the untaped side of a hand, went, *"Ahhh,"* in disgust, and began banging it on the top of his desk like Khrushchev at the U.N.

"What're you doin'?" Matt asked. He asked it rationally, but also carefully. Reasonable question though it was, he couldn't be sure that Grazer had reason within reach.

Grazer jumped up, exasperated. "He dusted up my *shoes!"* He stepped out from behind his desk. His beige pants had a dingy gray residue clinging to the cuffs. "He didn't do much for my slacks either, *but the shoes.* One-hundred-fifty-dollar white suede and he just barrels right into me with a loaded broom."

"Who?"

"Albert Einstein, who the hell do you think?"

Under most circumstances, if a man claimed that Albert Einstein had sabotaged his wardrobe, you might safely assume that man had flipped over into the happy side. At the very least, that the man was being heavily sarcastic in referring to a particularly dim-witted fellow.

Bryon Grazer, though, was being entirely literal.

Albert Einstein, a youthful Newcomer, was the day-shift janitor at the precinct house.

"I'm sure he did not mean it," George offered.

"He *laughed,"* Grazer insisted. "He *schmutzed* me with this filthy broom and he *laughed."*

Matt shook his head.

"No. Sweet, naive Albert laughed? Usually, after an accident, he gets on his knees to denounce his unworthiness."

"Sure, get on his knees," growled Grazer, "why should he screw up *his* pants?" He paused, as if listening to a private little tune, cocking his head curiously, and suddenly giving a single, decisive little nod. "Ah-*hah!"* He strode past them to his office door, threw it open. "Hear for yourself."

And, sure enough, like a delicate *obligato,* riding above the din of general office noise, came the sound of dizzy laughter.

"It is unlike Albert to behave in such a fashion," George commented.

"Gets worse," Grazer snarfed. "This morning he left an entire box of fresh jelly weasels on the radiator too long."

Jelly weasels were Newcomer snack food, rather akin (in intent, if not in content) to the doughnuts ingested by humans. Like any other meat-based product suitable for Newcomer consumption, jelly weasels had to be consumed raw. Tenctonese physiology not only thrived on the nutrients and enzymes in raw meat, it was, furthermore, unable to digest meat in any other condition.

"Cooked 'em," Grazer exclaimed. "Just enough to cause damage, not quite enough to be noticed by a preoccupied officer until the first bite went down." Grazer flapped his arms in frustration, the shoe on his hands describing a wide, and possibly dangerous, arc. "A dozen of those disgusting things, twelve potential cases of food poisoning."

Sikes wasn't sure what it was that Grazer found disgusting: cooked jelly weasels or jelly weasels as a concept. Probably a toss-up.

"I assume Albert found *this* amusing as well," George guessed.

"On a scale of one to ten, he thought it was a twelve. Better than the shoes. If May hadn't caught it, we'd've been knee-deep in Newcomer barf."

As if on cue, a young, pretty Newcomer girl showed up in the doorway. She was the sandwich girl, formerly May O'Naise, more recently May Einstein, Albert's wife.

"What?" Grazer snapped by way of greeting.

"Captain, I wanted to apologize for my husband."

"Forget apologies, can you calm him down?"

"I've been trying. I don't know what to do."

"Hi, May," Matt said, lightly, trying to diffuse a bit of the tension. And then: "Hey, you're a little lighter in the bread basket there, aren't you?"

It was true. Where previously she had been pregnant, full with the pod which would gestate into her first child, now she was her former slim-waisted and flat-stomached self.

"Oh, yes. Albert assumed the pod last night. It was beautiful."

George exhaled, as if relieved about something.

"Of course," he said, almost to himself; and then, to Grazer, "Did you not notice that Albert was suddenly pregnant?"

Grazer pursed his lips and snorted. "I'm a *cop,* Francisco, of *course* I noticed. But after he broadsided me, I wasn't too keen on offering congratulations."

"What I am trying to get across, Captain, is that his current . . ."

—Albert's laughter floated across the squad room again—

"*. . . giddiness* is directly attributable to his condition."

"Well, now, how the hell was I supposed to know that? I mean, when *you* were pregnant, it didn't turn *you* psycho."

"I dunno, Cap'n," Matt put in. "George had some remarkably pissy moods."

Matt pointedly ignored George's brief glare as Grazer poutily responded, "You know what I mean."

May seemed sympathetic.

"I really don't understand it myself."

Grazer made a face that eloquently translated as, *There! Satisfied?*

"I at least know what you mean, Captain," George conceded, and Matt did not miss the implied dig. "But I'm a *gannaum,* Albert is a *binnaum."*

"And my great-grandfather was a *moyel* in the old country, what does that have to do with anything?"

"*Binnaums* have a somewhat different body chemistry. They are built so that they can incubate a pod to term, but it is a feature few *binnaums* actually utilize. A small number of *binnaums* have even been born without a pouch."

Grazer's inflection took on a long-suffering quality. "The point being . . ."

"That by accepting the pod into his system, Albert triggered a chemical change, and a fairly emphatic one. In order to create a safe environment for the pod, several of his glands have kicked into overdrive."

"You telling me he's on a nutrient rush?"

"That . . . is one way of putting it. But the imbalance is only temporary. Once the activity normalizes . . ."

"Oh, great. But until then, he's a PMS time bomb. Any way to speed the process along?"

George turned to May.

"May, have you tried having Albert ingest large quantities of soda water? If he belches a lot, the release of carbon dioxide may calm him considerably."

She smiled gratefully.

"Thank you, George."

George smiled back hugely. "No thanks needed. I am, after all, the *gannaum*. It is my responsibility." Matt observed the moment with the slight residue of a discomfort he should long since have shed. But it was weird, still, to think that it took *three* Newcomers to make a baby: a female, a *binnaum* to catylize her, and a *gannaum* to fertilize her. Well, no, that wasn't what was weird. What was weird was that the Newcomers were just hunky-damn-dory with the idea. Albert had been the *binnaum* to George's daughters Emily and Vessna. Less than four months ago, George—in what would turn out to be his last pre-*Gahsec* hurrah as a fertile male—had returned the favor. It was considered an honor. A big one. Sacred ceremony and everything.

In the background there was the sound of something falling, the sound of someone cursing, and Albert's drunken, soprano laughter.

May turned to Grazer. "Captain, I'd like to fix the damage done to your shoes, if I may."

She reached for them with such guileless innocence that Grazer didn't have enough reaction time to reflexively pull them away.

"That'd be great!" he smiled. And then asked, "How?"

"Albert has about five bottles of Wite-Out in his locker, I can just—"

Quickly, Grazer snatched the shoes back. "*On*—second thought . . . You have enough to do, kiddo. See to your husband. That takes first priority."

"You're very kind, Captain," she said—incredibly enough, meaning it—and hustled off.

Grazer stood by his open office door, wearing his shoes on his hands, shorter than usual in stocking feet, muttering, "Wite-Out on suede . . ."

He looked up at Sikes and Francisco, as if noticing them for the first time.

"What're *you* hanging around for?"

Matt bobbed his head back and forth in tiny increments for a while, and said slowly, "To report on the *case,* Bry."

"What? . . . Oh, *that.*" He brushed past them, on his way back to his desk chair. "Yeah, sure, get to it."

He wrapped his fist with tape again and the two detectives filled him in on the morning's progress as *crinkle* and *thwop* punctuated the information. The sound effect slowed only near the end when George's sense of outrage resurfaced briefly. The heightened emotion seemed to snap Grazer into some kind of sober awareness, and he dislodged a hand from a shoe, lifting a cautioning finger.

"I need not remind you, gents, you're in a gray area. The doctor's activities, however abhorrent, are not illegal. Right now, all you get is a ticket to ride"—making reference to the prescription—"which expires in less than forty-eight hours if you can't get a lead on the *specific pharmacy* used by your actress friend. I can't spare the time it would take for you guys to scam every fishy drugstore in L.A."

"But, Captain—" Matt began.

"I thought we had an understanding, Sikes. I applaud your efforts so far, but don't push your luck. Get it?"

A long pause.

"Got it."

"Good." Grazer glanced at George. "Francisco?"

"Of course."

"Fine. Thanks for the tip on Albert. Now get outta here."

They left the office and crossed to the adjoining desks, the sound of *crinkle-thwop, crinkle-thwop* fading behind them.

The timing couldn't have been better.

No sooner had Sikes's fanny hit the chair than a khaki officer told him there was a call waiting on line three.

"Sikes here."

"Matt, it's Cathy."

"Cathy! How are you?"

"They set up a cot for me in the nurses' dorm."

"Yeah, but . . . how *are* you?"

"Oh . . . you know."

He didn't. Rephrased the question. "Get any sleep?"

"Enough to function. Hasn't been that much to do . . . until now."

"She's awake?"

"You could call it that. One minute of rationality for every five of delirium."

". . . What's her condition?"

"Good news, bad news. Order's up to you."

"Let's go out on a win. Start with the bad."

"The delirium probably signals the beginning of withdrawal. It'll be rough."

"How can you tell?"

"Weren't you paying attention last night?"

". . . You sound angry."

"Do I?"

"A bit."

"I'm not."

"You sure?"

"Ma-att . . ."

" . . ."

" . . ."

"Okay, right. What's the good news?"

"Provisional. I got her to come up with the name of a pharmacy. Took a lot of shouting, but I think I got through. The one she named was *See Gurd Nurras* in Little Tencton."

"See Gurd what?"

"Nurras."

"You spell that?"

"Phonetically only. Like it sounds, but that may not do much good. Pass it on to George, he'll know what to make of it. It translates as 'The Drug Runners.' "

"Cute."

"I thought you'd like it."

"She give you an address?"

"You're lucky to have *that.*"

"Never mind, we'll look it up. And it is good news. What's provisional about it?"

"She's not connecting much. I can't guarantee that's the right name or that such a place even exists."

"It's better than nothing. We need an excuse to roll. If George and I can't be in full-tilt boogie by tomorrow A.M., the case turns into a pumpkin."

A short laugh escaped Cathy then. "I actually think I understand that," she said. It was the first time in the entire conversation that she sounded remotely like the Cathy he knew. The moment passed too quickly. "Well," she sighed, "no doubt you'll be checking in. I'll let you know if the information gets more specific, or different."

"Of *course* I'll be checking in. Dammit, you *are* angry."

"No, really. Just . . . just gearing up."

"You're sure."

"Yes."

"Really?"

"Matt . . ."

"Okay." A beat. And then, softly, awkwardly, because he wasn't always comfortable with it, even though it was the truth: "I love you, you know."

". . ."

"Cathy?"

"Boy, you'd better," she said, and hung up.

He drew the phone away from his ear at the sharp *click!,* fighting an impulsive desire to speak her name into the mouthpiece—*"Cathy?"*—and retrieve her.

What checked the impulse, curiously, was a comedy bit he'd once heard on a scratchy old vinyl album featuring Mike Nichols and Elaine May.

In the bit, Nichols plays a poor schnook stranded on the road, trying to call for help from a phone booth. But his call has gotten cut off, and the phone has eaten his last dime (and the days when a phone call cost a dime were also the days without touch-tone dialing and calling cards, so this guy is stranded but *good*). He manages to connect with the operator, played by May, who won't reconnect the call but assures him that if he *just hangs up the phone,* his dime *will* be returned to him. Which puts Nichols into a panic since he has no doubt that the dime has long since dropped into the phone's innards; there's no *way* to reroute it to the change basket. The operator argues that he will indeed get his dime back, and then Nichols really becomes desperate. He swears to her that he distinctly *heard* the decisive *clunk* all pay phones make when they swallow your change—

—and, adding to that with the anguish of years, he cries, "I *know* that sound. *I've been hearing it all my life!"*

Matt felt like that now. One part of him not quite understanding, wanting to play the conversation with Cathy back, get it right, make amends for—whatever the hell it was he needed to make amends for; the other part saying, Forget it. She's hung up on you.

I *know* that sound. *I've been hearing it all my life!*

"Matthew?"

Sikes looked across his desk toward George at the desk opposite.

"Is anything wrong?"

Yeah, something's wrong, thought Matt. *That open innocence of Cathy's seems . . . seems, I don't know what, diluted. Compromised. The woman whose face lights up at the tactile sensation of theatre tickets in her hand is not* quite *the same woman I just spoke to on the phone.*

And then Matt thought, *Business first,* and snapped on a tight smile, holding aloft the piece of paper upon which he'd scribbled Cathy's information.

"Maybe not, partner," he said. "Maybe not."

CHAPTER 6

Cathy Frankel racked the receiver, leaned back in the chair, and sighed. Anticipating exhaustion. And worse. Dr. Steinbach had been nice enough to give her access to the phone and whatever else she might need in Dr. Casey's office, and she wasn't shy about accepting the offer.

A soothing office, Casey's was, in soft earth tones, the swivel chair comfortable, with a substantial cushion for lower back support. She snuggled into it looking abstractedly at the office door. Closed now.

Procrastinating.

As long as she didn't cross to the door, open it, face what was outside, she was safe. Safe from everything but her own thoughts, at least, which inevitably turned toward Matt.

Matt asking if she was angry. And her various responses: the noncommittal silences; the *no*s that meant *yes.* She hadn't exactly been fair to Matt, but—

—as if prodded by electric shock, she shot out of the chair, walking purposefully toward the door. Safe from all but her own thoughts was not safe at all. She'd do better confronting the task at hand.

She threw open the door, began making her brisk way toward Fran Delaney's room.

When she rounded the first corner, *they* were there.

"Ms. Frankel," said the older woman, "my name is Iris McGreevey."

"And I'm Dallas Pemberton," the smaller, shaggy man said.

"Producer—"

"And director—"

"Of *A Doll's House,"* they finished together, managing, by sheerest chance, to fall into a rhythm that sounded rehearsed.

"Hi," Cathy responded, smiling in as kindly a manner as she could.

"If you need anything—"

"Anything at all—"

"We're here . . ." finishing together again.

"That's very good of you," Cathy said. "I'm sure Fran will appreciate it."

"She's great friends with her other cast members," Dallas said. "Should I arrange a visit or—"

"That," Cathy advised, "would be premature. In fact, it would be best if you didn't spread this around just yet."

"Well, what *should* we do?" Iris asked primly. "There's a performance tonight."

Through a short laugh that was mostly shock, Cathy said the only thing she could think of to keep her anger in check. "I'm sure that didn't come out the way you meant it."

Pemberton interposed gently, quickly, "To be honest, Ms. Frankel, I have a feeling that . . . whatever we say under the circumstances, some of it's bound to sound like insensitivity. You must know, we weren't remotely prepared for anything like this. On the one hand, we don't know what's proper. On the other hand, there are pragmatic considerations that are unavoidable."

Good save, thought Cathy—then, upon a better look at Pemberton, thought that perhaps it wasn't a "save" at all.

He was genuinely confused, trying to make sense out of an insane situation. What was that colloquial expression Matt would have used? *Welcome to the flub.* Because we have all flubbed. Yes, that sounded right.

Cathy was less sure about the sincerity of Iris McGreevey's concern. Cathy didn't much like her flinty-eyed expression. *There is a coldness to this woman,* she thought. But the little man beside Iris was so pitifully distraught, so open in his vulnerability (and his willingness to admit it), that he balanced out the equation.

That decided her.

"Walk with me," she said, heading toward a bank of elevators, setting the pace, speaking as briskly as she walked. "You need to keep in mind that Fran did not enter into this situation lightly. In order to express herself, she had to deny herself, the very *idea* of herself at a fundamental Tenctonese level. You can't tell anybody yet; she's too ashamed."

"I don't think there's a person in the company who won't empathize," Dallas said. "I think they'd rally to her support."

They reached the elevators, and Cathy punched the Up button. She studiously kept watching the indicator lights above the doors. Some odd impulse she was unable to articulate made her want to look away from this nice man. They were on the first floor. The indicator read six.

"Even worse," she sighed. "Empathy from those she set out to fool would probably only increase her shame . . . or reinforce her initial convictions. Both very dangerous during withdrawal."

"What," Iris asked, "would be so terrible if her original convictions were reinforced?"

"Iris," Dallas said warningly.

Cathy kept her eyes glued to the indicator. Five now. Why, oh, why were hospital elevators so slow? Again, she spoke without turning.

"I assume by that you mean, Why can't she just take the good stuff—pure Stabilite—and continue as before?"

Behind Cathy there was a palpable pause. She imagined that Dallas must have scowled at Iris in disapproval, because she was suddenly defensive. "Well, that *is* what I meant."

Cathy said, "She can't go back—"

Four now from the indicator.

"—because she has to thoroughly detox before any more foreign chemicals can be introduced into her system. And in order to detox, she has to revert. After that, assuming she *wanted* to do it all over again—even if she could afford to, which she can't—she'd have to start from the beginning."

"New surgery, too?" Dallas asked, stunned.

"Yes," Cathy replied.

Holding on three.

"God," he whispered softly. And then added, "I can't help but feel responsible."

Cathy hadn't expected that. She sort of didn't want to deal with it.

"You're not," she said, keeping it simple.

Holding on three. What in Andarko's name were they *doing* up there?

"I wouldn't have cast her if she'd come to me as a Newcomer."

Bingo. *That* was why she didn't want to face him. Because, nice as he was, *that* would always be the truth. She could hear in his voice, though, that it was not an admission he was proud of. And so she offered him a little slack . . .

"Ask yourself this. Given what you've learned in the last twelve hours, would you cast her now?"

Holding on three.

Ding!

Behind her.

It *would* be an elevator from the bank in the opposite wall that came first. Which meant she had to turn—and face him for his reply.

To his credit, he looked at her squarely.

"I can't answer that. I'm sorry."

She wanted to say, *Congratulations.* Now *you're responsible.* But that seemed harsher, more judgmental, than she had any right to be. So she opted for the neutral standby.

"I'm sorry, too," she said, walking past him and Iris into the waiting elevator.

"Ms. Frankel," she heard Iris's voice—that woman, *I don't like that woman*—and faced forward, holding the Door Open button, wishing other people had been waiting for the elevator so she'd have a reason to excuse herself. But no . . . it was just her. And them. She didn't prompt Iris, merely waited for her to continue.

"Fran Delaney's situation does raise inevitable business questions. About whether or not we can continue to run the show with an understudy. About whether or not to look for a replacement. About what kind of damages, if any, Ms. Delaney is liable for—"

"What?" Cathy blurted, only a millisecond before it came out of Dallas's mouth as well.

"She signed on to do a job. One she was clearly in no condition to complete. The entire company is at risk, not just the production. I've been left holding the bag, as they say, and I need some barometer by which to gauge matters. You being on the case, I thought—"

"Think again, Ms. McGreevey. The answers to those questions are between you and your soul." Cathy released the Door Open button, the elevator began to enclose her, and she just had time to add, before the sliding doors broke their gaze, "If you can find it."

On the third floor, a nurse told her that Fran had been moved to the fifth. Room 503, to be precise.

Already? Cathy thought. *All I did was leave to make a phone call.*

And she headed back toward the elevators.

The fifth floor was the psychiatric ward. Its west wing

contained the patients with bent minds, who needed constant supervision, or restraint, or continuous medication—

Or, like Fran Delaney/Fancy Delancey, isolation.

The elevator doors opened, and Cathy was treated to the background noises that permeated the air like ceaseless, sad underscoring—intermittent cries of despair, muffled gibbering. Not nearly so profound or unsettling as they might have been in a specialized medical facility—this was, after all, but one part of a comprehensive hospital complex—but what she heard was unsettling enough.

She was almost used to it, though.

She'd spent enough time getting used to the layout last night.

Young Dr. Steinbach—it suddenly struck her like the name of some iconographic movie character, *Young Dr. Steinbach;* it was good to smile at that; it would probably be her last unburdened smile for quite a stretch—was waiting for her to return from phoning Matt.

"She's a little more coherent now," he began.

"You fellows don't waste a minute," she said, by way of greeting.

"I've learned that as soon as they come around, you gotta move them from an unsupervised bed to a detox cubicle. They need the bouncing-around room. Besides, she's burning off the effects of the sedative unusually fast."

"Does that mean anything?"

"I *think* it means her metabolism has unleashed itself, now that the cycle of Stabilite has been broken. I've seen withdrawal take anywhere from a week to two, but if she's become conscious this quickly, my guess is the process is going to rip through her like a tornado."

"Why doesn't that sound encouraging?"

"Because it's not. She's going to be hit with every kind of trauma there is in a very short period of time."

"Are you saying she won't survive?"

"If I knew that for sure, I would've put you in a cab and

sent you home. All I'm saying is, I've only had one other patient in accelerated withdrawal . . ."

". . . and she didn't make it."

"He. And no, he didn't." A beat. "On the other hand, he didn't have another Newcomer to take him through it minute by minute. Like what *you're* about to do." Another beat. "You're sure you *know* what you're about to do?"

"Yes. And no. But mostly yes. I think."

"Well, either way, you're braver by far than I."

"I doubt that."

"Don't."

He reached into a pocket of his lab coat, held out a wrist band.

"Here it is. Do I need to take you through it again?"

"No. The green button alerts the on-call nurse at the desk to check the closed-circuit monitor, in case there's something I want you guys to see. The red button is the alarm for an emergency. If I need help getting out."

"Right. Now, for leaving the cube on your own steam, do you remember the code?"

"Yes, 3051, and I'm to cover the keypad with my palm so the patient doesn't figure out the sequence."

"Okay."

He strapped the band to her wrist and, when he was done, held her hand a few moments longer than necessary. She didn't mind. It wasn't a romantic gesture but rather an acknowledgment of admiration for her courage. She nodded, and he let go.

Then she moved to the door, looked through the small, wire-enforced window. *Studio apt, 1 rm, unfrnshd, padded,* she thought.

At first glance Fran wasn't visible. Just the rubber-colored walls and floor. In the opposite right corner, a toilet and sink were installed. Cathy almost said, "I can't see her," and then remembered to look at the high left corner, to the rounded mirror behind the wire mesh shield, which gave a fun-house perspective of the whole room. It showed that Fran was huddled in the corner on Cathy's left, against the wall that was flush with the door. (What it didn't show was the video camera behind the mirror, which was, of course, a two-way affair.)

Fran's position relative to the door meant that Cathy would have to exercise caution going in. As she'd been briefed, the cell door swung inward, left. Sometimes "they" liked to spring at you when you entered, using the door as a nice, versatile weapon. "They" could ram it into you if you were behind it; ram you into *it,* if *it* was behind *you;* sandwich you or any part of you between the door and the frame . . . a door could do all kinds of serious damage.

Not that Fran seemed poised to attack. She was seated. Leaning up against the wall, head back, dark circles under closed eyes, looking a little wasted, as if she'd merely slept badly. Feet apart, knees bent, in repose.

Attractive, human, unremarkable.

Except for the straitjacket.

Cathy reached for the control panel on the side of the door, punched in the code, and the electronic lock *snicked* open.

Steinbach waited until Cathy had entered the cubicle. Waited while the hydraulic loaded door had hissed shut behind her and the lock had *snicked* shut. Through the window, he saw her wince slightly at the sound.

Then he walked to the nurse's station to check the monitor and make sure the camera was working properly.

It was.

He was watching Cathy speaking with Fran when his superior, Dr. Casey, showed up.

"How's she look?" asked the big, basso-voiced Newcomer.

Steinbach guessed he meant the patient. "Too soon to tell," he replied. "Every indication of being a rough ride, though."

"How rough?"

"Industrial strength."

Casey signaled the head nurse, addressed her and Steinbach both.

"Our Ms. Frankel is a noble volunteer, but you pull her out at the first sign of danger, I don't care *how* vehemently she insists she has it under control. You're not to make a judgment call, you're to err on the side of caution."

Steinbach and the nurse nodded soberly.

Fran's head turned slowly to meet Cathy's gaze.

"I know you?" Voice a bit dulled, still druggy.

"We've been touching base, on and off, since last night. I don't expect you to remember."

"What am I doing here?"

"Has nobody told you?"

"I need my medication. I tried to explain to them."

"Your medication is why you're here. I'm here to help you with your *Leethaag.*"

Fran's eyes went wide at recognition of the Tenctonese word that meant "The Healing." She tried to cover the recognition by shaking her head emphatically. It looked more like she was trying to shake off the last vestiges of sedative.

"No," she said. Then with each rock of her head, "No, no, no, no, no, no, no, no. I don't know what that thing is you say. I have high blood pressure. I need—"

"Fran, this is a *hospital.* You're surrounded by *doctors.* You can't keep it up, not in here."

"I need my medication," she repeated hoarsely.

"No, that's the last thing you need. It was killing you."

Fran Delaney beat her head against the padded wall three times. "They told me it was *saaaafe,*" she whimpered.

"I know. They lied."

Fran buried her face in the padding of the wall, sniffled a while. Cathy tried another tack.

"I saw you perform last night. You were magnificent."

Fran's eyes closed, shutting back tears. She sniffled, did not turn away from the wall.

"Thank you." A long pause. "Looks as if you caught the farewell performance."

Cathy moved in closer. "It doesn't have to be like that."

Sharply, suddenly, head whipping about: *"What would you know about it?"*

The abruptness startled Cathy. Alerted her, too, that despite any appearances to the contrary, normalcy was simply not a guest in this room.

"I know that our people can do anything," she replied, quietly, choosing to ignore that the question had been rhetorical.

"Civilians," muttered Fran disdainfully.

Then she looked up at Cathy, really looked at her for the first time. Taking her measure.

"Tell you something, civilian," she said, and this time the word did not sound unkind, "I used to be pretty like you. Now I'm pretty like this. . . . This is what pays the bills."

Cathy crouched down at a slight distance.

"I don't think it was ever about paying the bills for you, Fran. At least not *primarily* about that. I *saw* you last night, I *saw* how . . . how you transformed yourself. Not cosmetically. I mean the *other* way. It's a remarkable gift. And it must be a remarkable release, borne of a remarkable need. I can't imagine what it would be like to have such a gift and . . . and feel as if you couldn't share it, express it, use it."

One corner of Fran's mouth lifted.

"Yeah. Yeah, you can. You're pretty smart for a civilian."

"Thanks."

"You a doctor?"

"In a sense. Biochemist."

"You don't have patients, then?"

Cathy allowed herself to sit.

"Just you," she said.

"And *what* is so special about me that you feel compelled to guide me through a *Leethaag?*"

Cathy considered the various ways to answer that question.

She could mention being here on behalf of Matt Sikes. But Matt had been vague about the nature of his relationship with Fran. And Fran had bolted from Matt at the theatre last night. Big gamble, with those facts in evidence, to assume that Fran held Matt warmly in her hearts. The bond she'd created with Fran was fragile enough. Any mention of Matt might undo it completely, with no chance of repair.

I'm here on behalf of a friend. Another possible way to answer Fran's question. But such a response would certainly arouse Fran's curiosity, and it might complicate matters later.

The best answer was a no-frills truth.

"I'm a volunteer," said Cathy. Probably Fran would assume there was some kind of official program.

"Oh," responded Fran. "A do-gooder."

Fine. Let her.

"Curious phrase, do-gooder," Fran continued after a while. "It always sounded backwards to me. Shouldn't it be good-*do*er?"

Cathy laughed a little. "I take your point."

Fran laughed too.

Moment of connection. The first.

"I was a do-gooder once," Fran said wistfully.

"Tell me?"

"Might," Fran replied easily, so easily that when she slipped in, "Think we might take this thing off for a while?"—talking, of course, about the straitjacket—Cathy was barely aware of the desperate manipulation.

They will do anything to get loose, Steinbach had warned. *That's a step removed from getting out. And that's a step closer to the drug.*

And this one's an actress, Cathy reminded herself. A great one.

"Let's see how it goes first," Cathy replied, just as casually—but, wow, did something go hard in Fran's eyes, and, wow, did it happen fast.

"Sure, I know what that's about." Fran said it calmly, but with a layer of frost, and made a tacit point of looking away.

Cathy reached out hesitantly to touch Fran. Lightly, barely a brush, nothing too familiar, just . . . an overture. Something. Damage control.

"I'm going to have to earn your trust, I know that. But if it's anything to start with, I am in this for the long haul. I'll be here for you . . . all the way."

Fran shrugged under the straitjacket.

"Good," she said.

Yes, he'd better love me a whole lot, thought Cathy.

And on that note the *Leethaag* began.

CHAPTER 7

THE STORYBOARD LAID out like this . . .

PANEL ONE: Start out with a Tenctonese businesswoman in a swank restaurant; she's as classy as her surroundings, a genuine stunner in a form-hugging business outfit, just sexy enough to raise eyebrows, though not so revealing that you get any vibe from her other than top-of-the-line smarts. It's lunch hour, and in the background, with all the suits, attaché cases and cellular phones around, we know this woman is a serious player.

PANEL TWO: The waiter serves her prelunch cocktail, a sour-milk-and-strawberry daiquiri.

PANEL THREE: And as she starts to raise it to her lips—

PANEL FOUR: A glimpse of her earlier in the morning, huddled with a human male client, poring over paperwork, real face-to-face stuff. (This panel is shaded in sepia, the idea to indicate that, on film, we'd cut from full-color steadicam shots to hand-held cinema verité stuff, the better to instantly distinguish between the restaurant and the rest of her day.)

PANEL FIVE: Back at the five-star feed, and now starters

are being served, raw beaver tail in an endive sauce over purple cabbage with slices of carrot and raisins.

PANEL SIX: She starts to eat, delicately forking a slice into her mouth and—

PANEL SEVEN: Another part of her day, she's at a department store, the jewelry counter, the salesgirl helping her adjust a very elegant earring, and, as before, the faces are close and—

PANEL EIGHT: The restaurant again, an over-the-shoulder angle on our heroine, as the main course is placed on the table: a half weasel covered in a special, cold orange glaze and we proceed to—

PANEL NINE: —and in this one we don't see her chow down (because we've seen her eating twice now, no need to be artlessly schematic), we just see her beautiful face turn up to thank the waiter, and if we're alert (and if all goes well, we should be), we're starting to detect a pattern. She's eating some pretty odiferous stuff—at least by human standards—and yet she has to interact on a *constant, face-to-face basis* with humans. And, to make the point emphatically—

PANELS TEN and ELEVEN: She races for, and gets into, a crowded elevator, a *seriously* crowded elevator, and as the doors close, we return to—

PANEL TWELVE: —the restaurant, one last time. Our heroine is spooning the last of her dessert from a parfait glass. This time we don't *see* what she's eating, but chances are it's just as Newcomer-specific as every other course. And that explains why—

PANEL THIRTEEN: —she reaches into her pocketbook and her hand emerges holding—

PANEL FOURTEEN: —a tiny breath-spray vial and—

PANEL FIFTEEN: —she opens her sensual mouth and gives herself a discreet little spritz.

PANEL SIXTEEN: Insert of the product in its various forms. Bottled mouthwash, breath spray, breath mints. Especially prominent is the logo design. It resembles a famous work of art in one respect: looked at one way, it's the silhouette of a goblet (and one might imagine that goblet filled with sour milk). Looked at another way, it's the silhouette of two faces, nose to nose. Difference between the logo and its famous progenitor is in ours the goblet shape appears engagingly uneven. That's because when your eyes invert the silhouette to perceive faces, you realize that one face is the silhouette of a human, the other the silhouette of a Newcomer. The product name, underneath, in a Chicago-based font, reads: **TENCTON-EASE.**

PANEL SEVENTEEN: The last. The Newcomer businesswoman exiting the restaurant, returning to the hustle and the bustle of the streets, the fast-paced rhythm of her consequential life. And over this, the slogan, the moral of our story:

"Tencton-ease. It helps. Face it."

"Well, it couldn't be finer," Jonathan Besterman said. "I like it a lot. And I *love* the logo."

Jonathan was one of Susan's coworkers. He was slim, brown-haired, good-humored, managing to be very friendly while staying a little bit remote; an interesting fellow from Chicago (just like the logo font), whose speech was flavored with that city's characteristic broad *a.* It was rumored that he was homosexual, and it was rumored that he was not, but he never betrayed his preference either way, not at work. He was no less an enigma to Susan than to anyone else in the office, but she tended to gravitate toward his energy, which was positive and enthusiastic. Very *much* so, right now.

"Yeah. Classy. Understated. To the point." A beat. "A little *fun*ny . . ."

Susan blinked. A bit defensively, she said, "I didn't *mean* for it to be funny."

Jonathan held up a soothing hand. "I know, I know, and that's *okay.* I just want to prepare you, that's all. You're gonna get some smiles, and they shouldn't throw you. Smiles are good if you're hip to them."

They were standing in the plush, blue-carpeted office of

one of their bosses, account executive Keith Berries. Neither Keith, nor the client for whom Susan's pitch was designed, was there at the moment. Susan had been allowed this advance time to set up her presentation. Jonathan, a more experienced hand at the ad game than she, had volunteered to help her with some last minute refinements. And encouragement.

Or at least what *should* have been encouragement. The "smiles" part was throwing her.

"Why should anyone smile?"

Jonathan spread his hands, shrugging in a way that made him resemble Tevye the dairyman in *Fiddler on the Roof.* "Like your slogan says, face it. You're about to show a coupla white guys a woman eating weasel in a five-star restaurant. To most of them it's a total incongruity. And, even though they'll be too smart to say anything, you can just bet they'll be making off-color jokes to themselves about the appetizer."

"What kind of jokes can they make about a simple appetizer of—"

"I'll tell you later. But, as I say, that shouldn't be a problem. If you know it's gonna happen, you can roll with it. Keep in mind that the ad is directed at Newcomers, not humans. Make sure *they* keep it in mind, and I think you're gonna come outta this smelling like money."

She pursed her lips. "I don't know that money smells like anything much."

"As long as it smells like something they want." Jonathan took one last look at the easel holding the storyboard sketches, made a *Here, help me* gesture, and they grabbed the easel on either side. "Move it a bit more to the left where the light is better, if they're gonna be sitting where those chairs are."

He stood back, appraised everything once more.

"Beauty."

There was a tap on the door, which then opened, with no pretense at waiting for a response. Keith Berries stuck his head in.

"You ready?"

As always, the voice was soft, but authoritative.

"Willing and able," Jonathan said on Susan's behalf, for which she was grateful.

"All right, veddy good," Berries said lightly, and entered.

He was a tall, solidly built man with close-cropped red hair and a fashionable mustache. He was renowned, justifiably, for his brilliance at the ad game; for being one of those uncanny fellows who could look at a problem from five different angles simultaneously, drawing upon not only the perspective of his own long experience, but the history of media advertising in America, which he knew cold. "Cold" likewise described the impression he left on most people. The same objective detachment that allowed him to function so effectively at his job also limited his personal appeal.

Whereas Jonathan was private, Berries had no particular secrets. Yet it was Jonathan who was emotionally accessible, while Berries treated everyone with clinical bemusement. It was said that on a passion scale ranging from one to ten, Berries' personal barometer stopped at approximately seven.

Berries' entrance was followed by that of a shorter, dapper, slightly stocky fellow, dressed in the kind of clothes that are made to appear casual while seeking to draw attention. He had longish blond hair swept back over his ears, which were unusually large, and the air of someone who was industrious but somehow lazy; someone who survived on great personal charm and unrefined instinct more than intellect; someone who was arrogant, and knew it, and liked it. This was Kent Allman, the client, who also happened to be vice president of the company that manufactured Tencton-ease.

"This is where I do my graceful exit," Jonathan whispered, and winked. "Good luck."

He left as Berries made the introductions and the two men took seats, Berries behind his desk, Allman in a new-wave swiveler that allowed him to alternately face Berries or Susan when she was at the easel.

At a nod from Berries, Susan began her pitch.

Not an easy thing to do, pitching, not for Susan, anyway, and it was her least favorite part of the job. It wasn't enough that her idea was good, she had to tell it well, *sell* it well; and no matter how much she'd rehearsed it in the privacy of her office or home or car, there was an intangible *something* about the live bodies in front of her that changed the equation and altered every preconception. The energy in the room could be up, or down; the people listening could be enthusiastic or bored and could change from one extreme to the other like *that.* She had to concentrate not only on her proposal, but *their* level of interest, and she had to modulate the presentation accordingly. If she was losing them, she had to get to the good stuff, cut to the chase. If they started asking a lot of questions, or became needful of reassurance, she had to be prepared to pad with extra material, or worse, to improvise. (She had no particular desire to perform, but on occasions such as this, she admired people like that actress Fran Delaney, for whom it all came so easily.)

In addition, pitching was heavily political, requiring a certain amount of guile which was not part of Susan's natural makeup. On some fundamental level, she liked to believe that the work—the art—should speak for itself. But she'd picked up some skills and instincts through osmosis. Her genuine enthusiasm and personableness tended to carry her the rest of the way, as did her life experience. Simply being a good parent, sensitive to the incremental changes in her kids, had trained her to deal with the capricious shifts of people in the business arena. So a pitch—while still somewhat frightening, and always a little loathsome—was something she could accomplish intelligently.

Most times.

This pitch, however, was difficult.

She had known in her hearts that it would be, the minute she'd begun. Berries kept listening impassively, of course, and she had long since gotten used to that—but Allman. Allman was scowling. Not unhappily, but rather like a man trying to decipher a foreign film without aid of subtitles. And his expression didn't change even to produce the brief smiles Jonathan had predicted.

It so unnerved her that in the middle of the pitch, she broke stride—something she had learned *never* to do—and said, "Do you want me to go over any of this again?"

Allman gave a short shake of the head and a brief, two-fingered wave. "No, no, go ahead, I'm with you."

Clearly, then, he *was* being attentive. So what was that expression on his face *about?*

It wasn't until Susan was nearly through her spiel that the image came back to her—a man trying to decipher a foreign film without aid of subtitles—and she suddenly understood Allman's expression. It was the face of a man trying . . . to figure out a problem.

She exposed the final panel, wrapped up . . . and waited.

Allman nodded once, briefly, said "Good work," his cursory tone indicating it was less a compliment than an acknowledgment, and before she could even smile a thank you, Allman swiveled to face Berries, got up, leaned over Berries' desk, and whispered to him.

It was a stunningly rude thing to do. Berries, of course, took it blithely, his voice so naturally soft-spoken that he seemed to be whispering back, which didn't help.

She could make out none of what they were saying, merely the rises and falls of hushed inflections; and she stood there getting hotter and hotter in the face, knowing nothing except that they were talking about her. Or at least her work, which was a part of her and, therefore, amounted to the same thing. They might at least have asked her to leave the room. It wouldn't have made her any less nervous, but she would've *understood*—

Her thoughts were interrupted as Allman turned and sat back down.

Berries spoke first. As usual, his compliments were maddeningly understated, and he sometimes inflected declarative statements as if they were questions.

"I don't really have a problem with it?" he said. "I even think it could work on a couple of basic levels? My biggest issue is that it's a bit familiar—which is okay if that's what you're going for. Audiences often respond well to what they know."

"Uh huh," she said, noncommittally, just to hold up her end of the conversation. She dared not ask what made Berries think any part of it was "familiar," certainly not in front of the client. To do so would indicate the impolitic truth: that she had sincerely thought she was onto something unique.

"But," Berries continued, "Mr. Allman has some bigger issues that . . . sort of make a lot of sense to me?"

Allman nodded.

"Right, right. First of all, *good* presentation, really *good.*"

Bletro, thought Susan. A Tenctonese word which, in this context, translated roughly as "Yikes."

"It's just—here's the thing, okay? Kimchee."

Susan blinked. It had sounded like a sneeze, but clearly it had not been.

"I beg your pardon?"

"Kimchee. It's a Korean appetizer. All kinds of kimchee, but the most popular kind is a white cabbage in this intense red sauce. Not just spicy, *deadly.* Like ingesting paint thinner."

"Okay . . . ?" It was the best she could offer. She had no idea where this was heading.

"Thing is, this red sauce has a heavy garlic base. As strong as it is hot."

"Oh?"

"Yeah. See . . . let me work backwards from what I really responded to, okay?"

Ah. There was something he liked.

"Sure."

"I'm a New York boy, and I'm thinking of this neighborhood where my grandmother lived, in Sunnyside. All along Queens Boulevard, like from Thirty-eighth Street to Forty-ninth, Korean restaurants. Kimchee palaces. And parallel to Queens Boulevard, there's the elevated train station, gets you on the number seven, which I used to take to Manhattan."

"Right, right," she said. As if she had a clue. Still waiting for him to connect with the thing he'd "responded to."

"Well, you get onto a crowded subway car with a bunch of Koreans after they've had their daily dose of kimchee? Whoo, man, I gotta tell ya, it's like being in the sardine can from hell. No way out, no air to breathe except this yukky garlic fog."

And now she had to say it. "I'm sorry, I feel like I'm missing something."

"No," Berries chimed in, with one of his rare, toothy smiles, "you're not. The point is about to be made. Could you go back to panel number ten?"

"Which one is that?" *She* didn't even know them by number, only by graphic.

"Uhh, the elevator, I believe?"

She brought it forward. "This?"

Allman practically grabbed it out of her hands.

"Yes! Right! Here it is! The key to the campaign! The elevator bit!"

"Bit?"

"You've got the seeds of great comedy here. Comedy scores points. That woman on an elevator after her lunch of beaver and curds? Picture it. People around her could be just, like—*hurling* themselves against the walls, anything to get out."

"Why?"

"Because her breath—"

"No, I mean, why make the point so broadly when you—"

"Because, trust me, honey, *comedy sells.* People *remember* it."

Honey? Susan thought. Not judging it yet, just noting it.

"I tend to agree?" Berries added. "I mean, the campaign

you've laid out here would be ef-*fec*-tive"—drawing out the word to express his reservations—"but it's a little upscale, when really the product should appeal to a broader range."

"Exactly!" from Allman.

"Well," Susan began, "what if the main character wasn't a businesswoman? We could change the career. We could even do a series of ads, focusing on dif—"

"The thing is," Allman interrupted, "I've *always* had good experiences with comedy. Comedy spots for toothpaste, cough drops, even deodorant. It sends a message. Not only is the product good, it's *entertaining*. And the more you exaggerate the consequences of not using the product, the more self-conscious the buyer is about not having it in his or her arsenal."

It was said with such assurance it sounded true.

"I mean," he continued, "I was looking at those face-to-face panels and I felt as if I wanted to laugh . . ."

(So *that's* what was going on, thought Susan, *that* was the problem he was trying to figure out. How to turn something serious-minded into a lampoon. *He was rewriting me even before I was done.* And *now* she began to judge him a little, the verdict getting harsher as he spoke.)

". . . And that feeling of wanting to laugh and not laughing—I think it confuses the audience."

Susan looked toward Berries for some sort of support or, at least, guidance. He pitched his chin a bit forward, his eyes seemingly focused on his own thoughts, and casually bit his lower lip. "Uhhh—ye-ah," he said, softly. "I don't know that I'd articulate it quite like that, but I will say the impact of humor can't be underestimated." In other words, Berries was choosing his battles, and debating a client over a fine point of philosophy was not one of them.

"You know what?" Allman said, swiveling to face Berries, away from Susan, his voice rising as if divine inspiration had finally struck. "Better than the elevator! I mean, that's closed, a box, right? Visually not very interesting. Let's get a little motion into it, a little light and color like—like me with the Koreans. Set the thing on a subway car. Same principle, but heightened production values. Picture it. People cowering from the bad breath, then as soon as the train reaches its next stop, the doors slide open and the entire complement of passengers clears out in a mad stampede (we speed up the film for that), leaving our heroine alone. Adrift. Asking herself, 'What's wrong with this picture?' "

Much as I am now, thought Susan. . . .

"The problem there is?" Berries said gently, "Los Angeles is not known for its public transportation? Subways are an East Coast phenomenon."

Totally unflustered by his own careless gaffe, Allman said, "A bus then. Better still. Outdoor locations, movement through the windows. People trying to *open* the windows and we *know* how hard those bus windows are to open! Yeah, that could be really funny, who wouldn't identify with *that?* Everybody screaming at the driver, anything to get some fresh air. Picture it. The bus stops and even the *driver* gets out. Yeah. That'd work fine. I mean, I'm *sure* you guys have *buses."* He swiveled back to Susan. "Yeah. Put her on a bus!"

"Well, I can't put *her* on a bus," Susan said.

Allman's face darkened.

"Course you can, why not?" Spoiling for a fight now. He had gotten all juiced and she was raining on his parade.

Berries smoothly interposed:

"I think what Susan is saying, correctly, is that her campaign's particular character, in *this* city, is a bit too high up on the social ladder to take buses. Cabs or a car, most likely." A beat. "But I think what Kent is saying, also correctly? Is that we don't need the woman to be that character anymore. In fact, if we're going comic, what *can* she be?"

"Housewife?" A banal, knee-jerk solution. Allman's, naturally.

"I think we can be more memorable than that."

"Waitress?"

"No, it makes a false issue of her job."

"Librarian."

"Hmmm."

It was like some kind of surreal Ping-Pong match in which she had suddenly become merely a spectator.

"Librarian," mused Berries. "Not too subservient, not too powerful. Nice balance. Easy career to put across in costume. I could see her prim, in glasses, carrying a couple of books with those drab library bindings. And no question a woman who deals face-to-face with people all day, so we're covered for symbolism." He tapped his desk with the palm of his hand a few times. "All roighty. That's the way we're going to go."

It had happened so fast that Susan was barely able to absorb it. And there was more yet to absorb.

"Okay now—how do we feel about the logo?" Berries queried. It was a "we" Susan didn't much feel a part of. But she dutifully pulled out the correct panel without being asked.

"I was meaning to ask about that," Allman said. "It looks"—squinting at it—"sort of like a cup." He looked up at Susan. "Why is it a cup?"

Susan was now beginning to wonder if she should even bother. But she gamely pointed out that it was a positive-negative use of space, a fairly standard technique of pop art. It took Allman a disturbingly long time to grasp the concept, recognize the silhouette of faces.

"Oh! Ah. Right, faces. Close together, *I* see . . ." Clearly not sold, though. "Now, about the cup . . ."

Just as gamely, Susan explained that she meant it as a connection with mealtime.

"Hm," said Allman. "Yeah, I don't—"

"It is a bit of a reach for me too, Susan," Berries sighed, "because the metaphor is indirect. A cup implies drink, not food—and not every drink goes with a meal and . . . well, I think you can do better, is the thing."

"Actually," said Allman, "I think it's there already. Forget the cup, go with the faces. Except not silhouettes. Fill 'em out. A happy, smiling Newcomer facing a happy, smiling human. Bright colors, bold outlines. Comic book style, simple and cheery. *That* I could go for."

Berries raised his eyebrows, wrinkled his forehead, smiled playfully, and spread his hands. "Well . . . there it is." He nodded at Susan. "You know what to do."

Allman got up, clapping his hands together. "Great. Just great." To Berries, he said, "I'll stop by tomorrow, then?"

Berries to Susan: "That give you enough time?"

"Well, to *rough* it, sure, but—"

"That's all we'll need."

Allman shook Berries' hand, pantomimed a gunshot at Susan, and he was gone.

Susan stared, a bit dumbfounded, at the door long after Kent Allman had made his exit.

"Susan?"

She turned. Berries was rising from his desk.

"Everything okay?"

"Fine, Keith. I think. I guess."

"I think I know what's troubling you, and I understand it? You thought the assignment was one thing and now it's another?"

"Partly that. Partly something else."

"Oh? What?"

"I'm not sure yet. I mean, I guess I can get behind the new approach, but—"

"Then that's all that really matters?"

"I suppose . . ."

"This was not a disaster, Susan; the client saw something in your proposal and ran with it. You tried for something classier, he wanted to go another way. He *is* paying the freight and he *did* have a point. It happens?"

"Yes, but . . . his way, the main character is a buffoon."

"So's the Maytag repairman. And Ronald McDonald is a clown. I think the lesson to keep in mind here is? We're in a noble profession, and performing a valuable service, but ultimately? We're not curing cancer. We're just selling stuff." He looked at his watch. "Anyway, I have a lunch appointment. So take your time clearing out. I'll speak on ya later." And he strode out of the office.

Susan fell into a chair, covered her eyes with a hand, and sighed heavily, trying to collect thoughts that stubbornly clung to the back of her mind, which refused, for the moment, to come out of hiding.

Jonathan Besterman poked his head into the office.

"So? Sing me a song of victory."

She looked up at him, smiled weakly. "He . . . e . . . lp," she sang tunelessly, the word drifting through several sickly sounding pitches.

Jonathan entered, his face showing concern.

"Oh, no. What happened?"

"That's just it. I don't know! The whole thing just . . . got away from me. I don't know how, and I was standing right here!"

"Uh-oh. One of Those." A beat. "Did you get your smiles?"

"Worse. The client wants to go comic altogether."

"What?"

"I know."

"What'd Keith say?"

"He said we weren't curing cancer."

Suddenly Jonathan was furious. "I *hate* that. I *hate* that attitude. I don't want to hear somebody telling me what I do with my life isn't curing cancer, isn't as *important* as curing cancer. What we do takes brains, taste, training, craft, talent, and it *means* something."

And she loved him right then for that little speech, for his passion, for hitting ten on the scale, where Berries, today, hadn't even neared his usual seven.

Jonathan closed his eyes, calmed himself.

"I'm sorry. I'm not angry at you."

"I know that."

"Replay the meeting for me."

And she did. Blow by blow. When she was done, Jonathan was very quiet. At length, he said, "So you left it with Berries that you could get behind the new approach."

"I thought so."

"But?"

"But I really don't think it's all that funny. And it's making me . . . tired. *Literally* tired."

Another long silence from Jonathan.

"What?" Susan prompted.

Carefully, he said, "Your conscious mind is trying to protect you from your unconscious thoughts. The truth is too painful. You have no reason to be tired. Your body's shutting down in lieu of an anesthetic. What you're feeling isn't fatigue. It's passive rage. Believe me, I speak from experience."

She looked at him. Surprised. "You know . . . I *am* angry. But I still don't know why. It's not like pitches haven't turned around on me before."

"There's a reason why this one's different . . . a reason why the new approach isn't funny."

"Tell me."

"I don't think I have to. Koreans and kimchee? People cowering from a Newcomer in an enclosed space? *You* figure it out."

That's when the penny dropped.

"It's racist," she said softly.

And now her anger was a very real thing.

And she had no idea what to do with it.

Because she needed her job.

CHAPTER 8

MOSTLY, THE PLACE reminded Matt of an infected needle.

He didn't know why that should be; sensibly, you'd think a guy running a shady business in public would want to deflect suspicion by making the environment as pristine as possible. But *See Gurd Nurras*—The Drug Runners—was unmistakably a dump.

For one thing, it had the signature smells of neglect: must, overapplied disinfectant, corrosion and age, combining to create a thick, sweet, ubiquitous odor like stale, rotting wood. For another, the shelves had been wiped down only cursorily, front ledges primarily, and that only a half-assed nod toward the niceties. Anyone chancing to move around some merchandise on those shelves and peer into the back rows of boxes might be likely to find everything from the odd dust devil to an evenly spread dust blanket, sometimes obscuring product names entirely.

Best, though—or worst, if you couldn't retain your mordant sense of humor—was the condition of the merchandise itself, which included water-stained boxes, some broken safety seals, and expiration dates that had already come and gone.

A quarter of a pad's worth of citations. Easy.

The drugstore had not been easy to find, even with the address. In that maddening way of many commercial businesses, the street number was not displayed on the door, the window, or the minimal awning. Furthermore, it was in the shadiest part of Little Tencton, a seventeen-block stretch known by law enforcement types as The Badlands (and, among the less enlightened, Slagtown). Humans—or, as they were most commonly referred to in this area, "Terts" —didn't often show their hairy heads during business hours, and *never* after dark, if they knew what was good for them.

This area had the highest concentration of Newcomer prostitution, street gang crime, and drug traffic in all of Little Tencton. It was also the area in which violent crime stood the least chance of being punished because so much of it was random.

Even on the widest possible street, even out in the open, you still couldn't escape the claustrophobic depression. On all but the cruel faces (and there were many of those, many) hung the haunted, desperate look which tacitly cried for a way out: The Badlands was filled with free civilians who were indistinguishable in mood from prison lifers. And among them, every now and again, had been an angry Newcomer actress.

Matt silently tried to understand. The woman had been a PACT worker, a crisis trainer—naiveté did not figure into the package.

What the hell had she been *doing* here? What had driven pretty, talented Fancy Delancey to *this* goddamn place? To *this* neighborhood, which seemed so utterly alien to anything in her artistic nature; which seemed to willfully suffocate any attempt at growth, at self-expression; to actively camouflage any sense of specialness, of . . . ?

That, of course, was the answer. She wanted to bury her personality. No chance of recognition here. She'd pass through, anonymous, unnoticed, unremarkable, unfamiliar but for being another Tenctonese face. He did wonder, though, how she managed to pull off the same parlor trick once she had "changed" into Fran Delaney? Obviously she came back to this pathetic place for her refills. How did she remain neutral? Or did she?

Maybe he'd get the opportunity to ask her. Sometime.

Business first.

Matt Sikes affected an apprehensive, slightly nervous posture and Business began in earnest.

Working at the scale with the old rubber gloves on, measuring out a wee tincture of this, a teensy dram of that, humming rum-te-tum under his breath, Bob Sled, owner, operator, and head pharmacist at *See Gurd Nurras* cocked half an eye at the curved mirror high up in the corner overlooking the store. Not a lotta customers here today.

Two women, checking through the over-the-counter feminine stuff; one guy, suit (didn't get too many suits in here, hmmmm), biggish nose, plastic basket on his arm, moving his methodical way through the aisles, working off a shopping list (list pegged him as a regular hubby, though, out on errands, Wifey's Will Be Done), and—

Hey-hoo, what's this?

A Tert.

Fewer Terts than suits this neck of the woods.

This one wearing a gray jogger's sweatshirt with a hood. Hood over the head. Pretty odd for indoors on a warm day.

Bob Sled looked back down at his scale. Mix the powders carefully, rum-te-tum, tap the mixture into a bottle, rum-te-tum, lay out the empty capsules and fill those puppies later, tum-tiddle-um-tum, and belly up to the counter, boys, survey your domain.

"Help you, Chief?" he said.

Bob Sled was a short, chunky Newcomer wearing a white shirt, sleeves rolled up over his elbows, a tie loose around his collar, and glasses in a black frame. His stature was somewhat mitigated by the fact that the floor behind the counter was elevated: Everyone had to look up to him, tee-hee, pun intended. His was the kind of face that, had it the ability to sport facial hair, would've worn a jaunty mustache. So disarming, really, that you'd never know he had already opened a drawer behind the counter, which gave him easy access to a loaded gun. He'd been robbed before, but never again. And not by a Tert for cert.

This Tert seemed genuinely unsettled to be addressed, like he wasn't quite ready yet; eyes were darting uncomfortably; didn't want to make eye contact, this boy.

And mumbled when he talked.

"Yeah, um, got a prescription here . . . somewhere."

The Tert dug into several pockets, the pants, the sweatshirt, pulled out a piece of paper, all crumpled, like it'd been clutched for security. Already Bob had a feeling what was on it, took the prescription off the man and, *right the first time, wotta guy,* hey-hoo, Stabilite.

Another look at the Tert. The ersatz Tert.

'Splained the hood right enough. Hair not all grown in, cranium still probably looking funky.

Hell of a nice job on the face, though. A fooler.

"Usually I can tell," Bob Sled said, a short nod of approval.

"Yeah, um, wouldja mind? I mean . . ." The ersatz Tert gestured lamely at his surroundings, not wanting this conversation overheard or even interpreted. Not that Bob had said anything that could remotely give away the game.

"Hey, Chief, what, I say somethin'?" He looked at the prescription again. Using the generic nickname for the Newcomer equivalent of Alka-Seltzer, he hinted as artfully as his wit allowed, "You know this ain't eggzackly Fizzenbelch, now."

Adding a visual aid, he ran his thumb along the surface of the paper. Back and forth, back and forth. The ersatz Tert shifted uneasily.

"Well, sure, I can *pay,* but—"

Bob waited for it.

"—I heard this was a good place for a . . . discount."

Bob made a little show of inspecting the ersatz Tert's altered features.

"You're already pretty far along. What happened to your old place?"

"Uhh . . . no discounts there."

Bob Sled took another gander at the prescription. Name on it was okay: LeBeque. Recognized the hand. Story sounded legit enough, too. Money ran out, couldn't support the brand name goods. Needed a new outlet.

Bob made his decision. What we're here for—service with a smile.

"Can't attract new customers, you give no discounts," Bob Sled grinned. "We want your patronage."

He turned, bent to one among several closed cabinets behind him.

"Think we have what you need here." He started rooting around, moving big plastic canisters of tablets, capsules, powders, liquids. "See, I was mixing a prescription myself just now . . ." He turned to glance over at the ersatz Tert's altered face. ". . . but that's rare, ya know? Mostly, pharmaceutical outfits give you everything you need already made. So the challenge of running a pharmacy isn't about filling up bottles with pills . . . ah-*hah,* here's the sucker." He lifted a medium-size plastic canister out of the cabinet; capsules rattled around inside—not many dosages left. "While supplies last," he muttered.

He straightened, reached for an empty plastic vial.

"Safety cap or no?" Bob Sled asked the ersatz Tert.

"Do I need one?"

"You got little kids?"

"Nuh-uh."

"Then you don't."

He got a regular twist-off cap to top the vial once it was full.

"See," Bob Sled pontificated, "it's *that* kinda stuff makes a pharmacist." He went for a label next, scrolled it into his industrial green typewriter, an old but sturdy IBM Selectric II. Started to type. "Knowing to ask about little stuff like that. It's not about drugs, this business—*whoops,* typo there, lift-off tape is a wunnerful thing—it's about *information.* It's about scoping the needs of the customer."

Label done, Bob Sled scrolled it out of the typewriter, peeled the backing off and pressed it stickum-side against the vial.

"It's a *people* business, really. It's not a drug business. It's a people business."

He set about loading the correct number of capsules into the vial, closed it with the twist-off cap, bagged it, stapled it, pleased with the sound of his familiar riff, and turned to hand the package to the ersatz Tert.

"That'll be fifty ninety-eight," he said, noting that the suit-and-shopping-list Newcomer husband had gotten in line next, an impatient expression on his face, as if not in the mood to wait through idle chat.

He extended the bag to the ersatz Tert, who reached for it and then, curiously, kept reaching *past* it, got a purchase on his forearm instead, and yanked him gently but firmly forward. No time to think, no clear way to reach for the gun in the drawer, his belly now flat against the countertop, Bob was in the unusual position of having to look *up* at a customer for a change.

Only, of course, it *wasn't* a customer.

It wasn't even an ersatz Tert because it shook off the hood, revealing a Tert head, a *real* Tert head, too small to be otherwise. And the Tert was handing the Stabilite to the Newcomer behind him, the shopping list husband who, of course, was no such thing either, opening his jacket to reveal a holster and a badge.

"Don't you just love it when they make it easy, George?" the Tert said.

"You have the right," the one named George began, "to remain silent . . ." which was enough to clear the female customers out of the store.

Helluva note. You think you know people and then—
Hey-hoo . . .

The back room, not being open to the public, made not even a pretense at being presentable. Dust was everywhere. Bob Sled, having been made to flop the sign on the front entrance door from OPEN to CLOSED, sat in a hardwood swivel chair, squirming, as George and Matt inspected the back room's surroundings.

A curious anomaly was a placard that hung on the wall over the pharmacist's office-work table. It was the Code of Ethics Preamble as laid down by the American Pharmaceutical Association.

"Interesting document," George opined coldly, as he examined it. He read the first principle out loud:

"'A pharmacist should hold the health and safety of patients to be of first consideration; he or she should render to each patient the full measure of his or her ability as an essential health practitioner.'"

Matt looked at Bob Sled with an air of faint disdain. "So question number one becomes: Are you fundamentally a schnook or do you really think you're doing the best you can?"

Bob Sled audibly *ulp*ed.

"It goes on," George continued, "'A pharmacist should never knowingly condone the dispensing, promoting, or distributing of drugs or medical devices, or assist therein, which are not of good quality, which do not meet standards required by law, or which lack therapeutic value for the patient.'"

"Question number two," Matt announced. "What the hell *business* are you in?"

"Hey-hoo, guys, *guys,"* Bob Sled said, trying not to stammer, "I admit, a coupla short cuts, here, there, but I take all that stuff on the wall seriously. Nobody gets ripped off, not at *See Gurd Nurras."*

George turned from the wall and crossed to Bob's chair.

"My good sir," he began, clearly meaning the opposite, "do you think us blind, or stupid? The condition of your over-the-counter merchandise alone is appalling."

"Look, no expiration date is gospel, the stuff ain't like milk products. There's always a wide margin for error before the chemicals actually lose their potency. I don't believe in waste, is all."

Matt joined George in a narrow gaze at the once jaunty pharmacist.

"What my friend's telling you is that you're gonna go down. There's no way you're *not* gonna go down. It *starts* with revocation of your license. Whether or not it finishes with a long stay in the House of Many Doors—that's up to you."

"I kn-know what you guys are doing. You're t-trying to play good cop, bad cop on me."

"I'm curious," George said. "Which one of us gave you the impression that he was being good?"

Bob Sled *ulp*ed again.

"We played good cop, bad cop this morning," Matt offered. "Gets old, you do it more than once a day. Right now, we're playing bad cop, worse cop."

"We haven't quite decided who plays which yet," George added. "Although, personally, I'd like to be the one who rams your own poison down your throat."

"Wait a minute. Poison? What are you talking about? Stuff's a little old sometimes, but it's all bona fide."

Something in Bob Sled's voice caused Matt and George to exchange a glance that said, *He doesn't know. He honestly doesn't know.*

"The discount Stabilite," said George. Slowly. Looking at the little man in the eyes.

"Stuff's fresh as a daisy! No expiration problem there at all. I mean, I get regular refills and—" His voice caught, and a dull, horrific realization clouded his face.

"It's bad?" Almost a hushed whisper. "It's *bad?"*

Briefly Matt told him *how* bad.

"I thought it was just—just *surplus* or something."

"Something?" George gritted.

"Or maybe somebody was copying the formula, like they do with generic drugs. You gotta believe me, a coupla short cuts, here, there, but nothing that would *hurt* people *ever.*"

"It's the short cuts do it," Matt said blandly.

Bob Sled sat. Unmoving. Just sat and stared at his hands.

"I worked the infirmary in the slave ship. They conserved everything there, the Overseers, and maybe I learned that lesson too well. Shouldn't be keepin' the old stuff on the shelves, I guess, but I do check it periodically. I don't hurt people. What they did on the ship, that was hurting people.

"I kept that in mind when I applied for pharmacology school, four and a half years ago. You know, Terts—I mean, humans—they have these training programs, five, six years. Us Newcomers, faster brains, obviously more experience with our own body chemistry . . . put *us* through an accelerated *one*-year program, they couldn't get us out into the workforce fast enough. There was a need. I came to this neighborhood, I figured, here's where I'm needed."

"Don't waste this on us," Matt sneered, "save it for the jury."

But George raised a hand. Matt read the gesture. His partner wanted to hear the rest.

"Not the neighborhood for altruism," Bob Sled continued. "I let it lower my standards. Got held up one too many times. Insurance rates? Hey-hoo, whattaya think the short cuts are about? Affording the payments! Any wonder I got selfish?

"This Stabilite thing, though. The drug is so expensive. For the public, I mean. So when this guy brought the knockoff to me, I thought, hey-hoo, sure, there's something in it for me. But in a way, I'm back to helping people again . . . give 'em something they couldn't otherwise afford."

"Heard enough now?" Matt asked dryly.

George nodded. The druggist's rationalization for his

own moral decline was a Byzantine, tortured path of denial. So ingrained now, so rote-learned, that nothing they could say would make him see the light. In fact, pure moral righteousness would only confuse him more.

Bob Sled looked up piteously. "This goes easier on me, I cooperate, doesn't it?"

It would come down to that in the end.

"That," George breathed, "is usually the way it works in such instances."

The little druggist nodded. Relieved to be small-fry when the hunters were after Big Game.

"So cooperate," Matt prodded. "Who's your connection?"

"Don't know him by name."

"Aw, cummon. Fit this guy for cuffs, George."

"No, really! He showed up here one day with a sample and a sales pitch. Thirty percent to me, seventy percent to him, all off the books. And I'm only one of four dealers in L.A."

Matt and George exchanged another glance, this one accompanied by tight smiles. Their job—maybe—had just gotten a little easier. This revelation seemed to imply that the bum Stabilite was coming from a single source. As they had hoped.

"What else can you tell us?" George queried.

"Well," Bob Sled replied, "I'm expecting a new shipment tomorrow . . ."

Tomorrow. Well within Grazer's forty-eight-hour deadline. And given the new evidence, Grazer might even pitch in a little more manpower. Tomorrow. How nice.

"Ask me what's the secret of comedy, George," said Matt.

George peered at his partner strangely, but complied. "What is the secret of co—"

"Timing," Matt interrupted.

CHAPTER 9

IN HER HEAD it was perfect. In her head it would be almost like some movie musical. She'd lead the way, the others would get into the groove and follow; and soon enough, with choreographic precision, everybody would be in step.

Doing the step.

It would be beautiful.

It already was beautiful. In her head.

As Emily Francisco smiled her way through the junior high school day, entertaining twelve-year-old notions of success and renown, she looked more and more forward to the gym club. It was generally a good day because her spirits were so high, but every hour or so, she'd entertain the fantasy of What It Would Be Like when she taught her clubmates the great new step she'd devised, and the vision would divert her attention. She was caught daydreaming by her math teacher, but being a good student, she was not too embarrassingly rebuked. Scary moment, though, and she overcompensated the rest of the afternoon, sitting up straight and forcing herself to be especially alert.

But then, at the end of social studies (a misnomer she

never understood; really, it was only history), the class bell rang, and she bolted out of her chair.

She ran all the way to her gym locker, hearts pounding with anticipation. The run seemed to take forever, and then once she was at her locker, she barely remembered it at all as she dialed her combination, opened her locker, and proceeded to change into her gym duds.

Her other clubmates trickled in, their energies varied, depending upon the kind of day they'd had, good, bad, or indifferent. They exchanged greetings, and it disappointed Emily that they weren't picking up on her rush of energy, and that some had even forgotten it was *her* turn to teach a routine to everybody. But that was okay, she consoled herself. How could they know how way-cool this thing was until they actually *saw* it? After all, only Emily had been living with it all these hours. When the full grandeur of it was unleashed upon them . . . then they'd know.

There were two gyms in Emily's junior high school; her gym club assembled in the smaller of the two, which also doubled as the cafeteria. Great, long tables and benches were hinged and folded up in wall recesses behind collapsible doors at regular intervals. The residual smells of lunch—macaroni and cheese, baked chicken, mole strips, vegetarian plate—lingered pleasantly in the air. Despite the obligatory jokes, the food here wasn't bad, really, not at all.

Ms. McIntyre, the gym teacher who usually supervised, had left word that she would be late due to a faculty meeting, and that they should just begin without her. Emily felt a bit let down; she would've liked Ms. McIntyre to see her nifty new dance routine, but she quickly adjusted her fantasy. Ms. McIntyre would come in late, see Emily leading the pack, and, awed by the sight of fourteen girls looking tight as a kick line, praise her ingenuity.

They gathered around in their usual semicircle and arranged to do things alphabetically. Two other girls besides Emily were also scheduled to teach dance steps that day, both of whom had last names that came before Francisco. It was only right to acknowledge this as fair procedure, but again, Emily felt a twinge of disappointment. She'd wanted to burst upon the scene and wow 'em. However, the fantasy adjusted itself easily enough. *Save the best for last,* she thought. Why burden anybody with having to top her creation?

The next twenty or so minutes crawled by for Emily as she dutifully joined her clubmates in learning two routines that seemed particularly bland and uninspired. At one moment, her best friend, raven-haired Jill Molaskey, caught Emily rolling her eyes heavenward with impatience.

"What's the matter?" Jill whispered as they went through the same dull step for the tenth dull time.

Bo-ring, mouthed Emily, and as they turned in unison, Jill said something that startled her a little.

"Watch that."

At long last it was Emily's turn to strut her stuff.

"Okay," she announced, "I call this the Emily Seven, because it took six previous versions before I could get it right." She had expected laughs or smiles of appreciation at this. But the few smiles they sported were polite; the rest of the faces were impassive, a few even vaguely uncomfortable. Jill, looking right into her eyes, mouthed *Emily Seven?* as if to say, *"Oh, come on!"* Well, it was true . . . no one else had actually given a *name* to her step, let alone a name that announced how much work had gone into it. Maybe that information should've come *after* they'd learned the Emily Seven and seen how great it was; maybe she'd been a bit too—what was that big new word?—*pretentious* in making a show of it before the fact.

Right, Jill, you're right. Just get on with it.

"Anyway, this is how it goes," Emily said.

She crossed to the right wall, leaned against one of the huge doors behind which a lunch table was stored, and then she

took a single hop, bounded up several feet, landed

Thump,

deep bending at the knees, arms up, uncoiling like a spring, arms at the side now, pirouetting full in midair, landing,

Thump,

kick-starting a forward tumble,

de,

landing on her hands,

thump,

bending at the elbows, uncoiling again, pushing herself into the air, somersaulting backward until she was again erect and landing,

Ka-flump!

with a flourish, arms outflung, breathing hard, a big smile on her face as if to say, "There! Now, how did you like *that?"*

Thirteen faces stared at her in stupefaction.

Emily's smile hung there and died.

Some of her clubmates were shifting their feet; and Jill, of all people, was shaking her head slightly.

This was not the fantasy. This was not even close.

"What?" Emily said, finally, through her deep gulps of air, breaking the interminable silence. "What?"

A girl with long brown hair, Leslie DiMeo, was the first brave enough to speak.

"We can't, like, *do* that, Emily."

"Why not?"

"Because we're, like—*human,* Emily."

Emily had stopped gulping air to compensate for the exertion. But breathing was suddenly just as difficult.

"Hey, now, Leslie, I've *seen* humans do stuff like this!"

Mei-Mei Harada, an Oriental clubmate, said, "Where? Where've you seen humans pull that off?"

"Don't you guys ever watch the Olympics on TV?"

Responding as a collective for the first time, the thirteen human girls groaned.

Jill said, "Emily, those are the exceptions. Those athletes train for *years* to get that kind of dexterity. But this is a gym *club,* for godssake, not a professional training program. We're just a bunch of kids here, trying to have a little fun."

"But it *is* fun!"

"No," said Joannie Delahanty, a redhead, "it's fun for *you* because you're a Newcomer. For us it's work. It's more than work. Frankly, it looks a little dangerous."

Boldly Emily strode over to Joannie and took her wrist. "No, it's not at all," she said. "Come on, I'll show you."

"I don't think I want to do this, Emily . . ."

"What, are you chicken?"

As soon as it was out of her mouth, she knew it was the wrong thing to have said. Her fantasy scenario had long since expired, but with that choice phrase, she had pounded the final nail into its coffin. The discomfort in the air coalesced into a faint but unmistakable haze of anger directed at her. And in the back of her mind she felt it. But Emily was twelve, concerned with peer pressure and being right; and the dare had been articulated. It was out there in the ether. And, fighting her instincts, bowing to her frustration, she stood by it.

Joannie was twelve too. And nobody's chicken. She said so, and followed Emily to the starting position against the wall.

"Okay," said Emily. "Just do what I do."

She did the initial leap, bounding several feet in the air, landing bent at the knees. She looked over her shoulder as Joannie took a running start, bounded up, not quite as high, and landed clumsily, one foot shooting out from under her, causing her to land hard on her rump.

"Ow!" she said, and there was a frozen moment in which everybody, including Emily, thought Joannie had done something serious, twisted an ankle or something. The other girls started to inch forward as if to offer aid, but then Joannie rose, rubbing her hindquarter, clearly not in much pain. Even Emily had to breathe a sigh of relief.

Jill stepped forward. "You know what I think the thing is, Em?" she said.

Emily looked at her by way of response.

"I think," Jill said, "that maybe you're right. We can do this, but you're just so good at it we've become self-conscious. Why don't you show it to us once more and then leave us alone to practice it for a while, okay?"

It sounded odd to Emily . . . but it also sounded reasonable. And after all, Jill was her best friend.

"Okay," she said.

And back to starting position.

Grimly this time, the joy of it seeming to have vanished, Emily took a single hop, bounded up several feet . . .

. . . and went through the motions of the routine again, ending, as always, with a flourish. But no smile. No, her expression was very serious now.

"Should I . . . do it . . . again?" she breathed.

"It's real clear. I think we've got it," Jill said. "Right, girls?"

There was a general mumbling chorus of assent and accompanying nods all around.

"Give us about five minutes," Jill added.

"Five?" asked Emily. "Really? That's all?"

"We're quick studies, I think."

Emily crossed to the exit, thick silence following behind her. She turned at the door, tried to smile encouragingly. The faces looked back, unresponsive.

With a cheer she didn't feel, Emily said, "It's easy. You'll figure it out." And then she left to wander the halls for a while.

It was after class hours, so she didn't need a pass, didn't have to justify herself to a hall monitor, just strolled around, occasionally peering into the windows of empty classrooms, trying to process a general feeling that was . . . ungood, somehow. Trying to true up the sequence of events that had just transpired with the fantasy she'd harbored all last night and all day today.

Maybe, she thought . . . maybe it's all happening the way it's supposed to. Maybe the step *was* too hard, maybe they *did* need to practice without her eagle eye on them every second.

She liked the reasonableness of that, and her optimism grew from there. Yeah, sure, they just needed time. And when she got back, she'd open the door and . . . there they'd be, doing the Emily Seven and having the time of their lives. It was the latest configuration of the fantasy, and it was the best one of all.

Just to be a good guy about it, she waited an extra minute before making her way back to the cafeteria-gym. And when she pushed the door open . . .

They had left. All of them.

Only Ms. McIntyre was there, holding a piece of ruled notebook paper in her hand. At Emily's entrance, she lifted her blond head and held the paper out at arm's length.

"Emily," she said soberly, "I believe this was left for you. Do you think you can explain it to me?"

With mounting dread, hearing nothing but her pulses pounding in her ears, Emily Francisco took the longest walk of her life to where her teacher stood. She reached for the paper. She had to read it twice; the first time it was so hurtful she couldn't truly believe her eyes.

The handwriting was Jill's, the note printed with meticulous neatness.

Emily,
It's easy.
You'll figure it out.

And they had all signed it.

Meanwhile, in another part of the school district . . .

The teachers would ask questions, Buck's hand would go up; maybe they'd call on him, maybe they wouldn't. If they did, he'd have an answer—the right one or at least a *good* one. After he volunteered a response once per class (twice if the instructor was an especial hardass), it was just amazing how content his teachers would be to leave him alone for the rest of the period. He was barely conscious of any individual question he might've been asked, or any individual answer he might've given; only aware that by paying the ritual this little bit of homage, he was buying more time to be with himself.

To concentrate on the important matters.

Today to the outside world he was Buck Francisco, participating high school student; but secretly . . . he was Buck Francisco, Senior on Autopilot.

In a way, it was like operating on two different levels of consciousness at once. Before beginning his studies with the Kewistan Masters—an enclave of Elders whose philosophy marked them as distinctively as if it were one of the many Tenctonese religions—it might have been a difficult feat to pull off, being partly in class and mostly in his own head. But one of the first things the Kewistans had taught him was *Kewisto,* the essential skill of abstraction, which allowed one to live in the moment and observe it at the same time. Buck was by no stretch an adept—that came with years and experience—but he applied the basic philosophical principles and was able to affect a rudimentary posture. Which was okay. Today it was all he needed.

But his thoughts were too big, too consequential, to remain in his head, unarticulated. He *knew* things. Since studying with the Elders, he had *learned* things; and he hadn't yet come anywhere near mastering the discipline it would take to hold in the dilemma that now plagued him. He needed to speak his mind. He'd once read a name for this condition: Information Compulsion. It was apparently one of the most powerful and least understood drives of sentient beings. Knowing that, he knew he had to *do* something about it.

So when his free period at long last came, he made straight for the one person he'd be able to talk to, who would give him unconditional tolerance, unconditional love, and free rein to unleash the bubbling cauldron of thoughts inside his head. Without consequence or compromise.

This person was to be found in the school's day care center.

Babies and small children were tended to here; some were the offspring of teenage students who were determined not to let premature parenthood stop their secondary education; others, like Buck's baby sister, Vessna, were the offspring of working families who could not afford private home care.

It was Wednesday, Buck's day to be responsible for the baby. Other days she'd go with her mother to the day care center at her workplace, less often with her father to the day care center at his.

Buck approached Marlene, the middle-aged volunteer worker at the center.

"How was she today?"

The question was more than just an amenity. Vessna could be cranky when too long away from her supply of *Yespian* . . . but today, apparently, there was no such problem, because Marlene replied, "She was gold. Precious gold."

Buck scooped Vessna out of a playpen and informed Marlene that he was going to take her outside for a while.

"Beautiful day for it," Marlene said, adding, "Make sure you keep her head in the shade." Buck didn't have to be told, but he was fond of Marlene for caring enough to remind him, and nodded as he took the burlap bag with the baby's supplies.

Buck exited the school, emerging with Vessna into the fine, bright, warming sunlight. He walked with Vessna snug against his chest, periodically stopping to hold her out at arm's length and lift her high into the air, keeping eye contact with her. Then he'd smile at her, she'd smile back in response, maybe even squeal, and then he'd bring her back down into his embrace. It wasn't much of a game, there was no winner, no loser, but neither of them ever tired of playing it.

He walked with her out past the sports fields and parking lots to a slightly wooded area just on the fringes of school property. And there, under a lushly leafy tree, the better to keep the baby's head in the shade, he settled.

He spread a small blanket on the grass, and over that a disposable paper sheet. Over that, in turn, went Vessna, and then began the routine of checking to see if she needed changing (she did), and dealing with it: disposing of the disposables in a sealable plastic bag, wiping the baby down with special damp nappies, and preparing her anew for the next onslaught. Throughout it all, Vessna was quiet and cooperative in a way she usually wasn't, even with her parents.

Somehow she connected to Buck. For all his rebelliousness, for all the anger he sometimes held within him, she found him fascinating; and even Buck had to admit that he could be tender and gentle with Vessna in a manner that most who knew him would find uncharacteristic.

But he knew a secret about that.

A secret he shared only with Vessna.

He was most naturally, comfortably himself when Vessna was near. Tender and gentle were the things he liked being above all else.

Until recently, it had been his most intimate secret.

He knew he could trust her to keep it; and he knew, therefore, that he could trust her with the bigger one he now held, that he felt compelled to share.

"Neemu," he began softly, "I'm not sure, but . . . I may be going away."

Vessna, crawling toward a rattle, looked up at him and cooed inquisitively.

"It's not that you'll never see me again, but . . . I'll be different. I've been studying with the Kewistan Elders, you know that, and they've taught me the basics of *Kewisto.* I guess you know that too. But . . . have I told you why *Kewisto* as a philosophy is so important?"

Rattle now in hand, Vessna banged it soundly against the ground and looked up proudly.

"It's the basis of everything the Kewistans do. They're the collectors of knowledge for our people. They observe the progress of our race from a remove, never getting directly involved, save to offer advice when asked. They feel it's their mandate to keep a historical perspective at all times, apart from extremes of emotional involvement. I don't mean to say that they're *un*emotional. Actually, they're not, but—"

Vessna was sucking the rattle now. "Mmmmm?" she asked.

"You're right, it's a very complicated idea. But it's not the point, really. Here's the point."

He took a deep breath.

"I think I'll need you in my lap for this one," he said, and he reached under her stubby arms, lifted her, her feet pedaling the air with barely coordinated joy, and he brought her in close, nestling her head against his chest.

"The point is . . . I'm the most accelerated student they've had since we've been on Earth. Also, they tell me, the most eager. I've been pushing for a full initiation into the order and . . . well, my Elder-Master tells me that if I think I'm ready, I've earned the right to my *Tighe Marcus-ta.*"

He paused then, putting his hand to Vessna's cheek, lightly brushing his fingers over the delicate swell around her ear. He loved touching his baby sister, holding her. The innocent sensuality of it was a constant wonder, and often overwhelming.

"It means complete absorption. It means I, too, would learn to watch the world from a remove. To be able to watch daily events as if they're living history and fit them into the larger context of our heritage."

He rested his chin on her head, savoring the warmth of

her, enfolding her with both arms. Normally Vessna had a slight claustrophobic streak, and such an all-consuming embrace would have made her restless. But the connection between her and her brother was strong now, so she merely said "Ab-ab-ab-a," and sighed.

"But in order to do that, I have to 'untie' myself from the outside world. It's not as severe as it sounds, not a counter-productive act of anger, like becoming reclusive or going to a Tenctonese compound. Those things cut you *off* from the world. When you're taken in by the Kewistans, you make all beings equal in your sight. You put yourself in *harmony* with the world. So that no people are better or worse than others, or held in higher or lower esteem. What I mean is, I'd have to look upon you, Dad, Mom, Emily . . . just like I'd look upon—"

Buck glanced up idly, spotted a mailman on the other side of the school fence, and adjusted Vessna on his lap so that she could see him too.

"—that mailman," Buck continued. "You couldn't be special to me. Or that mailman couldn't be *un*special to me. Do you see?"

Vessna squealed delightedly at the mailman, who heard, from half a block away, and waved at her.

"That's why I came into the house last night to think. I wanted to see what it would be like to observe the family from a remove. I wanted to find out if I could distance myself even while I was among you." He turned her around, put his forehead to hers. "I couldn't even work up a small *Kewisto.* Emily started that damn jumping around and . . ."

Vessna made a long "Ehhhhhhh" noise.

"You're trying to tell me that's my answer right there, I know. Yeah, I thought of that. I'm not so sure you're right. The Elders tell me that separating from the family is the hardest thing. They even say it *should* be because retaining your compassion is a big part of the process."

He kissed her forehead. "I want to do it, Vessna. I want to keep the knowledge of our people; add to it, monitor it, help it grow and endure. I mean, it's a larger, nobler, greater concern than the individual need for family. And yet . . ." He rubbed his nose against hers. She smiled, laughed. "This. You and me, here, just doing this. How do I not miss *this?"* He lifted her higher, rested her head on his shoulder, moved his cheek gently against hers.

"Tell me, Vessna," he asked in a choked whisper, closing his eyes, "how do I not miss *this* most of all?"

Vessna dribbled lovingly onto his neck, and *urgled* softly into his ear.

CHAPTER 10

MATT'S FIRST STOP, once he entered the hospital that evening, was the gift shop. Typically for such a business, their selection of merchandise was limited and overpriced, but Matt had been too antsy to browse and shop elsewhere; once he was off duty, he felt the need to see Cathy as soon as he could.

He settled on a heart-shaped box of candied cauliflower. As it was being wrapped, he idly scanned the store's limited stock and a paperback title on the solitary carousel book rack caught his eye. *Black Like Me,* by John Howard Griffin. "35th Anniversary Edition," the cover proclaimed, and it was a nice cover too, embossed, the title big and prominent, gold letters upon a black background.

The book Dr. Steinbach had mentioned the night before.

Matt—never much of a reader, but an acute observer of his surroundings nonetheless—was a little surprised it was still in print, *very* surprised to find it stocked in a hospital gift shop, where potboilers, *Star Trek* novels, Tom Clancy thrillers, and Stephen King clones usually held sway.

Further thoughts on the matter were interrupted and

forgotten as his package was returned to him, wrapped, and he paid the damage. Next he made a quick stop at the main desk to get his visitor's pass and find out Fran Delaney's floor.

He took the elevator to the fifth floor, went to the nurse's desk, and announced that he was there to visit Cathy Frankel. Matt was advised to take a seat in the waiting area nearby, and another nurse was dispatched to pass along the message. Matt didn't see the first nurse look up toward the monitor view of Fran's room, only heard, as he sat, "It may be a little while."

It was eight or so minutes before the second nurse returned and told him, "She'll be with you as soon as she can."

He tried reading magazines and had no more success at it here than he had had in the emergency room the night before. Less, really, because the sounds on the ward were too distracting—sometimes even harrowing.

He tried just looking around, but whenever he did, he found himself making unwitting eye contact with one or another of the psychiatric patients who were, with minimal supervision, allowed to roam the ward. And the minute they caught his gaze, they would start to move forward, *toward* him, to engage him in conversation. Matt had a certain intellectual appreciation of their loneliness, but it didn't stop him from getting the creeps when they approached, even if there was no outward manifestation of mental dysfunction. Fortunately, the nurses were old hands at running interference, and Matt never got cornered for too long; but in short order, he learned to keep his eyes away from all faces but those of the hospital staff, never glancing above the chest of any person who wasn't attired in an official tunic.

And thus, a long, dull, unnerving forty-three minutes transpired before Cathy put in her appearance.

He was prepared to vent his anger, but as he saw her approaching, his beautiful light bulb, the anger seemed to retreat, to become less important. She was in borrowed clothes, hospital issue save for her shoes, and she seemed intently preoccupied. He rose to greet her with an embrace. She returned the embrace . . . but only briefly. She let go first and slipped quickly out of his grasp.

"What's *that* about?" he asked.

"I'm sorry, Matt, I should have called you. I didn't fully realize how this would go until I was into it. You mustn't be here now."

A little anger advanced into the forefront. "Cathy, you had me here waiting almost a whole hour and now—"

She held up both hands, clenching her jaw, a quick, clean gesture that silenced him as efficiently as if she'd told him to shut up.

"Matt," she said, with dangerous calm, "this isn't . . . about . . . you." He didn't feel he had quite deserved that, and his expression must have said as much, for she added, *"Or* me. It's about what we're trying to do for *her.* What you have to do is what you've been doing. What I have to do is get back. I'm sorry I kept you waiting so long. Couldn't be helped."

Her gaze shifted to his hand and the wrapped candy box he held uneasily. Her eyes softened momentarily.

"Oh, Matthew," she said.

He shrugged, handed it over, very little of the intended romance in the gesture. "You're, uh, welcome," he said.

"Sweet," she nodded, and tucked it under her arm. "Might even be useful," she said. Then she put a hand briefly to her temple. "Oh, God, so soon?" she muttered. Then, directing her attention toward Matt again, said, "Next time call first. I'll leave a message at the desk." She gripped his arm lightly, kissed his cheek perfunctorily, and strode briskly back up the hallway, turning a corridor, out of sight.

And that was it.

The whole goddamn visit.

Matt walked over to the nurse's desk, irritated enough not

to wait for the nurse to finish what she was doing before saying, "Excuse me. I'd like to see Dr. Steinbach."

Not dropping a stitch in her poise, the nurse said, "I'm sorry, he's off tonight."

"Well, in that case I'd like his number, please."

"Sorry again. We're not allowed to give out that information without the proper authorization."

Matt Sikes reached into his pocket, pulled out his ID, flipped it open, revealing the badge.

"Proper enough?" he asked.

She had left Fran in a fitful, sweaty sleep. It hadn't lasted long, nor had it proved very restful. When Cathy slipped off her shoes, which she left parked to one side of the doorway, and reentered the detox cubicle, Fran was awake—as Cathy knew she would be—eyes bloodshot with fatigue and trying to contain her shivers.

"I thought y-you'd g-gone." The remark had been meant to sound brazen, but fear of abandonment was clearly beneath the surface.

"Not me," said Cathy. She sat cross-legged, close to her charge.

"Glutton for p-punishment."

"If you can take it, I can. How you holding up?"

"C-cold. Strange feeling in the p-pit of my stomach. Can't t-tell if I'm hungry or nauseous."

"To be expected."

Fran's eyes flicked to the heart-shaped box Cathy had absentmindedly carried in and set beside herself on the floor. "Hell is that?"

"Oh, gee!" Then Cathy shrugged. "Something handy if you turn out to be hungry. Later."

"Heart-sh-shape. I g-gather that means you've got a honey?"

Cathy looked down, smiled a bit, blushed a little.

"Yes. Yes, I do."

Fran nodded tightly, fidgeting in her straitjacket. "That's good. That's nice. Couldn't get the hang of romance mys-s-self."

"What do you mean? Why not?"

"Human only from the waist up."

Fran offered a small, crooked smile. Cathy gave an acknowledging nod. Under her composure, however, she was rocked by the import of those six words.

By choosing to pass as human, not only had Fran denied her heritage . . . but her very sexuality. The outward appearance of her skin and her face had been altered, but she was still a Tenctonese woman underneath, with a Newcomer's body and a Newcomer's desires. And she'd felt herself free to indulge neither. Intimacy with a Newcomer would have meant risking shame and ridicule. Intimacy with a human would have meant certain discovery—even danger for the unsuspecting male. For, as Cathy and Matt had themselves learned, interspecies relations were impossible without meticulous preparation and training.

Enforced celibacy. That particular wrinkle to Fran's elaborate masquerade—an additional level of loneliness—hadn't even occurred to Cathy before. Now it seemed depressingly obvious.

"I bet lots of men made passes, too," Cathy said, hoping it sounded like a compliment.

"Fair share." And then, with a hollow nonchalance she added, "Actors, mostly." And then, unexpectedly she asked, "What's *your* guy d-do?"

"Works for the city," Cathy replied. Knowing instinctively that if she didn't change the subject right there, right away, Fran would ask, *In what capacity?* and she'd be honor-bound to reply *Cop;* and Fran would ask, *What's his name?* and she'd have to reply *Matthew;* and Fran would say, *Matthew, as in Matt? What's his last name?*—and that was a road Cathy did not want to travel down—

—so she quickly said, "How did you handle dining out?"

The segue wasn't graceful, but as the subject of hunger had just been raised, she hoped it wouldn't seem like too big a leap.

"You mean with members of the company?" Fran asked, and when Cathy nodded, the actress answered, "Easy one. In public I was a strict vegetarian. T-took care of raw meat protein in the morning or the evening, p-privacy of my own home."

"Buying groceries must have been a problem."

"You'd've thought so, but no. People just assume you're entertaining friends. Don't g-go to the same st-store too often in a row, and nobody's the wiser."

One more little compromise, though, Cathy thought.

"Why're you so fixated on food?" Fran asked, tone changing. "You hungry?"

The question surprised Cathy, and the answer even more. She hadn't, in fact, eaten since the *Leethaag* began, and she suddenly realized she was famished.

"Actually," she said, "I am."

Fran pointed her chin at the box. "Go on ahead."

"I thought I might save this for us until . . . after. Use it to celebrate—or whatever."

"You're expec-t-ting a whole lot of me, C-Cath." In the midst of this bizarre situation, it did not escape Cathy that that was the first time Fran had addressed her by name. "Forget c-celebrations. Have a bite."

"Feels rude. Feels funny. Especially since you can't have anything until . . . until we're done here."

"I'll watch you and live vicariously. T-tell me how it t-tastes."

A little gratefully, a little sheepishly, Cathy unwrapped the box. She lifted the lid. The assortment looked wonderful, and the smell of chocolate was strong.

Too strong for some, as it turned out.

Suddenly paler and swallowing, Fran gasped, "Well, at least I know *I'm* not hungry," and Cathy leapt to her feet, the candy forgotten, rushed to grip Fran by the shoulders and all but dragged her to the toilet.

Without a moment to spare.

In the end, a reasonable compromise was reached: Rather than give Steinbach's number to Sikes, the head nurse dialed it herself. As it turned out, this was a more expedient route, for when there was no answer at his home, she dialed the code that would activate his beeper, wherever he was.

Within a few minutes, the phone at the desk rang. Steinbach checking in. Quietly the nurse informed him that there was a Detective Sikes wanting to speak with him and, no, it was not a medical emergency. From the expression on her face after that, Sikes got the distinct impression that Steinbach was angry at having been interrupted for an ancillary matter.

Well, tough, thought Sikes. *It's important to me.*

The nurse handed him the phone, tight-lipped. Well, all right, there was some sympathy in Sikes's soul—for *her*—so he opened the conversation by saying, "Don't take it out on the help, Doctor. I didn't give her much choice."

"Sikes, no mistake, I think you and your lady are nobility incarnate, but I've got me and my lady to consider, too. Do you know how long it's been since we've been able to just cool out and see a movie together?"

"I'm sorry to have pulled you away from the big screen. What were you seeing?"

"*Batman Five.* Right near the end, too."

"The end? He wins."

". . . Thanks." And a sigh. "What's up, Sikes?"

"Actually, that's *my* question. As far as I know, Cathy and I haven't had any rocky times recently, but since she's been taking Fanc—I mean, Fran—through detox, she's irritable, dismissive. It's like she doesn't want to *know* from me. It's not like her and I don't get it."

As the words left his mouth, they sounded petty to Sikes.

He had felt Cathy's rejection profoundly, still did; but giving voice to the frustration seemed to diminish it, made it sound as if he wanted help with a domestic squabble. He started to regret having barged into Steinbach's evening and fully expected the man to say, "You called me up for *that?"*

But he didn't. Instead, with quiet import, the intern said, "Sikes, I'm sorry. I thought you understood."

Aware that the conversation had taken a more serious turn than he had ever anticipated, Matt unconsciously straightened, stiffened.

"Understood what?"

"Let me ask you something first. When you spoke to Cathy just now, aside from her being brusque with you, anything odd happen?"

"Yeah. She touched her head, said 'Oh, God, so soon,' and then goodbye."

"She knew she was needed. She's beginning to bond with Fran. It's part of the process."

"What are we talkin' about here, some kind of psychic connection?"

"Yes and no. Look, we don't understand *everything* about Newcomers. They have a lot to learn about themselves, too. But as far as we can determine, this is a physiological phenomenon of the species. You know about humming, I guess." Matt grunted affirmation. Humming preceded the act of love between or with Newcomers; its purpose was to work into a mutual vibration. "Well," Steinbach continued, "shared stress induces a sympathetic reaction, too, not unlike the sympathy pains a husband might have for his pregnant wife."

Matt vividly remembered the day he helped deliver George's baby, Vessna. The sweats, the desperate need to keep panic at bay, reaching into George's pouch to turn the baby around—and the vague pain in his own abdomen, seeming to echo the infinitely more acute agony George must have been feeling. Matt swallowed, collected his thoughts.

"How . . . how intense do these 'sympathy pains' get?"

"Varies from case to case. If Cathy's withdrawing from you, I think she expects it to be pretty severe. What she's doing is tuning out distraction, keeping her mind clear. She has to focus on Fran's emotional and physical wavelengths —ride them, the same way you might ride the levels of a tape recorder at a rock concert."

"Ride the levels?"

"Sikes, there are two things going on here. One is the actual purging of poisons from Fran's body. Concurrent with that is the purging of poisons from Fran's mind. Unless and until her body readjusts, the deprivation of Stabilite is likely to cause a temporary psychosis. Attempts at emotional manipulation. Possible attempts at physical abuse, too, though I'm less worried about that. The room's on twenty-four-hour monitor, and we're prepared to pull Cathy out *stat* if any of that shit happens."

"Are you telling me Cathy's in some kind of danger here?"

Steinbach articulated his next words slowly, pointedly. "Not if she stays alert. And objective."

"How's she gonna do that with all this 'sympathy' stuff going on?"

"That," said Dr. Steinbach, "is the trick."

Matt thought about that for a moment. Then said, "Cathy knew this goin' in?"

"Most of it. We cautioned her about the rest."

"She's here because I asked her to be, did she mention?"

"I gathered."

"She never let on . . . Not to me."

"What can I tell you, Sikes? She must love you a lot."

"Yeah," said Matt softly, and lowered the receiver back into its cradle.

The manager of the hospital gift shop—a portly black woman with a name tag that identified her as Valerie—was just locking up for the day when Sikes was making his way out. On an impulse, he changed his trajectory and approached her.

Used to dealing with last-minute wheedling, Valerie launched her patented preemptive strike even before Matt could say a word.

"Ah'm sorry, the register is closed. Come back tomorrow an' thank you."

Clearly, she would brook no argument—he'd only invite abuse if he tried—and yet he ploughed ahead. "Please, if you would—"

She had locked the door, she was reaching to slide down the protective gate, and without missing a beat or dignifying him with eye contact, she announced, more loudly, "Ah *tol'* you, this store is *closed fo' the day*. You a smart fella, you should understand that."

"Look, I know exactly what I want, I won't take up any—"

Now she turned, not used to this much resistance. "It don't *matta* you know what you *want*. How'm Ah gonna take your money when *the register is closed?"*

"Please," Matt implored, "it's not a lot of money, just enough for a book, maybe you could hold the cash overnight and put it in the register tomor—"

She cut him off. "What book you talkin' 'bout?"

He looked into her round, black face, taking in the archetypal southern cadences of her rich, black voice, and he felt his mouth go dry, embarrassed to say it. She caught the hesitation.

"You connected with Dr. Steinbach?" she asked when he couldn't answer.

"Uhh . . . yeah. How did you know?"

"Been here a long time. Ah know what you want."

She unlocked the door, went inside to the bookrack, made a point of choosing the spankiest copy of *Black Like Me* in its rack, and emerged again, handing the book to Matt. She relocked the door, proceeded to tend to the gate as Matt reached for his wallet and the appropriate amount of money.

"He's an interesting boy, Dr. Steinbach," Valerie said. "Makes us keep that book in stock." Finished, she faced Matt and accepted the money. "Ah like him," she concluded. She blinked at him, offering a very nice smile, one that seemed to say, *I don't do this for just everyone.* "'Joy it now," she added, and then she was on her way to hearth and home.

Matt stood there looking at the book's cover for a while.

Then he went out into the parking lot, unlocked his car, slid behind the wheel. He put the key in the ignition but didn't turn over the engine.

It was still light out. He rolled down the window, letting the cool air in.

Then he opened the book and began to read.

CHAPTER 11

George threw himself into buying vegetables.

Usually, any old arugula would do, a carrot was a carrot, and a tomato was still really just a fruit. But today when he went to the supermarket after work, every detail suddenly had meaning.

The parsley would have to be just the *right* shade of green, the celery of just the *right* crispness, the shape of the yellow squash aesthetically pleasing, able to complement the curve of the plate upon which it would eventually find itself.

It all became vitally important.

He was going to prepare dinner tonight, treat his family to the closest approximation of a homemade Tenctonese vegetarian banquet Earth materials would provide.

Because if he could think about *that* thing, he wouldn't have to think about the *other* thing: the mutilation of self and spirit a young actress had so willingly inflicted upon herself. And the system that allowed such atrocity to perpetuate itself.

After all his people had seen and experienced on the slave ship at the hands of the Overseers, after all they'd encountered on Earth, haven though it was, from those who would destroy or suppress their glorious uniqueness, how could a proud and gifted being make the *conscious* choice to—

—the purple onions looked especially nice. Yes, the color was soothing. He loaded some into his wagon.

Fixate on the vegetables, George told himself. Just the way Matt is fixated on this Fancy Delancey.

And there it was again, only now he was replaying his last conversation with Matthew, just prior to their parting company for the day . . .

They had filled out the day's paperwork, gotten the okay to continue from Grazer, decided upon their procedure for tomorrow, and were walking to the station's parking lot to go their separate ways.

The events of the morning at LeBeque's office were still with him, the encounter with the druggist at *See Gurd Nurras* threatened to make him ill, and, infuriatingly, Matthew was optimistic about solving the *case* . . . as if solving the case somehow solved the fundamental *problem.*

"Lighten up, George," Matthew had said, sensing his mood. "It's not worth getting funked out about this issue."

"You do not understand."

"George, I understand just fine."

"How could you?"

"What, Newcomers have a premium on angst and suffering? Partner mine, you're talking to a once-abused child. I don't want to hear from you that I don't know what it's like to get beat up by authority and carry emotional scars. I'm sorry she offends your sensibilities, George. But I know a little bit more about her than you. She made a mistake . . . but it was the best she could do at the time."

"And if that is the extent of your understanding, my point is proven. The best she could have done was fight."

"Oh, for God's—"

"—*Instead of creating the scenario* for her own destruction. My Gods, even on the slave ship we didn't willingly walk into the hands of the butchers, we had to be *dragged.* Do you not see the distinction?"

"I see it, but I don't buy it. She hurt nobody but herself."

"No, no, no, she hurt *all* of us; she *paid money* to have herself altered, to perpetuate the myth that one race is inferior to the other. It's the kind of action that encourages class differentiation throughout the whole society. Look how many lives were touched by the ripple effect already. The doctor believes he's performing a public service; the druggist thought it a harmless way to augment his income; an entire theatrical company embraced her for her humanness first and her uniqueness *second.* Every such betrayal of our species and its heritage has negative consequences that increase *exponentially* with every single being it touches!"

By now they had stopped walking and were shouting at each other over the hood of George's car.

"Jesus, George, talk about your paranoid musings! The doctor is a dime-a-dozen opportunist, the druggist is a bargain basement slimeball, and the theatrical company was innocently duped. Yes, there's a societal bias to consider, but let's not impute conspiracy motives to simple scumwads and blatant racism to people who had the situation forced down their throats!"

"That's *exactly* the kind of rationalization that created the climate for your Nazi Germany!"

"My Nazi Germany? Oh, now you are really beginning to piss me off."

"Why not ask the person closest to you? See what *Cathy* thinks!"

"Cathy's at the hospital helping Fancy go cold turkey!"

The shock of that had hit George like ice water in the face.

"Cathy . . ." he had said slowly, "is guiding that . . . woman through *Leethaag?"*

"I don't know what that 'leapfrog' is. But if it means Cathy's by her side, yeah, she's doin' it." A beat passed. "I didn't mean to hit you with it, George. Cathy was with me last night. I guess I thought you knew we were together on the deal."

"Why?" George had queried in stunned wonder. "Why would Cathy lend that kind of support to . . . that woman?" It seemed to be the only way he could refer to Fran without resorting to uncharacteristic profanity.

"Among other reasons . . . because I asked her to."

George had stood there, breathing shallowly, blinking rapidly as if it would somehow clear his head.

"I will see you in the morning, Matthew," he had said at length, achieving an eerie, existential calm, and without another syllable, got into his car and drove away . . .

"Mister. *Hey,* Mister, you wanna share the wealth a little?"

Startled out of his reverie, George turned to see a slatternly housewife glaring at him. He realized he'd been blocking the avocado bin.

"Excuse me, madam," he said, grabbed four avocados randomly, loaded them into his cart without putting them through the grueling selection process, moved down the supermarket aisle.

More determined than ever to focus on the fine points of persimmons.

When George pulled up into their driveway, noting that he had arrived before Susan, he could see through the window of the RV that Buck was ensconced within. He climbed out of his car, strode to the RV, knocked on its door.

"Buck?"

"Yeah, Dad."

Good sign. His son sounded more solicitous than he had the previous night.

"Will you be joining us for dinner tonight?" George asked. "I'm making something special."

George was pleasantly surprised when Buck opened the

RV's door, willing to speak face-to-face rather than through the walls. He was further gratified to see that Buck held little Vessna in his arms.

"Sounds okay, Dad."

There was precious little enthusiasm in Buck's acceptance, but there was also no hint of resistance. He seemed open enough to the idea; and this evening George was happy to take his victories where he could.

"Think you might help me in with a few packages?"

Buck rubbed noses with Vessna.

"What do you say, Sis? You let me go long enough to assist the old man?"

Vessna gurgled happily and Buck replied, "She says it's okay."

"Good then."

Buck deposited Vessna inside the house, and then he and his father carried the groceries into the kitchen.

"Is Emily home?"

"Yeah, she was here before me."

"Wonderful! Would you tell her about dinner?"

"Sure. You need help or something?"

There was an unusual eagerness to the way Buck asked this, and George found himself touched by it. He smiled gratefully at his son. "Under normal circumstances, yes, but tonight I feel the need to play chef alone. Do you mind?"

"Sometimes you gotta be with yourself. Gods know I understand that." He made a vague gesture at the staircase beyond the kitchen. "I'll go speak to Emily."

Buck left the kitchen, and George paused to marvel at the mercurial nature of children. Just last night Buck had been morose and withdrawn. And today . . .

George put on his favorite apron—the one that read STAND BACK: DAD'S COOKIN'—turned his attention to the vegetables, unpacking them and lining them up in neat, ordered groupings, then laying out the various seasonings, including the Vaseline paste he would use as a base.

He started by slicing into a head of green cabbage. It was a large one, requiring a large knife to get through, almost as large as his own head—

(her own head, turned upward toward a mutilating scalpel)

—stop it!

He cut several large slices of cabbage and then chopped them vigorously, monolithically, chopping away the bad thoughts, chopping them into little pieces, chopping the cabbage so that it bore no further resemblance to

(a Newcomer's head)

—stop it, will you, will you just dammit STOP!

The knife blade slammed onto the carving board a mere fraction of an inch from his finger.

The initial shock of the near injury gave way almost instantly to a perverse blitheness.

All right. Apparently we're not *going* to get this out of our mind. Fine. Just fine. So we accept it. Good. Hmmmm. Now, what vegetable is *most* likely to be a reminder? Ah! I know . . .

George shucked an ear of corn, an *ear,* named not for the gentle swell on a Tenctonese head, but the big, fleshy appendages sported by humans. Let's mutilate an ear, he thought, and carved off several rows of kernels with a grim satisfaction.

He split open a butternut squash, seasoned it with powdered cinnamon from a shaker. Sprinkle, sprinkle, look at the pretty brown spots it makes; looked at a certain way, why, they're almost like the spots on a Newcomer's head. George then put his hand into the squash and spread the cinnamon evenly around along the moist surface of its meat. *Isn't that interesting, how easy it is to obliterate the spots,* he thought.

But because at hearts George remained a gentle soul, his spirit soon tired of the nastiness. Without knowing quite how it happened, or why, the mood left him. It had served its strange purpose, though. By giving in to it rather than fighting it, he'd found himself able to concentrate on the task at hand. Slicing, dicing, seasoning, proportioning. Even pausing to puree a small serving in the blender for Vessna. And soon there was nothing but the placating colors of the vegetables, the attractive shapes into which they had been sliced, the artful presentation on the serving platter, and the notion of sharing it with a loving and appreciative family.

As George was putting the finishing touches on his gourmet meal, he heard Susan's car pull up in the driveway, next to his own. Smiling now, really feeling good about things for the first time that day, he sprinted through the living room—where Buck sat on the couch, absorbed in a book—toward the front door and flung it wide. Looking, he thought, cute as a bunny in his apron, anticipating the light in Susan's eyes at the idea that dinner had been prepared, the homecoming smile on her face now that she was back home with the man she adored.

She responded with neither. She seemed to have dragged herself out of her car, carrying her portfolio in front of her, two hands on the grip, as if it had attained a mysterious dead weight.

"Hi, George," she said listlessly, patting him on the chest as she squeezed by him.

"I made dinner," he said, sounding helpless.

"That's nice, dear."

And she wearily began climbing the steps to their bedroom.

"It's quite an elaborate spread, actually," he called after her.

"I'll be down in a minute," she called back. "Did you put your gun away in the usual place?"

"Why?"

"I think I'll just shoot myself first."

"What?" said George, whose first instinct was always to take such statements literally.

A fraction of a second later, of course, he realized his wife was being ironic—she could hardly come down to dinner *after* she'd shot herself—but Susan, unaware of his delayed understanding, could only respond to what she'd heard. She looked down on him from the head of the stairs. "Oh, George," she said, tiredly. "Spin the wheel and buy yourself a clue."

He didn't understand the reference, but the meaning was clear enough. And, as Susan entered the bedroom, he heard Emily's voice call out,

"Mom?"

"Yes, dear."

"Save a bullet for me."

Petulantly, the expression on his face one of *Well, I never,* George put his hands on his hips and huffed in the direction of the second floor. He shifted his gaze to exchange a look with Buck, who said, simply, "I think they're bummed."

Bummed though they were, George and Buck managed to coax them to the kitchen at the same time, and at last, the family was together, around the table.

It was a nice image, a cozy image, the kind of Norman Rockwell image that Matthew would have called "kitchen" —this time, quite appropriately—but it was missing the signature smiles, the sense of anticipation.

George, never one to be insensitive, tried to get to the bottom of things.

"How was everybody's day?"

"Just long," from Susan.

"Average," from Emily.

And nothing else. No one could say he hadn't asked.

"Well, everybody," George invited, with forced expansiveness, "chow down!"

Defeated eyes returned his gaze. Buck made a show of taking the first serving, even forking the first mouthful. "Gee, great, Dad," he said.

"Why, thank you, Buck," George responded.

Silence. Nothing.

Then, seemingly out of a sense of obligation, Susan and Emily served themselves. One at a time. The serving spoon clanked against the central dish, with the ponderousness of hammer against anvil, the sense of a chore to be done, bereft of delight. The servings they took were small, obligatory.

And when they ate, it was without enthusiasm, the silverware playing with the food in the protracted spaces between listless bites. George managed to clean half his plate, and then even he was unable to continue with the charade any longer. He looked up, dropped his fork onto the table. It made a sharp noise which adequately expressed his disgust.

Vessna, in her high chair, had already been sensing the discomfort around the table, and the sudden sound made by George's fork startled her into expressing it. She began to cry.

"All right, that's it," George announced. "This has become preposterous." He folded his arms and leaned back in his chair, patriarch surveying his domain, as Susan got up, lifted Vessna into her arms, and tried to soothe the baby. When the baby's cries at last turned to whimpers, soft enough to speak over, George spoke.

"You know, I put both my hearts into this meal. Tonight I felt the need of a reminder that we were proud of who we were, of each other. A traditional Tenctonese affirmation of life. If my timing is so off that it doesn't warrant some appreciation, even a simple thank-you, I suppose I can live with that—but to behave as if it's a job to be here . . . that's a bit much to take.

"Now, how was everybody's day . . . *really?* We may not be the ideal family, but I thought at least we knew how to *talk."*

The sentiment was too compelling, too true, not to be dealt with.

"Some things aren't that easy to talk about, Dad," Emily said, at length.

"Susan?"

"I'm not even sure *how* to talk about it."

More gently, George suggested, "You ramble until you find your way."

And then Susan blurted, "They stepped all over my work, George. Distorted it to the point where it's not even mine—worse still, to where it *makes fun of us.*" As she tended to Vessna—quieting her, continuing her feeding, wiping her little mouth—Susan told the story of her meeting at the ad agency. She finished by saying, "And I feel as if I've sold my soul against my will. I agreed before I knew what was happening. And now I feel as if the train's already left the station."

In the silence after, Emily blurted in turn, "They hated my work, too." Her story about the gym club and how her friends had reacted to her came out haltingly, in contradistinction to Susan's heated frustration. Emily knew the truth of her tale—that her ego and expectations had been unrealistic, unfair—but she had difficulty confronting those issues head-on; so her narrative was clumsy, prone to backtracking over itself, emerging in uncomfortable pieces. But emerge it eventually did. "And I don't know what to do about it," Emily concluded.

George got up from his chair, walked to the sink, stood over it a while. He started speaking while looking out the window over the sink into the backyard.

"On the one hand," he said softly at first, "we should never forget who we are. On the other . . . they will never let us. Maybe . . . maybe there are some situations—*some*—in which no clear answer is at hand."

He turned, his voice rising. "But you two, you should know better. When it's *their* choice—that is when you have to defend yourself. When it's *your* choice—that is when you have to understand the other side.

"Susan, your job is important to you, to all of us, but it shouldn't be kept at the expense of your self-worth. Do you think I, or anyone else here, would think less of you for losing it if it meant you could live with yourself? You'll have to decide how far you're willing to compromise, but you have more power than you think. At any point, *you can stop that train!*

"And Emily, you should cherish and display your Tenctonese heritage and abilities, but not at the expense of your *friends'* self-worth. That kind of pride is only racism in reverse. I know it doesn't look like it, sound like it or *feel* like it to you, because I know you don't think in those terms, but every now and again you have to think in terms of how other people are perceiving you. Until our people are truly assimilated, until there is a formula for balance, *everything you do sends a message.* You must take the *responsibility* for it!"

He was reflexively free-associating, of course, to his outrage at *that woman,* because the issues were intertwined. Which, naturally, made him angry again; and just as he hadn't been able to tell quite when the anger had left him earlier, he wasn't quite sure how it had crept back in now. He only knew that it must have been fierce, fiercer than he'd imagined, for the aftermath of his speech was met with a deathly silence. Even from Vessna. Emily and Susan were regarding him with something like fear.

Buck's expression registered a rather milder surprise—if he hadn't known better, George might have labeled it a bemused detachment—that made him bolder, unafraid to speak. Buck, however, spoke cautiously, like one unwilling to shout at a snow-capped mountain, lest one bring down an avalanche upon one's smooth, spotted pate.

"And what kind of day have *you* had?"

"Fruitful!" George snapped. Then he exhaled heavily through his nose. Seeing at last that he had been no better than Emily and Susan, conflicted about his feelings and hiding them from the family. The girls had hidden behind silence. He had hidden behind food and a pretext of family ritual. The *real* family ritual, though, was the one that had just occurred, that he himself had set in motion: the open sharing of problems and feelings, the willingness to submit them for discussion.

"Fruitful," George said again, in a more reasonable tone. "But not good."

He told the story of Fran Delaney, a.k.a. Fancy Delancey, noting the different expressions on the faces of his listeners. Emily became increasingly rapt, as if being told a whoppingly interesting, brilliantly plotted intrigue. Susan had her mouth open; every now and again, throughout the narrative, her hand went to her chest, above one or the other of her hearts. The story, George thought as he told it, must have been doubly shocking for her—after all, she'd been at the theatre the night before, she had *seen* Fran Delaney's performance, had admired it greatly along with everyone else in that audience. Had been *fooled right along* with everyone else in that audience.

Buck's expression, no longer bemused, was harder to fathom. It kept changing in subtle ways George was unable to interpret.

No matter. Buck, ironically, had been the most even-minded member of the family tonight. He'd express his thoughts soon enough. Probably very soon indeed, for George was winding up.

". . . and so I came home hoping to lose myself in an activity that might reinforce my own grip on who I am—who *we* are—and how we're supposed to function on this planet. I am sorry to have shouted at you all, it was really not directed at you. I am frustrated by Matthew, for I do not think he is capable of understanding. I am bewildered at Cathy, for *I* am not capable of understanding the enormous sacrifice she is willing to make for one so eager to turn her back on her heritage."

"Saving a life, isn't she?" Buck offered.

"A life barely worth saving," George snorted heatedly. "A life that deserves whatever befalls it."

"Emily, your father doesn't mean that!" Susan said quickly.

"Susan, don't tell the child what I—"

"—Yo, Dad," Buck interrupted. "We're being a little . . . *fascist* here, aren't we?"

"Fascist? How dare you accuse me of that, Buck, you know—"

And now Buck rose, his composure cracked and his temper flaring.

"—What I *know* is that you're very smart about giving good advice to everybody else, but you have no perspective on your own problems. Gods, Dad, you're the biggest advertisement for Getting Along with the Man I know! You dress in their suits, you protect their laws, you live like they live, and you never make waves! And all of a sudden you're hot under the collar about some babe who's taken all that to the next logical extreme? How the hell can you deem her life worthless, whether she's right or not?"

"Buck, it was only an opinion, not—"

"Those are the kinds of opinions that *breed* fascism, Dad." George was fleetingly reminded of having hurled a similar accusation at Matthew not two hours before, but only fleetingly, because Buck was not finished.

"You know what I think, Dad? I think that actress punched your button. I think she reminds you of you, and you can't take it!"

"That is *not true!*"

"Isn't it? You don't have the ability to *detach*, Dad. You can't *abstract* yourself from your own cycles of behavior long enough, *just* long enough to see what's going on!" Then he expanded his attack to include his entire family. "*None* of you can! And that's why—"

Buck stopped. Cut himself short. Whap.

Maybe, George thought, *I'm not as objective as I like to think. But I can certainly tell this much. There is something lots bigger going on in my boy's head than the purview of this discussion.*

"Why what, son?" he asked softly.

Buck shifted his stance uneasily. At length he said, "Why I have to be alone for a while."

Buck turned to leave, and as he hit the kitchen doorway, George said, "Buck."

Buck stopped. Didn't turn, but stopped.

"You're free to discuss what troubles you, too, you know. I won't tell you wisdom is always at my command—but between all of us there should be something of value. And it's here whenever you want it."

Not looking back, Buck said, "I know that, Dad. Thanks."

And then he left the kitchen for the sanctuary of his RV.

There didn't seem to be useful words left after that. Looking at the rest of his family, George spread his hands slightly, dropped them to his sides, where they slapped audibly against his thighs, and returned to his seat at the table.

The rest of the meal was silent, save for basic amenities, but at least now there was some genuine eating going on. As if releasing dilemmas into the air had released hunger. Susan polished off a large portion, pausing every now and then to spoon-feed puree to Vessna, who stayed on her lap. And Emily went for seconds.

George ate methodically, thoughtfully.

Thinking about what Buck had said.

Thinking about what Matthew had said.

Unable to reach any satisfying conclusion.

Chewing over his own thoughts as he chewed his food.

Both having become quite filling—and rather tasteless.

DAY THREE

CHAPTER 12

MORNING. DAY SHIFT.

Albert Einstein belched his way through the police station's equipment room to get them what they wanted, the electronic gear they'd need to pull off their sting on the bogus Stabilite dealer. As he collected the individual pieces, he placed them in a special, padded carrying case.

"Here you go, Detective Sikes—*uurrrrrrppp!*—George."

They signed for the radio-controlled devices and he handed the case over to Matt, who slung its strap over his shoulder.

Being in charge of nonweapon material was a new responsibility for Albert, one that he shared with several khaki officers, and he took the job seriously, very much a stickler for procedure. He filed away the release forms with the corresponding authorization signed by Grazer. Next, he reached for a seltzer bottle he carried on his utility belt, and swigged a little, throwing his head back, putting into relief the very pregnant shape of his midriff. After which he winced, as if in pain.

"You okay, Albert?" Matt asked.

"Oh, yes, thanks to George's remedy. Sort of."

"Sort of?" George said.

Albert sighed. "May won't let me stop drinking carbonated water for the next week. The doctor said that three days would be sufficient to recreate a chemical balance in my system . . . but May's a—*uuuuuurrp!*—worrier. She doesn't want a repeat of yesterday."

"Look at it this way," Matt offered. "There's guys'd think it's pretty cool to be able to belch continuously and not worry about what anyone thought of 'em. It's purely medicinal, it's amusingly gross. Everyone here is in on the gag. What's not to like? Enjoy!"

"Oh, I do not worry about my manners appearing uncouth," Albert said. "It's just that . . . between the weight of the pod and all this water . . . forgive me for being indelicate, but—"

"You always have to pee," Matt guessed.

Albert nodded morosely.

"I can't perform any activity for more than six or seven minutes. I can't concentrate on a book or a TV show. I can't even sit still for a meal. All I can do is feel—*uuurrrppp-pup-pup*—pretty much the way I feel now. Excuse me."

He started to waddle off in extreme discomfort.

"Albert," George called after him. "Tell May from me that she needn't be so excessive. A little release of carbon dioxide will go a long way. There's no reason to go overboard."

Albert's hands went reflexively to his crotch.

" 'Overboard' is a very bad word to use right now, George. But I'll tell her. *Urrrrrrpppp!* Oh, I'll be only too happy to tell her. *Urp.*" And he continued on his quest for porcelain.

Matt turned to George.

"And how are *you* feeling?"

They had, in the normal course of things, greeted each other upon meeting at their adjoining desks nearly a half hour before—hellos and nods and amenities of on-duty procedure—but it wasn't until right now that conversation, *real* conversation, found its way back into their relationship.

"What do you mean?" asked George, knowing full well.

Matt shrugged. "Seems to me we both went a little overboard yesterday before we parted company."

There was affection for his partner in the half smile that came to George's face. "Oh, I don't know, Matthew. A little stimulating debate is good for one."

"It is, huh?"

"I believe so, yes."

"So?"

"So. How do I feel," George repeated. And thought about it because he did not immediately have the answer. "Not as smart as I thought," he concluded finally.

Matt, hearing the answer, became aware of the weight of the paperback he had fitted neatly into the inside breast pocket of his jacket.

"Funny you should say that, partner," he said.

More than just Sikes and Francisco were in on this now. Given the introduction of hard evidence into the case, stopping the spread of bad Stabilite had become an official Operation, whose active personnel would increase as—and if—the investigation progressed.

The first extra hand to be involved would be Bob Sled, the little druggist, himself. Some quick negotiating and plea bargaining between his public defender and the district attorney's office yesterday had created a "mutually satisfactory climate" in which he would work with the police to identify the Stabilite dealer in the act of making a transaction.

He was receiving his official briefing from George Francisco in the back room of *See Gurd Nurras* on what was very likely its last official day of doing business—under the current management, at any rate.

George handed him a palm-size black box, upon which was a little red switch.

"When your contact comes in," George said, "reach into

your pocket and slide the red switch up. Then conduct business as usual."

"And that's it?" asked Bob Sled.

"And that's it."

"Hey-hoo, pretty easy."

George thought it best not to comment that they'd kept it easy because they didn't trust him. Not that there was any more illegal activity he could get away with, but Matt had had the suspicion—and George had to agree—that Bob Sled was a panicker. He was too sweaty under pressure. Probably exhibit so many involuntary tics when the sting was on that he'd give away the game. So to minimize the pressure, he was given only one simple thing to do: Flip a switch to send the alert that the dealer had arrived. Matt and George had decided to let him think that was the depth and breadth of it.

And they didn't tell him the rest.

They didn't tell him about the microcamera and its built-in microphone in the scalp conditioner box, with a wide-angle view of the counter.

They didn't tell him that it was battery powered and remote controlled and would be activated by his flipping the red switch.

They didn't tell him that his most docile customer that day—a lazily browsing young man in a tank top, grooving mindlessly to the private sounds of his Walkman—would really be Paul Bearer, a Newcomer rookie; nor that the Walkman was really a two-way radio, whose left earphone received information and whose right earphone (which was really a camouflaged microphone, sensitive enough to pick up his voice through his auditory canal) sent information out.

And they didn't tell him about the very special *thing* that Paul could do.

They didn't want Bob Sled *looking* involuntarily toward the camera, or Paul. They didn't want him *trying to guide the conversation* between himself and the dealer unnaturally.

They wanted him to be as natural (or as unnatural) as he normally was.

Because that's how a sting got stung.

"Now, you say he usually arrives around ten-thirty?" George asked.

"Geez, Ossifer, I only tol' you that around forty-seven times."

Actually, it had been more like five. But that was okay. Careful reiteration of information was part of this business.

"Just clarifying," George said.

"Like clockwork. Ten-thirty."

It was nine o'clock when this conversation took place. But the cops would begin their surveillance *now* in any event.

Leaving nothing to chance.

Or so they thought . . .

Matt, in the front passenger seat, tried to hide the book when he heard George open the driver's side door of their unmarked cruiser. He didn't quite make it. And George didn't just slide into the car, talking and oblivious, as others might've done; that wasn't George's way. No, old George stuck his head in first, got a real good look at Matt's sudden furtiveness—

—and smiled. A smile that would have been infuriating if it weren't so warming; the proud smile of a teacher who discovers a student has been doing extracurricular work in *secret.*

"Matthew," he said, "you're *reading.*"

Matt made a tired flapping gesture with his hand. "Don't spread it around."

Settling behind the wheel and closing the car door, George asked, "What book is it?"

Matt exhaled quietly through his teeth. *Oh, Christ,* he thought, *oh, well, in for a friggin' penny . . .*

"I'll show you," he said, "but you gotta promise me something first."

"And what might that be?"

"Don't make me talk about it. Okay? No comments, no questions."

"Odd. But easy enough."

Matt held the cover of the book up and put it down quickly, as if it were a flash card. If the book meant anything to George, he gave away none of it on his face.

"Ah," he said, noncommittally, and Matt considered that a deeper act of friendship than George could possibly know.

They had parked their car across the street and half a block away from the drugstore. From this vantage point, they would conduct their surveillance, affording them a parallax view of the store facade. As for viewing the inside: There was a small remote television for that, on the seat between them, prepared to receive a program not even the best cable service could provide. Next to that was the walkie-talkie, which would connect them with Paul Bearer, the young rookie.

And now they would watch and wait. Mostly wait. Until they got the signal.

"Listen, ahhh," Matt said uncomfortably, "do you mind if I'm not great company for a while?" He somewhat guiltily indicated his book. "I'd rather not make conversation. I'm kind of into this."

"Nothing would make me happier than that you continue," George replied seriously, again, in such a way that Matt could draw no conclusions other than that his partner was willing to be solicitous. Or was he? For after he said it, George folded his arms and stared fixedly front, through the windshield.

Matt sighed, started to put his book away. "Well, if you're gonna be *that* way about it, make me feel like I'm *abandoning* you . . ."

With a look of surprise, George turned back toward

Matthew. "Oh, no, no, I did not mean to convey that impression. I was just, as I've heard my eldest daughter say, getting myself into Zen à la mode. Concentrating."

"That's 'Zen mode,' George. Concentrating on what?"

"A fascinating game I've discovered in the puzzle pages of the Sunday paper. I've become rather taken with the pun-and-anagram crosswords. I can't say I'm as proficient at them as I'd like to be. So many of the answers hew to colloquialisms that don't come naturally to me yet—'Zen mode,' I suppose, being an example of one such—but I've found that there are anagrams everywhere. On storefronts, awnings, passing cars, billboards, posters. And in moments when there is nothing to do but sit and wait, the game of anagrams is one I find useful and amusing. It relaxes and entertains the mind while keeping it active."

"Uh-*huh* . . ." Matt commented. And then, after a moment, because he knew he'd only pay for his ignorance later, "What the hell's an anagram?"

"I'm sorry, Matthew," George said with self-effacing charm, as if Matt's lack of knowledge were somehow *his* fault. "An anagram is the rearrangement of letters from a word, or group of words, to form *another* word, or group of words."

"Oh, yeah, I've heard of them," Matt said, relieved because he actually had.

"For example," George continued, "using the letters of your own name, Matthew Sikes, one could get 'Skis met wheat.'"

"'Skis met wheat' . . ." Dryly.

"Or 'Skim a stew,' provided you drop one of the *T*'s."

"Got it."

"Or, perhaps best of all, 'The Wet Kiss Ma.'"

"You can stop now, George."

"The title of your book there—*Black Like Me*—might be rearranged to produce, 'Lick 'em, Elba.'"

"Makes no sense. Elba's a place, not a person."

"Then how about 'Lickable me'?"

"Why, you little filth-monger, you. I didn't know your mind worked that way."

"The salacious ones are the most fun."

"Well, now you're talkin'. Can you find any others?"

Furrowing a bemused brow, George scanned the street. "In fact," he said, "there is a terribly suggestive anagram hidden within the name *See Gurd Nurras.* Only one would have to rearrange the Tenctonese letters, rather than the phonetic English spelling, and then translate."

"To arrive at—?"

George paused a moment, then shook his head slightly. "No, it's too dirty."

"Trust me, George, I can take it."

"No, no, I really can't. It would distract you from your book."

"George—"

"I insist, Matthew. See to the expansion of your mind. Don't worry about me and my frivolities. What you want to do is *so* much more important."

George faced forward anew, having once again betrayed no hidden agenda. But Matt was certain now, certain, that he had just been the victim of a subtle vengeance, and that if one were to look into the mind of George Francisco, one would find mischievous self-satisfaction.

In the face of which, what was there to do but read his book . . . ?

The remarkable, sobering, and deeply troubling thing about the odyssey of John Howard Griffin is that it never read as if it were a sociological treatise. Matt found it to be an emotional roller coaster with a novelistic power that tore at the soul, precisely because it wasn't *a fiction.*

The further Matt read, as Griffin's journey took him deeper and deeper into the South, the more often he kept flipping back to the passage at the front of the book that haunted him most of all. He'd read it so many times he very nearly had it memorized—and still it possessed him.

Griffin had planned on maintaining a cool journalistic objectivity about the task he'd undertaken. But that had been blasted away the moment he'd seen himself in the mirror, a white man utterly transformed into a black man.

"I had expected to see myself disguised," he wrote, "but this was something else. I was imprisoned in the flesh of an utter stranger, an unsympathetic one with whom I felt no kinship. All traces of the John Griffin I had been were wiped from existence. Even the senses underwent a change so profound it filled me with distress. I looked into the mirror and saw reflected nothing of the white John Griffin's past. No, the reflections led back to Africa, back to the shanty and the ghetto, back to the fruitless struggles against the mark of blackness. Suddenly, almost with no mental preparation, no advance hint, it became clear and permeated my whole being. My inclination was to fight against it. I had gone too far. I knew now that there is no such thing as a disguised white man, when the black won't rub off. The black man is wholly a Negro, regardless of what he once may have been. I was a newly created Negro who must go out that door and live in a world unfamiliar to me."

Matt wondered if Fancy, upon looking at her *transformation for the first time, had experienced the same feeling in reverse. Over and above all the things she'd have to sacrifice, had she felt . . .*

Control . . . ?

Power over her own life . . . ?

Permission to roam freely among the owners of the world . . . ?

Had she liked herself better, simply for knowing that now she would be liked by others, liked not in spite *of being a Newcomer, but liked without label or qualification?*

Yesterday, Matt had taken Fancy's side against George by saying that she'd "made a mistake" . . . but who the hell was he to determine that, any more than George had been to decide that she was irredeemably vile?

Every now and again, Matt found himself pulling back from the book a little, when it referred to the whites only restrooms and the back-of-the-bus indignities of the past. That kind of thing doesn't happen anymore, *he would think. And then he would remember . . . sure it did. Of* course *it did. But like everything else in this new age of technology and reason, it was just subtler.*

And so all-pervasive it could send you off the deep end.

Literally . . .

They got word about the jumper at exactly 2:37 on a Thursday afternoon. Matt remembered it clearly because Tuggle had been behind the wheel, and Matt had been the one to log it in on the clipboard, the better to reference it easily come time to fill out the paperwork. He had to be especially meticulous about writing it too, because Tug had just popped the bubble onto the roof of their unmarked car, hit the siren, and stepped on the gas, the sudden acceleration making Matt's hand shaky.

The destination to which they were racing was the Markell Tower, a skyscraper hotel in downtown L.A.

The crowd had gathered, of course. Guy wants to leap, you're gonna get a crowd. All types in the crowd, too, which was par for the course: concerned citizens, curiosity hounds, and that all-time fave—you know 'em, you love 'em, you can't live without 'em—the Cheerleaders.

"Jump!" they shouted. "Jump!"

Cheerleaders yer ass. Effin' Death Squad, if you asked Sikes, which nobody did. Idiots to boot. They thought it was like the movies: guy jumps, does his fall, dog-paddling through the air, screaming, hitting the pavement (*damn,* that smarts), cops and coroners and chalk outlines on the street. Telly Savalas sucking on a lollipop, asking hard questions; Danny Travanti, if you fantasized a cop from a younger, hipper generation, gritty and soulful, just like on the Hill.

What they didn't know, morons, was that unless you *really* dove when you took your dive—positioned yourself to slice through the air like a knife blade—the fall was a graceless thing, resistance from the air molecules causing the body in motion to cartwheel rather frighteningly, gravity pulling it back toward the building, against which it would bounce along the way. And as for the chalk outline . . . figure a humanoid body is, what, ninety percent water, something like that? Held in place by a particularly fragile surround of skin. Basic physics, folks. Ever see a water-balloon hit the pavement? You may get your chalk outline, but there's not a helluva lotta hope it'll come out lookin' too much like a thing that was once a person.

Sikes always wanted to rub this information into their drooling yahoo faces, but there was never time, not in a situation like this. He was always too busy trying to get upstairs before the jumper came down. This fella was very damn high up, too, thirty-second floor.

He and Tuggle waited very impatiently for the elevator, but when it came, at least hotel management had been smart enough to send a guy with a special key, allowing the elevator to pass all interim stops between L and 32.

When the elevator doors slid open, the hotel manager was there, Denis Markell himself, forty-eight, goatee, thinning hair line, subtle French accent.

"Are you *les gendarmes?*"

Tug, who had a reflexive need to lampoon pretension, strode out of the elevator a split second before Matt, saying, in his best black basso: "Dat be us."

"Avec moi, s'il vous plaît," Markell commanded, too high up on his personal food chain to give much of a *merde* about irony from a public servant, and spun on his heels with characteristic French primness, setting a long-legged quick-march pace which they followed.

"Ze man is a Newcomair," Markell informed them as they walked. "His name is Carl Orff, he paid cash for an overnight stay in our least expensive type room, and he brought wiz him a child."

As if there wasn't enough to keep them perky.

"A *child?"* Matt blurted.

"Oui. It is hard to know wiz Newcomairs, zey are so, well, *new,* but ze desk man informs me zat ze child looked to be about ten years old. I have not seen ze boy myself."

"Not much mystery about the young'uns," Tug said. "If he looked about ten, he was about ten."

They stopped at room 3206. A chambermaid was poised and ready with a key; a few other staff members gathered around also, waiting to help in ways they couldn't fathom and trying to control interference from onlookers as more and more guests stepped out of their rooms to observe.

From inside they could hear the wails of a young boy.

"Dahh-DEE. Please, DONNN'T! Dahh-*DEE!!!"*

And, more faintly, an adult voice:

"I just want you to *see,* that's all, Chuck, I just want you to *see* what your mother has done to me! And then you can *tell* her!" (The voice was fainter, not because it was any less intense, but because it was coming from outside, half its volume being whipped away by the breeze.)

It kept going on like that and had clearly been thus for quite a while. Every now and again the exchange would shift into Tenctonese, but there was no translation needed. Desperation made the same noises in any tongue.

The chambermaid, a young college student, unusually articulate and to-the-point for one in her job (sometimes God gave you a break in the detail work), said, "Every time I try to enter, even if it's only to comfort the boy, he threatens to jump. I don't dare call his bluff. He says he'll speak to cops, though."

"Sounds like he's willing to negotiate, then," Sikes commented, looking at Tuggle.

"I don't know," said the chambermaid. "Whatever his wife did to him, he's very bitter. He says he wants a cop to witness this because he knows it's a cop's job to get the facts right. A cop will deliver the message to her."

Tuggle frowned. "So what does he need the kid for?"

"To deliver the pain."

Matt ran a hand through his hair. "Mama Mia," he said. And then, "Hey, Tug, I fucked up Slag Psychology but good in PACT class. You wanna take this guy, I'll handle the kid?"

"Don't know 'bout no 'wanna,'" Tug replied. "But I'll do it."

He took the key from the chambermaid, knocked lightly on the door, started to open it.

"I'm warning you!" they heard from outside. *"I'm warning you!"*

"Stay away!" came the smaller voice from closer in. "Don't make my daddy jump!"

The door was open only a crack; Tuggle held it there, spoke through the narrow opening. "Son, we're two police officers. Tell your dad it's the police. He asked for us. Remind him that he asked for us."

They waited as the message was whimperingly conveyed. A minute later, Tug felt the doorknob moving within his grasp. He let it go, and the young boy, Chuck Orff, opened it.

"He says you can come in. Nobody else."

The boy wore a striped shirt, ripped Levis, ratty sneakers, and an expression of emotional devastation too deep for any ten-year-old to have to bear. Sikes knelt to his level, said, "C'mere," and the boy practically fell into his arms. Sikes held little Chuck tight, and Chuck returned the grip to match, as if Matt were a lifeline.

The room was, as Markell had said, a no-frills jobbie: twin beds, dresser drawers, a little side table, a chair, small bathroom to the right as you walked in, GE television with remote, and a phone. And, of course—now—an open window. Big one, pivot hinges, so it swung in like a revolving door.

Tuggle crossed to it, stuck his head out, looked left,

obviously spotting his man on the ledge, said, "Carl, I'm a cop, my name is Bi—"

And that was as far as he got before Carl's voice roared back from the ledge, "Not you! Not you! I don't want to speak to you! You're brown! I want one of the pink ones! I can only speak to one of the pink ones! Get away or I jump!"

A little spooked, Tuggle said, "'Kay, man, chill, chill," and backed the hell off. He turned toward Matt, with a look of dumb astonishment on his face.

"You believe this shit?" he said. "A bigot *Newcomer.*"

Little Chuck lifted his head from Sikes's shoulder, turned to face Tuggle.

"It's because you look like my other daddy," he said.

"Your other—" Tug began, and Matt interrupted.

"Wait a minute," he said, the tone of his voice implying that he was on to something. He cupped Chuck's chin in his hand and said, "Did your mommy leave your first daddy?"

The boy, ashamed of it, nodded silently.

"And . . ." Matt continued, "did her new boyfriend look like my partner? Brown, like that?"

Again, a nod. Sniffles.

"Hey, listen. None of this is your fault. None of it, you hear me? Now, let me ask you—"

"What's going on in there???" came Carl's voice from outside. *"Chuck?"*

"Hang in, Carl, pink one's on the way!" Tuggle called.

"You have to answer me quick, Chuck, so I can save your dad," Sikes said.

Sniff, sniff. "You promise?"

"Yeah, I promise," Matt vowed. Like a schmuck. And added, "Did your mommy take you to *live* with your new daddy?"

A nod.

"What's your mommy's name?"

"Bea."

"Does she know you're with your daddy?"

"Daddy said so."

"Said so when?"

"When he came to pick me up at school."

"Does he usually do that?"

"Nuh-uh. I go home on the school bus."

Great. Carl had kidnapped his kid, in addition to everything else.

"Chuck? Can I give you over to my partner? He's a really cool guy, he'll take care of you."

Chuck Orff, helpless among the bewildering world of grown-ups, nodded, and Matt handed the boy off to his partner.

Then he took a deep breath, trying not to freeze.

Tuggle creased his brow at Matt. His expression saying, *You got to do this, man.* Chuck's expression saying, *You promised!*

Matt squared his shoulders and crossed to the window, trying not to think about it too much. Just do it.

He stuck his head out, looked down. Yeah, you bet: long way. Too high up to hear the Cheerleaders, though. Their unamplified yells were snatched up by the breeze long before they could make the tall trip to floor thirty-two. And he could see that the emergency service trucks had arrived. Soon someone would be up here with a harness—for the cop, not the jumper; some rescues had actually been carried out by catching a leaper just as he started his fall—and down there they'd be pulling out a giant air mattress. Maybe. If it seemed worth it or practical, which Matt doubted. Pretty big gamble, calculating the angle of descent from this high. And no guarantee that if he landed where he was supposed to, he wouldn't break his neck anyway.

The harness guy would probably be an expert crisis negotiator, too. But Matt was the one who had done Slag Time. He didn't think he ought to wait anymore.

Man . . .

He turned to face Carl Orff.

Almost nondescript, really. Bookish. A thin, nice-guy face, small nose, open-necked blue denim sports shirt, gray slacks neatly pressed, rubber-soled black shoes keeping a grip on the ledge. Wasn't much of one either, ever so marginally shorter than the length of Carl's foot.

Carl's collar, and the pleat of his pants, flapped wildly in the breeze—had Matt thinking that if he blew in the guy's direction, a little make-a-wish-birthday-candle puff of air, that would be enough to do the guy but good.

"Hey, Carl," Matt began, cucumber cool. "Name's Matthew Sikes. Call me Matt if you like. Need to see ID?"

"I'll take your word for it," Carl said. Nice of him.

"I hear tell you wanna talk."

"No, I want to send a message to my wife. I thought I had made that clear."

"Better if you deliver it firsthand."

"If you try to talk me down, I won't waste any more time with you."

"You have to do what you want, Carl. But I have a job to do. If it means anything to you, I'm not getting out there with you. I'm real happy from in here. *Real* happy. I just thought I'd mention that. It's a pretty nice place to be, relatively speaking."

"Maybe for you. I have nothing left in there."

"You have a son who loves you."

"No, he loves Hal."

Hal. Had to be the name of The Other Man.

"Maybe so," Matt conceded. "I wouldn't know. But he loves you, too. Children have an infinite capacity for spreading it around. Not such a bad thing, really."

"I can't face him now."

"Why, because you took him? He barely understands that. What you're doing now? A little tougher, I admit, but you gotta get it in perspective. *He* wants to face *you."*

"It's not just today. It's everything. It's my . . . bitch wife. We're supposed to have bonded for life, do you know that about us?" Matt clocked the pause before the word *bitch;*

Orff was uncomfortable with the word. Seemed to be a genuinely genteel personality who was so unused to channeling his anger healthily—so unused to even acknowledging he had it—that when enough was stored up, it cracked him open and emerged twisted, distorted.

"Tell me about Bea."

"Why don't I just tell you why she left me, and that'll save us some time. I can . . . get going and you'll know all you need to picture her clearly."

". . . I'm listening."

"We all had our functions on the slave ship. We were all bred to do specialized jobs. Me, I was a botanist. Well, Matt, nothing grows on Earth the way it grew in the ship or the way they say it grew on Tencton. I couldn't find work doing what I know how to do. What I love to do."

"That's rough. What did you live on?"

"Not much. The pittances I brought home from unskilled labor jobs. Those that I could keep. I tried washing dishes at a diner. Got sick smelling all that meat on the grill . . ."

"No offense here, Carl, but let me cut to the chase, okay? It wasn't enough of a life for Bea and so—"

"She was out, shopping for clothes at a garage sale. Met this guy. Hal. He made a good living, he was fascinated by her and . . ."

"One thing led to another." It was all Matt dared say. Interspecies relationships had not yet become common, and at this juncture they were not viewed as simply interracial but as a genuinely perverse aberration.

"She said it was because he was *happy*. He was doing what he wanted and it made him *happy*. She said I had become bleak. That I hadn't been happy since . . . since we'd been on the ship. Can you imagine that? Being happy on the ship? Funny thing . . . relatively speaking, she was right."

Ever so gently, Matt modulated his tone; it was not so casual anymore. He wanted to lay in a foundation . . . very carefully.

"People crack under pressure, Carl. It happens. Sometimes it's nobody's fault."

"How can it have just happened? How can I have just missed it? *I'm an educated man!*"

Matt didn't immediately have an answer for that one, and it disturbed him. Groping, he said, "And you think jumping tells your wife that she destroyed you? I'll tell you what it really does. It tells your son that your education is useless. That everything is hopeless. Is *that* the legacy you want to leave him?"

"His legacy is this world. This damn, damned world. It absorbs you—then it *takes* things from you. It starts with your name . . ."

"Let's say you're right. Hell of it, let's just say you're right. Who's taking Chuck's father away from him? You can make him *think* it's the world. And he'll go through life believing it, and who knows what *he'll* do when he gets to be as old as you. Assuming he does. But you and I both know, Carl, that the world doesn't *make* you go out on a ledge. This bit of injustice is yours. You *own* it."

"No, she *brought me to it!*"

"How, Carl? *You're an educated man!*"

The turnabout silenced Carl for a moment. Then he hung his head, chin touching his chest. The movement made Matt catch his breath. Under these circumstances, it could literally be enough to overbalance the guy.

"Marriage," Carl said softly, "is supposed to be sacred in the eyes of Celine and Andarko. She betrayed ours. But reverence for one's offspring is supposed to be just as sacred. And that's where *I've* failed." He blinked away tears. "I couldn't even afford to come here to do this today . . . I spoke to Chuck on the phone last night. He has a little toy safe. I asked him to empty it and bring the bills to school . . ." He sniffed and sighed hugely. "Ohhh, dear. It's time to do this . . ."

Carl began to shift his feet, and Matt shouted, "No, wait!

Wait!" And when Carl *did* wait, Matt said, "Talk to me about Celine and Andarko."

"It would take too long to—"

"No, I know who they are. I mean . . . what do they mean to *you* . . . right now?"

"They are . . . the ones who see what I have done. I can live out my life awaiting and dreading their judgment or . . . I can simply face it now. I'm useless to my son if I'm damned."

"Who says you're damned?"

"All the covenants I've broken. Can you imagine they'll forgive me?"

Matt's next words came out of his mouth with no particular speed; they were, in fact, meticulously formed on his tongue and teeth, beautifully modulated, elegantly delivered. But he barely believed he was saying them. He felt utterly detached from them, as if hovering three feet in front of himself, thirty-two storeys above the ground, watching his performance.

"Better than that. I think they'd approve."

Long silence now. Matt had seen jumpers go in just such silences. But Carl turned his head as far as it would go toward Matt.

"Why do you say that?"

Matt hadn't a clue. But the hook was in. He *sensed* it. And improvised recklessly.

"Look, what you did . . . the deed, I don't know, iffy, I suppose . . . but the *motive* . . . to send a message . . . about the sanctity of the family. You've *done* that. How can they not get *behind* that? And so far nobody's been hurt. It's called having your cake and eating it too. Doesn't happen too often."

It was bullshit. It was circular logic. It was nonsense. It was against every sensible fiber in Matt's body.

". . . okay . . ." said Carl in a very small voice, reaching out a hand for Matt to grab.

It was working.

Jesus Christ.

"Tug!" Matt yelled, and as he extended his arm out, he felt the reassuring grip of Tug around his waist, anchoring him, and he reached, reached, felt Carl's stretching fingers, leaned forward, came around with the other hand, gripping the belt line, guiding Carl back an inch at a time, and it seemed to go on forever, but when Carl was safely in front of the window's opening, Matt *pulled* for all he was worth and Carl fell in, on top of him. Whereupon everything seemed to happen very fast: Chuck running into his father's arms, the harness guy and *his* partner from emergency services, who must've been there through most of it, swooping down to collect Carl Orff and son, Chuck waving gratefully at Matt as they carried the boy out, and Tuggle helping Matt up, slapping him on the back, shouting, "You are one talk-'em-down mofo!"

And Tuggle was right. He was.

But the victory was both sweet and sour.

Because he knew he hadn't done it without help, and at that, help from the last person in the world he wanted to acknowledge or credit.

But he also knew that he would not be at peace with himself unless he found a way to do so.

In the right way, for him. And at the right time.

"Matthew, it's time."

Matthew looked up from the book, realizing he had been fixated on the same paragraph for minutes, maybe longer, not taking any of it in, his mind elsewhere. But George's voice had reached into his memory and pulled him back into the real world, where the immediacy of events came back to him in a liquid rush—

the stakeout

the drugstore

Bob Sled

the dealer

the case

the monitor

—and betraying no outward signs of adjustment, his eyes flicked to the small TV set between them, whose screen had just gone from snow to a black-and-white wide shot of Bob and the back of some guy at the counter. The guy carried a deep briefcase, suitable for the transport of pharmaceuticals.

They were speaking in concertedly hushed whispers, too softly for Matt and George to distinguish words from the camera's hidden microphone. George adjusted the volume on the set. It didn't help much, but it wasn't worth fretting about. The camera contained a Super 8 cassette, and the corner of their monitor screen said REC, so they knew it was all going on tape. The soundtrack could be electronically filtered and enhanced later. Right now all they needed to see was the exchange of goods and cash.

As they waited, George kept up a running dialogue with the young Newcomer rookie, Paul Bearer, who was in the store. . . .

"Can you see him from where you are?" George's voice crackled softly into Paul's left ear.

"Mmm-*hm,"* Paul answered, the object of his life to keep articulated speech to a minimum, to make any vocal sounds that issued from him seem as if he was merely gettin' down with the soun' of his mean tape machine.

"Anything seem to be happening yet?"

"*Mm*-mm," he replied, that one a negatory. So far they were just talking. The mark, as far as Paul could tell, wasn't especially remarkable: average height, not quite six feet; between thirty-five and forty; hair as black and shiny as the casing on a new stereo; gray jacket and slacks, white shirt, black tie. The conservative outfit implied a working stiff or a fellow who had little imagination. Not that the two were mutually exclusive, but you hadda remember, this guy was a maverick operator; his bailiwick was a designer drug; and that suggested he was capable of some mercenary invention.

Unless, of course, he worked *for* somebody. Somebody bigger. Couldn't rule that out, not yet.

Paul pretended to browse the shelves, shifted his angle of view enough to get a lingering bead on the man's face. Combined with the hair, the facial features bespoke black Irish or Italian, though Paul would have laid odds on the latter: intense eyebrows, cruel good looks (that is, his handsomeness did not seem particularly benevolent), and thin lips set in a constant, tight grimace when he wasn't talking. . . .

Which he seemed to be doing far too much . . . because dumpy little Bob was looking worried.

Paul retreated a ways and risked simple speech.

"Something's going on. Don't like it."

"Elaborate," George's voice said.

"Supposed to be a simple transaction. Right? Why the hell are they talking so long?"

"And you can't hear them?" A reasonable question. Paul, having a Newcomer's super-sensitive hearing, should have been able to pick up the conversation easy. But there was a detail they hadn't counted on.

"Fans."

"What?"

"Free-standing fans, two of 'em. They circulate the air great, but they're cuttin' out the highs." The "highs" were the higher frequencies that carried sibilants and hard consonants. "From here it just sounds like enthusiastic gibberish."

"Can you move in closer without being conspicuous?"

"Gonna try."

The dealer was gesticulating a little now. Previously he'd been a cool customer; he hadn't done anything like that before. Little Bob Sled was flapping his arms a bit too. But tight, like he was trying to keep a lid on things, control 'em.

Felt wrong, felt wrong.

Then Bob Sled shrugged with angry reluctance, and the

dealer followed him into the back of the store. Where Paul had no access.

"Fuck," he said in Tenctonese.

It didn't seem the time to discuss decorum with the young officer. Mentally marking that as a subject more appropriate for later discussion, George said simply, "We saw."

The two words were heavily weighted. The back room of *See Gurd Nurras* was not wired for sound, had, in fact, no surveillance equipment of any kind. And why?

Because Bob Sled had assured them that the exchange of merchandise and money always happened at the counter. The mystery man came in as a salesman and left as a salesman; to the naked eye, there was nothing untoward going on, just a normal restocking of supplies. Routine.

And now the routine had been altered. Whatever was going on back there, they had no way of knowing.

"*What do you want me to do?*" came Paul's voice over the walkie-talkie. Tinged with a little impatience, a little desperation, and with good reason. There was a serious judgment call to be made here.

Technically Bob Sled was now helping the cops, and that meant he was under their protection. But he had just walked out of their reach—unless Paul was to burst into the back room, gun drawn, and ID himself. Unless George and Matthew were willing to risk scuttling the investigation for the sake of Bob Sled's questionable life. And that meant assuming that the little druggist was even in danger. For all they knew, there was just a simple conversation going on in there, maybe not even a particularly heated one.

They could break in on it, but they'd never be able to prove what the mark had said to the druggist before they did, not in court; that would be hearsay. (Yes, there was the tape, but they didn't know what it would yield yet, and suppose it provided them with *nothing . . . ?)*

They could search the mark's briefcase, but they'd be on shaky legal ground without a warrant for that specific purpose. If the guy had the bad drug on him, and some bleeding-heart judge thought they'd violated his civil rights, the entire case was null and void: fruit of the poisoned tree. If the guy *didn't* have the drug on him, they would have just given him a warning to lay low, defeated their own purpose. Worse still, he could decide to be a troublemaker and sue for illegal search and seizure.

All this ran through the minds of George and Matthew in the space of a blink—and, once it had, George decided to forget chiding Paul for his expletive altogether. There was a poetic simplicity to the way he'd summed up a complicated situation.

George exchanged a look with Matthew, whose eyes reflected his own concern. A split-second decision was required. Gamble right, they could emerge heroes. Gamble wrong, they became stains on the escutcheon.

But Matthew's eyes reflected George's instinct, too. Reinforced by a tight, quick shaking of Matthew's head back and forth.

George spoke again into the walkie-talkie.

"Do nothing," he ordered.

Stabilite was a designer drug. And a very specialized one at that. They were gambling that the nature of the drug might indicate the criminal disposition of the dealer—unsavory but not lethal.

"But—" Paul's voice began.

"Wait, and proceed as planned," George said, firmly.

"Roger," said Paul, tightly, and proceeded to do just that . . . for seven minutes, minutes in which every second held the possibility of Bob Sled's body on the back room floor, in a growing pool of his own pink blood.

He was starting to wonder if he shouldn't just say to hell with orders, be a renegade, pull his concealed pistol, save a life while he could—

—when the dealer emerged from the back room—

—alone—

—two seconds later followed by Bob Sled, looking disappointed, but none the worse for wear—

—seen by George and Matthew on the monitor in their cruiser, and heard clearly for the first time, too . . . for as the dealer was leaving, he was saying in full voice, "I'm sorry it couldn't work out," and Bob Sled, hand raised in melancholy farewell, replied, "I'm sorry, too." Unheard by them, Matt, in English, used the same word the young rookie had uttered not eight minutes before.

"It didn't go down," he growled. "Son of a *bitch,* it didn't go down!"

Which was probably true, but nonetheless, George, his mouth poised over the walkie-talkie, barked the word *"Go!"*—

—and Paul Bearer moved into action. Looking the other way, he stepped into the aisle the dealer was exiting, and their bodies collided.

"Sorry, man," Paul mumbled.

It was a brief collision, no harm done, not particularly memorable as pedestrian mishaps go, but the dealer found it a little startling. He was either in a vaguely unpleasant mood or just generally a vaguely unpleasant fellow, for he pointed to Paul's earphones and said, "You know, if you took those damn things off, you wouldn't be so oblivious."

To which Paul lifted an earphone and said "Whut?" as dumbly as he could. Whereupon the dealer made a dismissive gesture at him and continued on his vaguely unpleasant way.

Never suspecting that a small device, no bigger than a cuff button, had been deposited into the inside right breast pocket of his jacket, traditionally the least used pocket of right-handed men (who tended to use their good hand to reach over to the left breast pocket), and therefore the last to be searched or emptied. The device would send a simple signal to a receiver in the car occupied by Detectives Sikes and Francisco. As long as they could stay within ten blocks of the signal, give or take, they would be able to follow the dealer anywhere he went.

Paul Bearer, while growing up on the slave ship, had developed into an expert pickpocket, which was sometimes of benefit to his nearest and dearest—and always a good way to confound the Overseers.

And putting something *into* a pocket was not really so different from taking something *out of* a pocket.

That was the special *thing* Paul could do.

Having done it, he closed in on Bob Sled to find out what had gone awry.

George kept an eye on the monitor while Matt tracked the dealer as he emerged from *See Gurd Nurras,* heading (they hoped) for a nearby car.

"Ask him what happened," George said into the walkie-talkie.

"I'm ahead of you, Detective," Bearer said respectfully, and George watched the black-and-white screen as the young rookie walked into the frame, flipped his ID for Bob Sled, who couldn't have seemed more surprised, and led the little pharmacist over to the shelf that displayed the scalp conditioner box in which the minicam was hidden.

"It's in *there?*" Bob said. "All this time I've been on *television?* Hey-*hoo,* Ossifer . . ." Bob leaned into the lens, and George got a good view of his nostrils.

"Just tell Detective Francisco what you told me," Paul said wearily, pulling the little man back.

"He insisted we go into the back to talk in private. So I knew somethin' was different. I tried to argue with him that someone had to watch the store, but he was gettin' steamed, and I knew if I pushed him too far, he'd get suspicious. So into the back we went. That's where he told me he was reconsidering some of his outlets. Our arrangement was over, thank you very much, and he appreciated our brief, but fruitful association."

As Bob was talking, Paul removed the earphones from his

head and positioned the earpiece between himself and the druggist so that both could hear George's questions.

"Did he indicate why? Did he feel there was any heat or pressure to—"

"He didn't say, and you can just bet I tried to ask him."

"And he evidenced no fear that you would try to blackmail him or turn him in?"

"With what leverage? I *still* dunno who the hell he is, and I was in on it, too."

"George," Matthew interrupted, an alert informing his tone of voice.

George shifted his gaze from the TV monitor to the street. The dealer was getting into a powder blue midsize '93 Mazda.

George turned on the ignition of their cruiser, let it idle as they waited for the dealer to pull away from the curb. Into the walkie-talkie, he said, "Close down the store, collect the electronics, and take Mr. Sled into custody. You performed nobly, Officer Bearer, and it will be duly noted on your record."

"Hey-hoo," said the young rookie wryly, and George turned off the monitor just as Bob Sled was giving his police guardian a comic look of surprise.

At that same instant, Matthew was activating the tracer. The beep it sounded was frequent, strong. The dealer's car pulled out into traffic. After a respectable pause, George did the same.

"Boy, I do not wanna go belly-up on this one in the worst way, George."

"I feel the same, Matthew. We can only hope the 'gentleman' leads us where we'd like to go."

"Question is, what the hell are we gonna do when we get there? *If* we get there? We got nuthin' to go on here. No probable cause, nuthin'."

"Except your conviction from the start that it needed doing. That is not nothing, Matthew."

Matthew looked sideways at him. "Thank you, George,"

he said with an unusual gentleness. And then, adjusting his tone quickly, "So you think that means I've earned the right to hear that damned anagram?"

"What, you mean the reworking of *See Gurd Nurras?*"

"Yes."

"Taken from Tenctonese and translated into English?"

"Yes."

"The dirty one? There are several oth—"

"Yes, George, the *dirty* one!"

George told him.

Matthew's face paled a bit.

"Jesus, George, that really is disgusting."

George kept driving, smiling.

CHAPTER 13

WHEN CATHY THOUGHT back on it, she supposed there was probably a reason why she'd forgotten to take off her shoes, a subconscious instinct that made her want to have something with her that was hard, that could do damage. She couldn't imagine, in the end, that it had been total coincidence, negligence, or even a simple, mortal mistake. The kind of efficiency her life-style and her career required, she didn't *make* those kinds of mistakes.

She'd spent the night on her cot in the nurses' dorm, as she had the previous night. She'd gotten to sleep shortly after dinner, which she'd had down in the cafeteria. A slow and carefully eaten dinner it had been, too, Cathy mentally battling the sympathetic nausea that lingered faintly from her last session with Fran. The symptom being psychosomatic, she was determined, while she could, to be stronger than *it* was. And because she had been concentrating so hard, dinner had hardly been pleasant . . . but it had stayed down. As it would have to. She needed, would be needing, the fuel.

She slept lightly and never for more than one or two hours

at a time. Twice she stirred awake, sensing that Fran had done the same. Groggy-headed as she was, the simple act of putting on shoes seemed the most onerous of chores, but it would have to be done. Exhaustedly, she would sit on the edge of the cot, holding her head as she bent down to reach for and strap on her high heels—the only shoes she had, not having been home since her night at the theatre—and then, zombielike, she'd go dutifully click-clacking down the hallway, into the elevator and, finally, down *that* corridor on the fifth floor to look through the window into Fran's cubicle.

But both times she arrived, Fran was curled up, asleep. It looked to be a sleep of dark dreams, but it was sleep nonetheless.

Either Cathy was being oversensitive (responding to signals that weren't Fran's or that were wholly products of Cathy's imagination), or Fran's periods of wakefulness simply weren't sustaining for very long.

Cathy didn't even remove her shoes the second time she climbed back into bed. If Fran needed her, she'd just be ready to go. And Cathy fully expected a third wake-up call.

As it turned out, ironically, Fran didn't stir for the remainder of the night—at least according to the night nurse at the desk who periodically checked the monitor—and come morning, Cathy woke before her charge, which left her the option of trying to grab either a few minutes more of rest or a quick breakfast. Feeling about as rested as she expected to be—not very, but enough—she opted for the latter, keeping it simple, dry cereal topped with fruit juice.

She was on her last bite when she felt a tightness in her chest, a sensation more like heat than pain; it was compounded by a vague woolliness at the back of her skull. And now she had no doubt. Fran Delaney was *absolutely* awake. Experiencing a drug-deprivation "hangover."

Cathy sat an extra minute at the cafeteria table, closing her eyes and waiting with dread for the sympathetic feelings to spread to her stomach, but they stayed where they were.

Good. Breakfast, like dinner before it, was safe, and she'd be fortified for the trial to come. Maybe.

She arrived at the door to the detox cubicle, punched in her code, opened the door, entered as it shut behind her—and toppled face forward onto the floor mat.

"Damn," she muttered over the sound of Fran's laughter, which sounded irksomely cruel this morning.

"Fantastic entrance there, Cath! Not much use for Ibsen, but wait'll they see you in Feydeau."

"You sound altogether too chipper for a woman who feels rotten," Cathy said. She struggled into a sitting position and shook her head slightly at her feet.

"I takes my entertainment as I gets it," Fran quipped, and laughed again.

Cathy unstrapped her shoes. She'd forgotten about the high heels; upon contact with the floor's rubber padding, they'd sunk right in and unbalanced her. She placed them by the wall behind her, under the keypad, not even pausing to consider her usual routine of leaving them without.

She slid over to Fran.

"How did you sleep?"

Fran smiled the charismatic smile of one possessed.

"You should *kno*-ow."

The mischievous inflection conveyed an ugly implication: that Fran, aware of the bond between them, had been deliberately disrupting Cathy's sleep pattern through the previous night. Why? To keep Cathy from being as fully rested and completely alert as she might be. To take *advantage.*

The notion that Fran would do something so malicious angered Cathy. Considering all she was *doing* for this woman, how *could* she—

Careful, a little voice reminded her, *careful. Fran's withdrawing from a drug, her erratic sleep pattern was entirely normal, no more consciously induced than breathing. She just wants you to* think *she did it on purpose. She wants to throw you off guard, get the upper hand,* manipulate *your emotions. Fully in keeping with that temporary psychosis Steinbach warned you about. Remember what he told you about this phase of it: "The only power she has is the power you* give *her."*

Cathy decided it was best not to banter with Fran, to avoid anything that smacked of competition, not that she had the patience if she'd felt otherwise.

"Nice try, Fran," was all she said.

Fran's face betrayed no disappointment.

"And you can't blame a girl for trying," she said airily.

So far, Cathy thought she had met two Fran Delaneys: a smart, sensitive artist and an embittered woman, too angry for her years. The actress swung from one extreme to the other, sometimes without segue or warning, and Cathy knew that was a result of the withdrawal and its concomitant depression. But the truth of who Fran Delaney *really* was lay in some combination of the two. Cathy wondered what the natural proportions were . . . wondered if she could possibly even *like* this actress-being once she was whole again (assuming she was *ever* whole again) . . . wondered what Matt saw of value in her besides artistry, which, alas, was not the sole province of nice people . . . found herself, for the first time, fighting a twinge of jealousy.

"I don't know what I can blame you for," Cathy said suddenly. "I don't know how much of your behavior is due to the withdrawal and how much is just plain old mean spiritedness. I don't know what my rights are here. I don't know when I'm entitled to be angry—or if—or when I'm supposed to make allowances for your condition. I only know that I don't like being treated badly. And I wish you'd stop and think about that. You may not be entirely responsible for everything that has happened or will happen—but you're alert enough right now."

Cathy found herself instantly proud of the speech—also feeling that it had been something of an inspiration. Rather than try and dance around the problem, she'd confronted it directly, labeled it precisely. For all the many types she'd met on the slave ship and here on Earth, Cathy didn't flatter herself as much of a psychologist; but she had learned that often the best defense in the face of attempted emotional manipulation was to draw a line in the sand: Define your space, refuse to let it be violated.

And now she had done so.

Fran seemed to take it all in stride.

"And if I abuse you again, what? You'll leave?"

Having an open and honest personality, Cathy was susceptible to attack—but also difficult to co-opt.

"I didn't say that, don't put words in my mouth. I told you I don't want to play mind games, that's all. What you do with that information is up to you."

"Maybe I can't help myself."

"Maybe that's your whole problem."

The split second it left her mouth, Cathy regretted the sentence. "I'm sorry," she said quickly, softly.

Fran, though she seemed to have been stung, covered it in a shrug restricted by the straitjacket.

"Nah, don't be. Maybe I deserved it." Then, after a beat, she blinked her left eye rapidly. "Dammit."

"What?"

"Something in my eye. Third time this morning. *Dam*mit, I wish I had my hands free!"

Cathy didn't know if this was a trick or not, but she doubted it. Among other things, it was too blatant, too unrefined, too—well, too stupid to fall for.

"Try to keep your eye open and don't blink," Cathy said. "If something's there, you don't want it getting trapped under your eyelid." She rose, crossed to the sink, moistened a paper towel with warm water, then moved to kneel by Fran, saying, "Hold still, now."

She positioned her thumb on Fran's cheek and, ever so gently, used her forefinger to hold Fran's eyelid in place against the bone above the eyeball, widening access to the surface of the eye. She moved in for a close look . . .

Saw it.

Pretty big offender too, as eye irritants went, though she wasn't quite sure what it was.

"Hold still," she said again, and, with an expert touch, dabbed once lightly against the eyeball.

She inspected the moist surface of the paper towel.

"Did you get it?" asked Fran, blinking, testing the sensation. "It sure *feels* like you got it!"

"Yes, it's here," Cathy replied, her voice toneless as she looked at what she'd removed.

"You make it sound like it's the proverbial plank," Fran commented. Cathy didn't understand the reference, didn't know the proverb, just recognized the stark shift in Fran's expression when the actress shifted her gaze to the paper towel and she, too, saw what the object was.

An eyebrow hair.

Third time that morning, Fran had said.

She was losing her facial hair.

The women looked at each other.

Then, in a hoarse whisper, Fran breathed:

"Fe dessa etoe nigebnog."

Oh, Goddess, it's starting.

For a moment Cathy thought it was a comment on the eyebrows beginning to fall away—then she realized Fran had been talking about something else altogether, as the actress's body tensed.

"Scalp itches," Fran whispered.

Cathy could feel it too, a sympathetic echo on her own scalp, a tingling that started to burn, not unlike the chemical heat from a medicinal ointment.

"God, I wish I could *scratch* it or *rub* it or *some*thing!"

"Here, let me," Cathy offered, quickly encircling Fran's shoulders with one arm, bringing her close, taking her free hand to Fran's head. She felt presumptuous scratching or rubbing without a specific directive to do so; so she tenderly did what seemed warranted and right—spread her fingers and passed them through Fran's thick hair like a comb, staying close to the skin.

Something felt odd.

She pulled her hand away.

Clumps of hair came away with it.

She shivered involuntarily, shook the hair off, and looked up to see the appalled expression on Fran's face.

"I'm starting to look like you," the actress said quietly, and it sounded like an accusation.

She scuttled about two feet away from Cathy, and then her eyes rolled up so far only the whites were exposed, and she moaned "Oh-*ohhh*-OHHH!" and a violent spasm threw her head back and arched her body. A wave of discomfort hit Cathy, too, but nothing that made her muscles act involuntarily, nothing like what Fran was experiencing; and then there were tremors that rippled through Fran's body, one, two, more, seemingly countless, and Cathy was about to press the emergency button on her wrist band—

—when everything stopped.

It was as if some invisible being that held Fran in its grip had suddenly just *let go,* and she collapsed limply onto her back.

Her shape looked funny under the straitjacket. Weird around the right collarbone.

Fran moaned softly in pain.

"What is it?" Cathy asked.

"Shoulder," came the reply in a strained, gasping voice.

It wasn't a pain that Cathy shared on any sympathetic level, but it seemed apparent enough what had caused it. The spasm had been so brutal it had dislocated Fran's right shoulder.

"Hold still," Cathy said, scooting to Fran. Gingerly she rolled Fran over, to expose the straitjacket straps.

"You don't want to do that," Fran husked. "Don't cause yourself trouble. Call for a doctor, I'll wait."

"No time," Cathy said, undoing the buckles. "It's dislocated. It has to be reset immediately or it'll swell up. In your condition, I don't want to chance that."

The buckles undone, Cathy set about gingerly unwrapping the sleeves from about Fran's body and even more gingerly maneuvering the straitjacket off, over her arms in short, gentle tugs . . .

The nurse at the fifth floor desk looked up at the monitor just at the point when Cathy was stroking Fran's head. *Good bedside manner, our Ms. Frankel,* the nurse thought, and turned away from the screen, having noted that things seemed under control.

Which gave her license to make a quick trip to the ladies' room.

Which left the monitor unobserved and unattended for three minutes and twenty-seven seconds.

Which was all it took . . .

Fran was sitting up, Cathy positioned behind her. Cathy put one hand on Fran's right shoulder, the other encircling the top of the arm where bone was supposed to meet socket at the joint.

"Relax now," Cathy said. "The sensation might be a little jarring, but it shouldn't hurt. Okay . . . one . . . two . . ."

As if by magic, Fran's shoulder snapped back into place all by itself, Fran brought her elbow forward, said, *"Three!"* and slammed it back into Cathy's gut. Cathy went back and bent inward at the same time, in pain, unable to catch her breath; and the next thing she knew, Fran was on top of her, pinning down her shoulders, trying to unfold her legs, the better for Fran to put her knees to Cathy's chest and *really* nail her guardian to the floor.

"Movement classes," Fran hissed triumphantly, "tool of the trade. D'you know, if you're particularly supple, you can actually learn to dislocate your shoulder at will? A gymnastic parlor trick. Who'd've thought it would come in handy?"

I should have known, Cathy thought in the split second after. The shoulder pain was the one she hadn't sympathetically felt. Because there hadn't *been* any pain. Oh, the spasms that'd racked Fran's body had been real enough. But those few seconds immediately *after* . . . It was both amazing and appalling to think that Fran had clearheadedly improvised a plausible ruse out of her own genuine suffering.

Cathy tried to struggle out of Fran's grasp. Fran reared an arm back quickly and slapped her so hard she heard ringing in her ears.

"That's for lying to me!"

"I . . . never . . ." Cathy gasped.

"Your boyfriend *works for the city??!!* You're here for *Matt Sikes,* I *saw* him at the theatre! As soon as you said it, I knew. I *knew!"*

Fran used her full weight to rock up and down on Cathy's shoulders; Cathy tried to slap at her, but Fran kept her head back, and most of the blows fell short or landed harmlessly on Fran's arms.

"He wants to keep me down, safe and Slag, just like before!" Fran raged.

"No!" Cathy shouted.

"Give me the code to get out of here or I'll kill you!"

"NO!" Cathy roared, and by now her wind was back sufficiently that her legs, bent against her chest, could piston out, and they did, pushing Fran off, sending her reeling back into the sink.

"Kata-be," Fran cursed, and Cathy got to her feet as fast as she could.

Fran was preparing to charge, and Cathy held her gaze, bobbing and weaving, back and forth, trying to forestall the inevitable. She had not forgotten her wrist band, nor the alert button. But she didn't want to press it, not yet. Matt would forgive her if she bailed out, without question; but Matt believed Fran was worth saving; and Cathy, after all this, needed to know that was true. She would never know any such thing, though, if she pressed that button. Steinbach's cronies would pull her out of here so fast the friction would burn away Fran's eyebrows before they could finish falling—and Fran would have to take her slim chances alone. Cathy couldn't let that happen.

And on that altruistic thought, she received Fran's next attack . . .

. . . as Dr. Steinbach, making his rounds, passed the unoccupied fifth floor desk, looked automatically at the monitor and saw . . .

. . . Fran around Cathy's waist, ramming her into the wall, as Cathy reflexively grabbed Fran's hair to pull her head away, push her aside.

But the hair freely gave way, entire locks of it loose in Cathy's hand, giving her no leverage at all. It was the *sound* of the hair leaving Fran's head that shocked the actress into a moment of vulnerability, however, or so Cathy thought, because with no other reason for doing so, Fran pushed away, horror-struck, and shouted, "What are you *DOing?* What are you *DOing?*" as her hands went up to feel the damage to her head, and she realized that she was *feeling* a great, patchy bald spot—

—and that unleashed an ululating wail of fear and outrage that grew in volume and rose in pitch . . .

. . . and Steinbach said "Mother of us all!" and yelled for an orderly, whereupon a big, muscle-bound fellow answered the call, and they both went bolting for the cubicle . . .

. . . and Fran came rushing at Cathy fingernails first, slashing. With a survival instinct that came from Cathy knew not where, Cathy ducked, weaved, got behind Fran, and pushed the actress into the wall, head first, where she lost her purchase and body-slammed onto the floor.

And that's when Cathy raced to grab one of the high-heeled shoes she'd left in the corner. Wielded deftly enough, a hard high heel can do as much damage as a stiletto, albeit more crudely; Cathy was counting on that; and as Fran was getting up, unseeing, she raised the shoe high.

She brought it down on the keypad control by the door, sending a shower of sparks flying.

She had seen, out of the corner of her eye, through the door's window, the faces of Steinbach and the orderly. She knew they would drag her out of there if she didn't come willingly; and since the door opened and closed electronically, she'd done the only thing she could think of that might buy her and Fran some more time together:

She sabotaged the lock mechanism.

Or at least she hoped she had . . .

. . . and her wish was granted, for on the other side of the door, Steinbach was punching 3051 frantically, over and over. He had seen what she'd done and blurted, "Jesus, Cathy, have you lost your *mind?"* but the door did not give because for the moment, the lock was well and truly jammed, and Steinbach, still trying the code in what he now knew full well was vain, muttered, "Come on, Cathy, don't do this to me," while the orderly waited nervously behind him, having no real purpose, shifting uneasily from foot to foot as inside . . .

. . . Cathy watched Fran trying to rise. And knew that if she was to have any chance here, any hope at *all,* she'd have to do something decisive, and fast, make a statement, set some ground rules—

—and then she knew what it was. Something out of character for her, something she would not like herself much for. But there wasn't a lot of choice in this room, and she could only work with what she had—

—so she swooped down, grabbed Fran's hospital gown by the nape of the neck with one hand, pulled up on the material around the waist with the other, and did exactly what she'd done last night, dragged Fran Delaney to the toilet, and put her face in it.

All the way in, into the water.

And held it there.

Despising herself, disgusted that it had come to this, held it there.

As Fran's arms uselessly flailed.

The flailing getting weaker.

Held it there.

For five . . .

. . . ten . . .

. . . fifteen . . .

". . . sixteen, seventeen, eighteen . . ."

(through gritted teeth, not even aware she'd begun counting out loud)

". . . nineteen . . ." seconds

and on *"Twenty!"* she heaved Fran's body up and flung it down as if it were no more consequential than a rag doll.

Fran landed with a *thump*ing sound on her back, spluttering and dazed. There was almost a full minute of coughing, blinking, breath-catching and face-rubbing before she was able to collect herself. When at last she did, she stayed where she was on the floor, looking up at Cathy in astonishment.

"You might've *drowned* me," she said.

Cathy returned the look.

What she thought was: *I would not have drowned you, no.*

What she thought was: *But I wonder if, in bonding, I've come to share not only your physical pain but your need to lash out, your violence.*

What she thought was: *Yes, I wonder . . . but I suspect it was after all just me being angry, feeling desperate, looking for a way to get through to you. Can't you see? If I want to get* through *to you, I am not about to* drown *you. I didn't even want to* hurt *you. I only want to help.*

What she *said* was:

"At last we understand one another."

And on that note, the *Leethaag* continued.

CHAPTER 14

TRAFFIC OUT OF downtown Los Angeles that late morning was gridlock purgatory, the worst for keeping up single-car surveillance on a moving vehicle. Sikes and Francisco had yet to discover that their man would be heading south.

The good news was that in a gridlock tail, the perp's car is always just as jammed up as yours is. Maintain a healthy distance and together you can crawl along or idle in neutral forever. Probably he'll never be any the wiser.

The bad news was that "probably" isn't always good enough. If the perp is especially on the ball, he'll notice the same car in his rearview mirror once too often, especially if his route is idiosyncratic. So naturally, part of the trick is deciding the precise parameters of "a healthy distance." You don't want to maintain *too* healthy a distance because you don't want to remain stuck in traffic when up ahead it's finally starting to clear for the car you're tailing; suddenly he takes off and you're stuck between a seventy-five-year-old grandma and a kamikaze computer operator from Taiwan, their horns blaring louder as the beep on your tracer device fades to nothing.

Now, if the traffic is *free-flowing* . . . well, then you have all kindsa tricks at your disposal—varying the car lengths between you and him, ducking onto and off of the main route, changing lanes, *any number of things* to vary the perp's rearview visual. But on congested streets, these strategies are simply not an option. You have to maintain a holding pattern, hope you can appear to be just as stuck and frustrated as everyone else (because all a perp has to do is catch your eyes to grok that you're being too attentive, that you care more about where *he's* going than about where *you're* going) . . . and pray.

Anagrams wore thin ten minutes into the ride, and the cruiser's air conditioner kept threatening to fail, so the trip managed to be boring and suspenseful at the same time.

But, in the end, it was a good day for prayer, at least where George and Matt were concerned, because after "twenty-five minutes of this crap" (as Sikes called it), traffic broke and they were sailin' smooth onto the San Diego Freeway, their man in the Mazda never suspecting.

Heading south.

Which caused George to muse, "I wonder where he's going."

On one level stating the obvious, that's the whole reason for tailing a suspect in the first place: You wonder where he's going.

But then again, they were heading south.

George spared a brief glimpse at Matt, who was reading his book on and off. "Matthew."

"Um?"

"Do you suppose he knows of our investigation? Do you suppose that's why he ended his 'business relationship' with Mr. Sled?"

It was, of course, the first question that had occurred to either of them the minute they heard Bob Sled's account of events. But neither had wanted to speak it out loud, to acknowledge the possibility that the investigation had been compromised.

"Hard to say," Matt replied. "It's not like we've been top

secret. Anybody who's learned what we're after could have alerted this guy. The hospital staff where Fran's staying, Dr. LeBeque, someone connected with the theatre . . . hell, people we can't even know about."

At the moment, they didn't even know about the guy they were tailing. They had called in the model and license plate number of his car, and DMV records had identified it as belonging to a sixty-eight-year-old woman, Anna Maria Corigliano of La Jolla. But there was no record of it having been stolen. Calls were being made to her home, to see about trying to get an ID on the driver—assuming the car had been legitimately borrowed—but so far there had been no answer. Other public records could be researched, based on this slim bit of information alone, but it was too soon to make that request of police department manpower; the two detectives, their hunches notwithstanding, simply didn't have enough to go on yet. This was a specialized case, nothing politically attractive enough to give it "sexy" priority, and unless the videotape bore fruit (which they wouldn't know for some hours), the fellow they were following could be officially suspected of exactly nothing.

And he was still heading south.

"Maybe it's coincidence," George hypothesized. "Maybe he felt the need to be represented by new outlets, precisely as the druggist reported, and we just happened to be there on the day he broke the news."

"Maybe. But I'll tell you what bothers me about that one. Why was he there at all? Sled couldn't identify him by name or affiliation, didn't have the wherewithal to track him down if there was no further delivery. The guy didn't owe Sled a *thing*. Why not just find a new outlet to do business with and screw 'im?"

"Because there are too many variables. The drug is predicated upon *dependence,* the customers who use it *need* it. They depend, in turn, upon Bob Sled to make it available. If we apply your scenario, though, our round little apothecary wouldn't know his supply had dried up since no one would have told him. So he'd advise his regular customers to be patient, thinking delivery imminent."

". . . and the customers would stay patient until it became too late?"

"Or they'd register complaints—with us or with the Better Business Bureau—about the way their druggist failed to make good on his assurances. *They* aren't guilty of anything, what have they to lose?"

"Their anonymity, if they're passing for human."

"Which they lose in any event if they can't get the drug. My point being that the clientele would become unpredict-aable, create too many waves that might be noted by the authorities. How much simpler to merely *tell* the druggist that you're moving on so that he can alert his customers to look elsewhere while they have time."

"That all makes sense, but it still leaves me with one big question. Bob Sled told us that as far as he understood, he ran one of only four phony Stabilite outlets in the Los Angeles area. I mean, maybe he did, maybe he didn't, the supplier could have been yanking his chain. But if we assume it's the truth . . . Sled doesn't know who the other current distributors are; the dealer isn't about to tell him who the *new* distributors are gonna *be;* he can't pass the information on to his customers. How the hell are the customers gonna find out where to go to get their stuff?"

"Big question, indeed, Matthew. Easy answer, I think."

"Enlighten me."

"The same way they found out about Bob Sled. Ask in the right—or the wrong—places. That kind of information is always available on the street if you want it badly enough."

"True," Matt nodded after a beat. "True."

And then he looked at his watch, registered that they had been driving for over a half hour since clearing the gridlock, noted by the road signs that Los Angeles was now officially behind them, gauged by the landscape that they were running out of United States territory in which to follow their man, realized that the term "jurisdiction" was threatening to become a cruel joke, and exclaimed:

"*Jesus,* I hate it that he's going south!"

Because it probably meant that their man could *afford* to go south.

In drug cases, suspects under surveillance, if they *knew* they were under surveillance, tended to do one of two things.

If they were low-level types, or scared, or stupid, they ascribed to what Matt Sikes called the cockroach theory: hit 'em with light, they scuttle for cover of darkness. That darkness was either their lair, full to brimming with damning evidence they would try to destroy before the cops got to it; or the lair of a perceived "protector," someone higher up in the operation. The flight toward darkness didn't always lead to immediate arrest but it almost always added to your chain of evidence, gave you new places and people to check out; and the more you had, the more opportunity there was for the Bad Guys to slip up.

But if they were smart, careful and cool . . .

. . . they simply went home. And south was a grand direction to travel if they wanted to go home. The scenery got prettier, the real estate values went up, the mountains were more impressive, you were closer to the ocean. And in that relative comfort, they waited you out. They kissed their wives, played with their kids, made like nice neighbors, and didn't give a shit about your impatience. Because they had all the time in the world.

The woman who owned the car they were following—DMV identified her as a resident of La Jolla. If their guy was behind the wheel legitimately, maybe he was taking the car back to La Jolla; maybe he *lived* in La Jolla. *Way* the hell south, rural and rustic, featuring two beautiful theatres run by a fellow named McAnuff just off a remote university complex, and brisk, briny sea air. Crime? What crime? Not a lot of drug action there.

Now, of course, La Jolla was a hop, skip, and a jumping bean away from the Mexico border. And there was so much drug action down *there* it made your teeth ache. But Mexico didn't seem a likely locale for designer drug operations. And if it was—what difference? Sikes and Francisco had no hard evidence. If their guy crossed the border and the drugstore tape showed nothing and his use of the car was legit . . . they'd never be able to get him back. They didn't even want to *think* about Mexico.

Better the guy should go home.

After Matt's comment, the next two minutes went by in silence and despair.

George and he were beginning to think, *That's it, endgame, over.*

And then their man got off an exit ramp that led into Carson County.

Exactly thirty-five minutes out of Los Angeles.

Taken by surprise, George nearly missed the ramp. He fishtailed a bit to adjust, suffering the angry car horn that blared past him down the freeway, and tolerating Sikes's sardonic, "Nice one, George, way to be circumspect," as his partner reflexively jammed both feet on an imaginary brake and leaned back into his seat. But the Mazda was too far ahead of them (George hoped) for the driver to pay any heed.

Carson was a suburban community. Just off the ramp were rest stops and fast food places, and a little further down, the residential section and a couple of modest shopping malls. But if you drove far enough, commercialism thinned out and gave way to open spaces, wooded areas, and a few large clearings.

Some of the clearings were occupied by smaller industrial firms that had made Carson their base. You could, Matt thought, work in worse surroundings. Nice to be away from the congestion of the city, but still be close enough for relatively quick access. *Now why didn't I ever think of that?* he asked himself. And then answered, *Because by the time you were old enough to appreciate the sentiment, it was too late.*

The Mazda crested the rise of a little valley, turned left into it; George slowed, pulled to the side of the road, waiting, not wanting to be spotted by their quarry; with the tracer device, there was no chance of losing the fellow, not in this semibucolic environment. After about forty-five seconds, he moved the cruiser forward again, crested the hill himself, turned left.

The road followed a gentle, unpaved, downward curve about a quarter of a mile, surrounded on both sides by trees and greenery. Then all at once, the greenery opened up and gave way to the entrance of a medium-size parking lot, fronting an impressively large two-storey building with a mauve and white facade, and an efficient, no-nonsense, no-frills architectural design.

Set just above the thick glass doors of the main entrance was a large, wide, flat metal awning. It jutted out about five or six feet, sheltering the walkway leading into the building. Today in particular its shelter might come in handy. There was a developing nip in the air, the sky was becoming overcast. It would rain soon.

Along the forward edge of the awning, metal or plastic red letters two feet high proclaimed the name of the company:

RICHLER PHARMACEUTICALS

George slowed the car, stopped. Staring.

Matt was staring too.

It didn't make any sense.

But there it was.

RICHLER PHARMACEUTICALS, the sign said.

Richler.

Which was, according to Steinbach, the authorized manufacturer of the legitimate, patented, *and entirely legal* Stabilite.

The last place in the world that might benefit or profit

from the sale of counterfeit merchandise—and faulty merchandise to boot.

What the hell was going on?

They watched as their man, having gotten out of his car before they'd entered the lot, entered through the glass doors, looking very much at home, nodded to the fellow at the security desk, who nodded back, and continued on his way.

Their guy *worked* here.

No sense.

No sense at all . . .

CHAPTER 15

THE ROUGH STORYBOARD preliminaries in the large spiral sketch pad laid out like this:

PAGE ONE: Our heroine, the prim Tenctonese librarian, is waiting for a bus. Little glasses sit on her nose, and one arm is laden with library books. The bus stop is in front of a fast food place that caters to Newcomers; with her free hand she's alternately wolfing down some raw weasel on a bun and looking nervously at her watch. The visual tells us right away who she is, what she's eating, where she got it, and how little time she has for the amenities of life. Clearly she's late for work.

PAGE TWO: From another angle: the bus pulls up and she boards, putting the rest of her sandwich in the fast food bag whence it came, juggling her books a bit to do it.

PAGE THREE: As she goes for her change, she asks the bus driver a question.

PAGE FOUR: The bus driver answers, trying his sincere best to be polite, but he can't help recoiling from her breath as he does so, and the look on his face is one of comic revul—

(Huge X marks are drawn through each of the four pages.)

The second draft laid out like this . . .

PAGE ONE: Start with the bus driver, close-up of him at the wheel, his expression turning to one of . . . rueful respect? Yes, try that. (Doesn't matter if it's too complicated to get right away, we'll understand it in about five seconds.) In voice-overs we hear his thoughts. "Oh, no," goes the first one.

PAGE TWO: His point of view through the windshield, as he comes up on the librarian at the bus stop in front of . . . make it a McDonald's or some generic fast food place, not a Newcomer specialty joint. Right, better. This is a place where *everybody* eats, but she just happens to be wolfing . . . gracefully eating . . . a McWeasel, say. And the driver's next thought is: "Gosh, that Ms. Jones—" (Jones? No, Eesana. A nice Tenctonese name. Meaning "giving," which is what librarians do.) And the driver thinks: "Gosh, that Ms. Eesana is such a sweet, pretty, special lady. Darn shame I just don't want her on my bus!" (There. Makes it about the individual, not the ethnicity. That way the driver not wanting her on the bus is . . . droll or humorous or something.)

PAGE THREE: Reverse angle as the bus pulls up and Ms. Eesana gets on.

PAGE FOUR: Ms. Eesana greets the bus driver. "Hi!" She puts a lot of air into the *H* so that it travels.

PAGE FIVE: The *H* and the breath that propels it hit the driver's nose and his voice-over thought, supporting his earlier trepidation, is: "She's got a *problem!*" And his face assumes an expression of . . . (Well, what kind of face would he make? What kind of face would a *Newcom* make after a human breathed saltwater seafood in *her* face? Goddess knows, it had happened often enough! Sure, Kent Allman wants to be broadly comic, but you have to wonder . . .

what kind of face did *he* make at those poor Koreans on the train? Very likely he made no face at all, at least none that they could see! . . . Hmm . . . Interesting point, maybe that's an angle.) The breath hits the driver's nose and we see it in his eyes, but that's all. Like any polite person in that situation, he tries to cover. Fine. That brings us to—

PAGE SIX: And as Ms. Eesana goes to her seat, *then, then* the driver makes his face, having enough respect for the woman to consider her feelings.

PAGE SEVEN: From the side, we follow Ms. Eesana down the aisle and continue the pattern, people are making faces *as she passes,* it's all happening *behind her back,* which is *naturally* funny because it *humanizes the conflict* and—

(A huge, squiggly line is scribbled fiercely over the last page.)

The third draft laid out like this.

PAGE ONE: Small letters: "Why do I have to 'humanize' anything?"

PAGE TWO: Larger letters: "I DON'T CARE *WHAT* THEY SAY, THIS ISN'T *FUNNY!*"

PAGE THREE: The largest letters, dashed off in a furious white heat: ***"I HATE THIS!!!"***

Susan slammed the sketch pad closed. Then she just sat at the desk in her office cubicle, holding her head in her hands. She had been hoping to meet the assignment by finding a more compassionate, personalized way into it. But no matter how she tried to mitigate it, the basic concept of Kent Allman's ad campaign was antithetical to compassion *at its very core.* You couldn't impose dignity upon an idea that was fundamentally undignified. To think otherwise was to operate from a false premise. The sketches in her pad were proof enough of that.

The fact that those same sketches had taken all morning

and part of the afternoon to execute was not insignificant either. Good work was never labored. Good work came easily—at *this* stage, in any event.

The wall clock read 2:55.

Allman had arrived ten minutes ago; he was already with Berries, chatting in Berries' office.

The meeting was supposed to be at three.

"What are you gonna do?"

She swiveled to see Jonathan Besterman at the entrance to her cubicle.

After a long while, she said, "I don't know . . . What do you suggest?"

Jonathan shook his head sadly. "I don't know either." Then he literally *shook off* the melancholy. "All right, wait, enough moping around. We're two smart people, right?"

She allowed herself a small smile. "Right . . ."

"We should be able to formulate some kinda plan here, right?"

"Jonathan, you have your own deadlines to—"

"Baloney, you'll do the same for me sometime, now answer my question. We can formulate a plan here, *right?"*

"Right!" Her smile was growing now.

Jonathan clapped his hands together.

"Okay. Here we go. The challenge is—"

And Susan's intercom buzzed.

Berries' voice said, *"Susan, we're ready for you to come in now."*

She exchanged a helpless glance with Jonathan, then replied, "Be right with you, Keith," and disconnected.

All hope left her. She just threw up her hands, and then quickly gathered up her notes and her sketch pad, and began a brisk, fatalistic walk to Berries' office. Jonathan was at her heels.

"Susan, slow down, give yourself a minute to—"

She stopped, pivoted on her heel, said firmly, "Jonathan! Thank you, but there's nothing to be done. I've given myself a minute. I've given myself every minute I've had since yesterday. Whatever happens in there, I have to face it. You're a lovely man for trying. I appreciate it."

She turned to finish the walk and behind her, Jonathan barked, "Just hold on!"

She turned again, exasperated, wanting to say *Please* stop, this is torture *enough,* but he had a stern finger wagging at her and a look of utter determination that stilled her.

"You wanted to know what I'd suggest? Here's what I suggest." He took a deep breath, then announced, "It's your party. Don't blink."

Whereupon he turned and walked away before she could ask him what he meant. Obviously he was speaking in euphemisms, she knew *that* at least, but she couldn't decipher them. *Party? Blink?* What—?

No time. She faced about, took the remaining steps, put her hand on the doorknob, and then, *sweet Celine help me,* there she was in the office. Berries and Allman were looking at her expectantly from the same positions they'd occupied yesterday, separated from her by only a few yards of carpet. But the separation felt to her like a chasm.

Widening at that.

With an anticipatory, but typically charmless, smile, Berries said, "Well, what have you got for us?"

Susan took a few steps forward, placed her paraphernalia on the chair in which she would have sat, and folded her arms—not as an act of defiance. She was, it would occur to her later, hugging herself for support.

"Here's the thing, actually, Keith . . . Mr. Allman . . ."

"Kent, please," Allman requested. (Great. Thank you so much for making this easier.)

"Kent . . ." Susan amended. "I . . . I need more time."

Berries leaned back in his chair, laced his fingers together over his chest. "The assignment was fairly straightforward, Suse."

"Yes, I know, but . . . as I was working on it last night and this morning, a few refinements occurred to me. Rather than show them to you half-formed, I'd really like to develop them for—"

"I can't say," Allman interrupted, "that I'm pleased to have made the trip here if there's no presentation. But"—he held up a conciliatory palm—"I do certainly understand that new ideas need to breathe. Provided we're all on deadline. Tomorrow, then, same time, same station?"

"In truth," Susan lied, "I was thinking more like three or four days."

Allman squinted, as if he hadn't heard correctly. Donned his hateful "figuring out a problem" expression. Swiveled to face Berries, exchanging a concerned look.

"Three or four *days?*" Berries echoed. "Listen, before we go any further with this, do you suppose you could thumbnail these 'refinements' for us?"

Susan looked away, bit her lip.

"I thought you told me she was good," Allman said ominously.

A dangerous edge crept into Berries' voice. "Susan, what's going on?" Emotional mechanic that he was, Berries didn't "get" angry like most people. He *chose* to be angry, and the control behind the choice made his anger a fearsome weapon.

And it would only be worse if she continued trying to bluff.

So she collected herself and in a very small voice said, "I'm lying."

"You're what?" said Allman.

"I was trying to buy more time, but the truth is, the real truth is, I don't need three or four more days. I don't need three or four more minutes. The truth is, Mr. Allman, your campaign ideas are . . . are just awful, and they can't be made to work."

"Susan," Berries said quickly, tersely, "I think you'd better leave? We'll discuss this later."

"Fine," she said, picked up her stuff and started to go. But going wasn't the answer either.

She turned back, clutching her stuff to her chest protectively. Her voice was a little shaky, and she couldn't steady it.

"But not until I tell you . . . this is wrong. I don't care about my idea not being to your liking. I mean, I do, but . . . it's different. Um . . ." She said "um" not because she was groping for words, but because she was terrified of the words that were, in fact, cascading out of her mouth, and she didn't want to cry. "And Kent, the fact that you can't envision things beyond your own life experience, um, um, that's limiting, not only to people like me, but to you. Um, your choice, though."

"I won't say it again," Berries warned. "Susan. Out. Now."

"What's important, um," Susan continued, the tears starting to form, her jaw trembling, "is that if you were doing a spot about Koreans instead of Newcomers and, um, they had eaten this kat-choo—"

"Kimchee," Allman corrected reflexively.

"Yes! Thank you! Kimchee!" and that was the burst of healthy resentment she needed to get her past the tears flowing freely now and the nervous shivers she no longer cared to control. "If you were doing *that* commercial and you did it the same way, made fun of their culture like you've tried to make fun of mine, how much mouthwash do you think you'd sell? Do you think the networks and pressure groups would even *let you get away with it?*"

And in the silence that followed, she added, "That was not a rhetorical question. You know?"

And now it was Allman's turn to say "um," albeit for entirely different reasons.

"So, if they wouldn't let you get away with it, why should I—or any Newcomer? Even the name of the product: Tencton-ease? By *itself* it's an insult."

Berries rose, his anger rising with him.

"I've warned you twice. You don't get a thir—"

Allman cut in. "Keith, let me handle this." The smaller man stood, flexed a bit within his jacket, as if about to enter the ring, and approached Susan. When he was nearly nose to nose with her, he said, "I . . . don't . . . insult . . . people. I've been in this business a long time, and I value my customers. Newcomer and human alike."

Wiping her eyes with a palm, Susan said, "Does your company manufacture a hair restorative?"

"You picked a poor time to make a joke." She held his gaze. Finally, he relented. "Yes, we've pioneered a mass market formula more effective than Minoxydil. It wouldn't work for you."

"As long as it works for humans."

"It works fine."

"And do you have a special formula for black people?"

"A minor variant. But we market it very differently."

"One moment."

She opened her large sketch pad, flipped to a blank page, produced a charcoal pencil from a small case and proceeded to execute a series of furious strokes that seemed to attack the page upon contact and fly off the surface upon completion. The strokes got smaller—she was writing something now—and then she was done, tapping the pencil point upon the page for punctuation.

"Now, then," she said. "Your hair restorative for blacks. In your wildest dreams, would you market it like this?"

She turned the pad around to face him.

It showed a rough sketch of a box. On it, was the happy, smiling, comic book face of a black man, exclamation points rising from the fine Afro on his head. Above him, the name of the product:

Allman laughed, a short, sharp bark, but it was the laughter of shock. And then his face went red with embarrassment.

"Which one of us is the most naive, Ke—Mr. Allman? I know what you're after. And I could have been your best friend." She looked over at Berries, who was looking out of his office window, his body tense, the symbolism evident: He had—metaphorically *and* literally—turned his back on her. She said to him what she had to say anyway. "Mr. Allman's all but a stranger to me. But I thought I knew you. You're smart. You should know better. You should have known before I did."

She left her pad in Allman's hands, crossed to the door. Didn't turn back as her hand touched the knob.

"A little sensitivity goes a long way, you know," she said huskily, her voice thick now for having tried to speak through her tears.

Then she was out of the office and moving. *Down the hall.* But she wanted her sketch pad back. Those terrible rough sketches were in it. All Kent had to do was flip a page to see them. *Past her desk, her pace increasing.* Didn't matter, she was done here, she had finished herself but good. *Past Jonathan, racing past, did that mean she was running, when had she started running, and was he calling her name?* Let them keep the stupid pad, let it be her stupid legacy in this stupid place. *Slamming the elevator button with both hands, just wanting out, just out, just air and—*

"Susan?" Jonathan called again.

But she didn't want to talk about parties and blinking, because whatever he had advised her to do, she had gotten it wrong, and not wanting his sympathy or sorrow, bolted for the stairwell, ran down five flights, and exploded onto the street, running she knew not where.

Jonathan was faster.

He caught her by the arm and turned her around. She

nearly beat him off in her fury, but then she realized that, no matter what, he was *not* the enemy, and settled for just pulling away. Hugging herself again. Only partially out of a self-protective instinct this time. There was a nip in the air; the sky was overcast. It would rain soon.

They were both gasping, out of breath.

"I don't want to talk about it!" she yelled.

"Then don't!" he yelled back.

"Fine!"

"Fine!"

Tense silence reigned between them.

Jonathan finally broke it.

"Were you this angry upstairs?"

"What if I was?"

Jonathan smiled at her. Slow smile. "Then . . . it was your party."

She started to laugh. And sob. Both. "I may have blinked a little, though. And I sure don't think I have a job anymore."

"As long as you got friends."

He spread his arms, and she fell into them, and he held her, and he told her how proud he was of her, and they clung, and it was just like in the famous song, "love, pure and chaste," not about anything but two points from entirely different circles finding the place where the circumferences intersected.

In the middle of the sidewalk.

In the shadow of the skyscrapers.

In front of the world.

As on either side, unheedful, unimpressed, or misinterpreting, the world passed them by.

CHAPTER 16

You could say this much for Maury Richler of Richler Pharmaceuticals: He was certainly a hands-on kind of fellow.

When Detectives Matthew Sikes and George Francisco flipped their shields at the guy behind the security desk, it was Richler's office he buzzed, and it was old man Richler himself who came down to the desk. No intermediaries, no henchmen, no flunkies, and no foolin'.

Richler's appearance was unlikely for the head of a firm that specialized in so meticulous a field as medicine, for the outer man was anything but meticulous. He was tall and galumphy, about fifty-five or sixty, pot-bellied, big-nosed, round-faced and hairy, the latter despite being clean-shaven. A Toscanini-maestrolike shock of brown hair streaked with gray was swept back over his head; his sideburns and eyebrows were big, bushy and unruly; and stray hairs popped out of every orifice that could reasonably support them. The backs of his hands were very close to being matted with gray as well. His clothes, jacket in particular, hung on him dutifully, but not particularly stylishly, and he wore his tie slightly loose.

For all his unruliness, though, he was not *slovenly.* He was simply unvarnished, a plain-spoken fellow of enormous intelligence whose veneer—or lack thereof—mirrored his candor, the impression that he had nothing to hide. It could be a deceptive impression, though. Sikes and Francisco knew that from long experience.

He introduced himself with a firm handshake, a fleshy, lopsided smile, and a deep, resonant voice.

"What seems to be the problem, gentlemen?"

They told him about their investigation into bad Stabilite.

"I'm aware of the situation, of course," he acknowledged, "and of course I'm . . . well, appalled puts it mildly. I'm furious and not just because it reflects badly on my business. I've offered my help to the authorities before, though, and it was duly noted, never accepted. What's caused the change of heart"—he nodded with dry, but genuine respect toward George—"or hearts, as the case may be?"

They told him that the investigation into bad Stabilite had led back to his company.

Until now, Richler had seemed a fairly unflappable fellow. Now—in his own understated way—he flapped. His jaw dropped, making his double chin conceal his neck completely, and his large eyes grew larger.

"Back here? You're telling me the road leads . . . back *here?* What specifically led you back here?"

They told him about the car they had been following, and they pointed to it out to him in the lot, whereupon the security guy, listening unobtrusively up to this point, said, "That's Max's car, Mr. Richler."

"Max?" Richler repeated. It was one syllable, but he managed to say it very slowly. His eyes stayed wide, so George and Matt had to figure the subtext was one of further disbelief.

"Max who?" Matt prodded.

"Max Corigliano," the security guy said. The security guy didn't know it, but he had just said a lot more than that.

"We maybe got pay dirt here," Matt said to George.

"Filthy money indeed," George agreed, missing the idiom but not the point.

"Do you know something about Max Corigliano?" Richler asked.

"Not as yet," George replied, "not conclusively."

"Hunch," Matt said evasively.

"Do you think you might amplify that for me just a little bit?"

"No offense, Mr. Richler," Matt said, "but we don't know you well enough yet."

"For the next little while at least," George offered, "it would be better if we could question Mr. Corigliano ourselves. And—if you're amenable—take a look around your operation."

"The implication being that if I'm not amenable you can get a warrant."

"That's the implication," said Matt. "Do we need one?"

"Quite the opposite, Detective. I just respond badly to not being trusted, especially in matters of law, ethics, or business." He appraised them coolly for a moment, then nodded to himself, having reached some sort of executive decision. He leaned over the security guy's desk, lifted the receiver on the phone, said, "Tim, would you hit the code for my secretary?" and then, "Thank you," once the security guy had complied. After a moment he said into the phone, "Norma? Call Max Corigliano, tell him I want to see him. Tell him right away. When he arrives, usher him into my office. Between you and me, I will *not* be there right away. You just let him sit, though. I want him to wait."

He hung up, turned toward the detectives.

"We'll do the tour first," he said. "It may not be what you want, but this is my sandbox. Long as you're here as my guests, we'll play by my rules."

They were introduced to an organic chemist, a biochemist, a microbiologist, a pharmacologist, a toxicologist, a pathologist, a pharmaceutical chemist, and a physician—

the chain of specialists, Richler said, required for the development of each individual drug.

They were escorted through several research labs, a research library, and the processing plant wherein the medicines were prepared and packaged for shipping. At all times the attention to detail seemed beyond reproach; every procedure, from the first experiment to labeling of the final package, adhered to strict double- and triple-checked regimens of quality control.

They noted that the general atmosphere around Richler Pharmaceuticals was, in the best sense, collegiate. There was a very definite team spirit at work; and Richler's employees clearly *liked* the work as well as the environment provided for it, which was clean, encouraging and—again, in the best sense—adventurous. Pioneerism suffused the *gestalt* of the place . . . and the fact that salaries, profit sharing programs, health benefits, and pension plans were all generous didn't hurt either.

In the middle of the tour, which had thus far occupied something over half an hour, Richler's secretary had him paged, and informed him that Max Corigliano was becoming impatient and fidgety.

"Good," Richler replied, instructing her to continue giving Corigliano the impression that he'd be right there.

Richler gave them the facts and figures. That each new drug cost between fifteen and thirty million dollars in research that generally spanned five to nine years. That during an average year in the prescription—or "ethical"—drug industry, about 170,000 chemicals were screened; about 1,000 of those were deemed worthy of investigation; and of those, only between 16 and 20 compounds actually made it into the marketplace with FDA approvals.

"It's not a racket," Richler explained. "The only way to make your money in ethical drugs is to keep the patient in mind. If helping people is your goal, you'll see a return. As for Richler Pharmaceuticals . . . well, I never quite realized the dream. We're not up there with Merck or Squibb. But I'm proud, at least, that we're considered the best of the smaller, feistier companies and that we're known for our integrity, not for fads."

"I don't understand," said George, and there was genuine sadness in his voice. "It is clear you are a person of honor, and your business does you credit. But—"

"—but if Richler Pharmaceuticals eschews fad drugs, how did we get involved with Klees'zhoparaprophine?"

George looked at him squarely. "Yes."

"And if research takes so long, how did we manage to get Klees'zhoparaprophine onto the marketplace so quickly when your people are barely five years off the slave ship?"

"And that."

Richler didn't flinch from the gaze, nor did he even seem especially challenged by it. He returned it as if taking George's measure.

Matt, breaking the moment, said, "You know, since this investigation began, you're the only person we've interviewed who refers to Stabilite like that."

Richler, in a curmudgeonly, professorial fashion, narrowed his gaze at Sikes.

"Because *that,*" he said, enunciating each word carefully, "is its *name.*" Returning his gaze to George, he said, "We have one more stop to make."

They entered the animal research lab. Though it was as clean and smoothly run as the rest, and though the animals (dogs, monkeys, mice, white rats mostly) seemed to be as well-treated as possible under the circumstances, it was a genuinely depressing place. Not, ironically, because there were animals on view who appeared to be suffering or unhealthy (though some were in a noncommittal sleep that may or may not have been drug induced)—but simply because the mere *concept* of the place filled the detectives with an ineffable melancholy.

Sensing their mood, Richler just said without preamble, "I know. I used to feel the same way, and on occasion, when I don't watch myself, I still do. But there's no other way. Comes a time you have to know if the idea's a good one or if it only works on paper. And you can't test on healthy human—forgive me, *humanoid*—volunteers until you've exhausted every other possibility of exploration."

"You test on *healthy* volunteers?" Matt asked.

"At first you have to. They're the ones with the strongest immune systems, the ones best able to ingest a new substance and give you a clear reading. A person in imperfect health can only give you imperfect data. The point to medical research is to dispense with as many variables as you can."

Entering an annex to the main lab, they approached a bank of cages. In front of it was someone in a wheelchair, back to them, wearing a lab coat, bent over an open cage in the bottom row.

"Someone I want you to meet," Richler said to George in particular. He lifted his voice, "Sotsta."

They heard the cage door closing, and the figure in the wheelchair unbent, revealing a Tenctonese head atop a frail body—or, perhaps, deceptively frail, as the thin arms that reached for the wheels and turned the chair around did so with rather remarkable strength and dexterity.

The figure—Sotsta—was male, by Newcomer reckoning somewhere on the dark side of middle age. Either that or prematurely older in appearance than his years, as his frailty (Matt thought of it as Ghandi-like) was particularly pronounced. And for a final distinguishing feature: He was walleyed. On his lap stood a beagle puppy, its forepaws against his chest, trying, with unbridled, and apparently uncontrollable, affection to lick Sotsta's chin.

"Now, now, Dogger," Sotsta chided, gently muzzling the dog with his palm. The frail Newcomer had a soft, almost ethereal voice. Dogger licked his palm until it became moist enough for Sotsta to wipe it upon his lab coat; whereupon Dogger happily went back to its prime objective: the chin.

"Sotsta," said Richler, "these gentlemen are from the police, Mr. Francisco and Mr. Sikes." He looked at the detectives. "Gentlemen, Sotsta is one of our topflight researchers. It is upon his work that the development of Klees'zhoparaprophine is based."

George stepped forward.

Chorboke is here, he thought.

Sotsta seemed to be about to offer his hand, a greeting gesture that had become reflexive for Newcomers over the years on Earth; but George, keeping his hands at his side, sidestepped any pretense at amenities and said, *"Won oot vot evin tew vostafless?"*

How do you live with yourself?

He hadn't really *meant* to say it, not in Tenctonese, and *certainly* not with such vitriol. But the words had just popped out of him. He was just grudgingly accepting the notion that Fran Delaney's actions might have extenuating circumstances and not be easily categorized as right *or* wrong. But here before him was the architect of her downfall, sitting in a wheelchair, petting a dog, personifying what post-World War II historians referred to as "the banality of evil."

And there was simply no excuse for *him.*

(Or so George believed right at that moment. He didn't see Matt behind him, about to step forward and intervene, about to diplomatically pull him away . . . nor did he know when Richler gently touched Matt on the arm, stopped him, lifted a quieting hand, and closed his eyes briefly as if to say, *Let this be. Let this happen.*)

Sotsta answered George's "greeting" in English.

"Live with myself. Ah. Well. One must. No choice, yes?" He smiled a brief smile that came and went without preparation, like a facial tic.

Between the walleyed expression and the air of abstraction, it was difficult to know how "present" the little scientist was in the room—difficult to know what he was looking at, if his mind was even on the conversation at hand.

"Do you know what you have done?" George asked quietly. "What misery you've wrought?"

"Done? Yes. Misery?" Again the spasmodic smile. "Knowledge is not ultimately controllable. Discover something. Look, see? It's there. And—*oh*—*in*teresting, it not only does *this*, it does *that*. Then the decision. *This* is desirable. *That* is, how can we say, a *wrinkle*. Better yet, a *ripple in the water* (much apter metaphor, in fact). And the ripple *once made* cannot be *unmade*. It travels its course. What ripples do."

"The hell is he talking about?" Matt said.

George, likewise, was utterly bewildered.

The puppy was starting to nip playfully at Sotsta's collar.

"Now, Dogger, now, Dogger," Sotsta chanted.

Richler stepped forward, put a hand on Sotsta's shoulder. The puppy leapt to lick at Richler's fingers. "Detective Francisco doesn't know the history, Sotsta. He doesn't know how it started."

Sotsta looked up at Richler—lifted his head, at any rate, hard to tell just where he was focusing—and three seconds went by in which the scientist's expression did not change. Then he gasped—suddenly—"Ah!"—as if the information had been delayed in reaching his brain, but had just now arrived. "Well, then!"

Without warning, Sotsta thrust the puppy into Richler's unprepared grasp—(producing the first and only moment in which George saw the drug magnate unbalanced, comically trying to adjust to the energy of the animal, which found his chin as interesting as Sotsta's)—and pulled the cuffs on both his legs up to the knee joint.

The feet above the sagging socks were prosthetic, as were half of each lower leg. Above the prostheses, the skin was scarred and pitted most hideously. Sotsta directed his gaze—his face, anyway—toward George. He spoke matter-of-factly.

"Experimental test subject. On the slave ship. Salt water. An attempt to seek immunities to its effects. Chorboke's idea, of course."

At first George couldn't process the information. It went so counter to his preconceptions that he was disoriented.

"You—" he said. Then swallowed. "You were a victim . . . of Chorboke?"

Sotsta nodded. "One of the few who amused him. He disposed of most failed tests. For me he actually created these prostheses. Consolation for services." He shrugged. "Walk on them, yes, sometimes, but not with comfort. The chair I like best."

"To the point, Sotsta," Richler requested gently. And, looking at George and Matt, added, unnecessarily, "He's a rambler."

"The point, indeed," Sotsta nodded. "The ship, Chorboke, I started to think there must be a *true* way to desensitize us—that is, you-me-us, Newcomers—to salt water. A way that could be achieved *without* suffering. No one should again have to . . ." He gestured vaguely at his legs, stamping them against the footrests lightly to shake his cuffs back down to shoe-top level. ". . . like me. Had sporadic access to Chorboke's lab, some files. Began working in secret, compiling much research, many years."

"Sotsta was far along in his discoveries by the time he got to us," Richler supplemented.

George was by Earth measuring seventy-five years old; Sotsta was older still . . . and Chorboke had been wreaking havoc on the slave ship for the better part of George's adult life. Sotsta hadn't indicated when he had been worked on by that monster, but it was easy to imagine that the "many years" of "much research" were far in excess of the five to nine cited by Richler as average for development of a prescription drug.

"Work went slowly on the ship," Sotsta continued. "Access to lab frequently impossible. No facilities, or stolen sometimes, clandestine experimentation. All the time in the world, though. Not fit for heavy labor. Too favored of the master to destroy. What else for a legless slave-victim but time, yes?" Then his tone became excited. *"But, then, boom.* Crash, and the ship is on Earth, and the Earth is four-fifths salt water and, this being our new home, I begin to hear the tick clocking, I mean the clock ticking. Ha!" The larger, open-mouthed smile that accompanied the brief laugh came and went as fast as its smaller predecessor.

"We were looking for Newcomer scientists," Richler said, continuing the tale, "to help in researching a market clearly about to expand. Sotsta was looking for the facilities that would support his work. We seemed rather right for each other."

"And how did you jump from lofty scientific nobility to Stabilite?" George asked Sotsta. "After what you'd been through—how *could* you?"

Sotsta looked toward his employer, his odd little face aswim with contradictions.

"The drug that will, we hope, desensitize Newcomers to salt water is still in the works," Richler continued, holding the fidgety puppy to his chest. "But in pursuing that goal, we discovered certain chemically-induced properties the Tenctonese physiology must have in order to survive exposure. Similar properties, as it turns out, to those Tenctonese physiology must have in order to maintain a radical cosmetic change."

"And so you just opportunistically—"

"No." Richler lowered Dogger, who dutifully jumped onto Sotsta's lap, and decided, for some mysterious dog reason, that the visitors were now interesting enough to observe. The animal nestled quietly, blinking at them soulfully, as Sotsta absently stroked his back.

Richler approached George. "We got wind of two other companies attempting something similar to what Klees'-

zhoparaprophine became. Neither one of those firms is as reliable and high-minded as we are (if they were, they wouldn't initiate that field of investigation in the first place), nor as proficient in research. We could sense that the FDA was willing to be a bit lenient where Newcomer drugs were concerned. There was a lot of pressure to get them out on the market, to avoid charges that they were ignoring the new citizenry, and clearly no other drug company knew as much about this issue as we did.

"Which presented us with a dilemma.

"Should we allow a competitor's inferior product to hit the marketplace and *really* do damage . . . or should we assume the responsibility ourselves—willingly create the lesser of two evils? You've already seen the consequences of bad merchandise."

"Mr. Richler's reasoning I understand," George said to Sotsta. "I still cannot fathom yours. How can you have sanctioned this? Participated?"

To which Sotsta answered, "Maury came to me. Asked. My people, my culture, what I thought. I told him"—again the now-you-see-it-now-you-don't smile—"not a responsibility I want."

"And I reminded him that it was my company," Richler said, "and *my* decision. But that I preferred to make it based on an informed opinion, not the standards I would choose to impose upon an unfamiliar culture."

"Suggested to him, this juncture," Sotsta said, "that of two evils, less is always better than more, yes?" He sighed then. Caught George's gaze. George did not want to feel compassion . . . but his soul had overridden his head.

"I am sorry. I didn't know."

The little scientist gave a shrug as brief as his smiles. "Not possible. Sorries? . . . Pah." (*Pah,* George suspected, meaning *"unnecessary."*) And then, *"Won oot na evin tew vostafless? Eon vernorocina, nos debah, u a heure."*

How do I live with myself? One minute, my brother, at a time.

The dog, restless now, looked up at Sotsta, who cupped its face in his hands and cooed, "Yes, yes, yes." Then he turned his attention to George and Matt again, saying sheepishly, "Animal test subjects. Not supposed to give them names, lest you get attached. Dog, I called this one. Then Dogger, because he is more like a dog than I am. Joke, that. Suddenly he responds to it. By default it has become a name. Dogger." He patted the animal's head. "Little dangers in any useful endeavor."

He swiveled his chair around then and wheeled himself back to where he had been when they found him.

They followed Richler out of the animal research lab. Nobody spoke until they reached Richler's office.

When they entered the office, Max Corigliano was there, as Richler had arranged, and bent out of shape about having been made to wait so long, as Richler had expected. Corigliano claimed he had been about to leave. What was the idea of treating him like this? He had a very important appointment with a client, and he was going to be late. And who the hell were *those* two guys? An instinct made Matt want to let Richler guide this little scene, and it was an instinct he was able to communicate to George with a glance.

Maury Richler explained that "those two guys" were the police. And that Max could solve his problem about the meeting by calling and canceling. "Use my phone," he invited. "Blame it on me. Say there was an emergency at work. Mention my name."

"My book's at my desk, Maury. 'S where I keep all my numbers."

"Fair enough. Back to your desk then. I'll just send Detectives Sikes and Francisco with you."

"For what? To tap my phone or something?"

"Now why would you say that? No, it's just they have some questions about you and I want them to see how you do business, overhear your end of the conversation . . .

eradicate the doubts." Richler turned to the detectives. "Max here is one of our crack MSRs."

"MSRs?" asked Matt.

"Medical Service Representatives. You might think of him as a field operative. He's one of the fellows who establishes a link between the company and the community pharmaceutical professionals."

"A salesman," George extrapolated.

"More than that, really. What we call a detail man, because he provides information and data along with product. His specialty is the independent drugstore. And he's damned fine at what he does." Looking at Corigliano, Richler said, "Max, I want you to show them."

"Come on, Maury, you're makin' me self-conscious here."

Matt's ears picked up the lilt of the street Italian in Max's voice. The cadences were subdued in these surroundings, but Matt imagined that in the pizzeria, Corigliano could be a real *paisan.*

"Nonsense," said Richler. "You could sell aspirin to the Bayer boys. Show these guys your mettle. And remember, mention my name to the client."

"I, uhh, don't think it would help a lot, Maur."

"For an independent druggist to know that the head of the company is himself abjectly apologetic for your absence? I'm not a salesman, but even I know that's sound business policy."

"It is, in theory, but I make it a practice never to put the blame off on others, you know? My clients, my responsibility. They respect that."

Richler took this in. Then said, "You know what? You're right. I'll call. Get me that number. We should earn some points with the druggist for that."

"Maury, I can finesse my own accounts, hah? Whatta we doin' here?"

And now Matt heard something else in Corigliano's voice. Guilt.

"I want the druggist's name, Max."

"Maury, he's a *liddle* guy, an *indie,* not worth your *time.*"

And now Matt spoke. "Like Bob Sled?"

Max's eyes started to dart from face to face suspiciously. "What is this?"

And George stepped forward. "Is Anna Maria Corigliano your mother?"

"Yeah, she's my mother, what's that got—"

And he stopped speaking. Just like that, stopped. His legs seemed to go weak. He stumbled for a nearby chair, lowered himself into it, held his head.

"Interesting question to get him so upset," Richler commented dryly. "You want to explain the dynamic to me?"

"His car is registered under his mother's name," George offered. "When we arrived here, we knew the name of the legal owner, but not *his* name. Learning from your security guard that the last names were identical suggested to us a certain . . . familiar refrain."

"It's a drug runner's trick," Matt added. "If the car you use isn't registered in your name, you're not legally liable for anything found in it during a search."

"Like bad Stabilite," George elaborated, pointedly directing the words at Corigliano.

"Moms are especially popular, bless their hearts," Matt added grimly.

"Max," said Richler patiently, "if these gentlemen *were* authorized to search your mother's car—would they find what they're talking about?"

"This," Corigliano said, wiping a hand over his mouth, "is the point where I ask for my lawyer." He looked at the cops. "Not that you have anything to go on. And not that I've done anything. But I've got a wife and babies, and I owe it to them to have counsel. Now read me my rights or whatever it is you do for a living. *Capice?*"

Yeah, Matt thought. *A real paisan putz.*

Despite Matt's rising irritation, it was George who tightened the screws.

"We have you on videotape, Mr. Corigliano," he said softly. "That's what we have. You and Bob Sled, huddled in conference."

Matt just managed to stop himself from turning toward George in surprise. Recklessly he added, "And we have your fingerprints on the package of last month's delivery."

Max Corigliano's mouth opened and closed several times, but no words emerged. At length, he turned away. "I knew I wasn't cut out for this. I told them I wasn't cut out for this. But they told me they'd double my salary."

The three standing men observed the one in the chair for a few heavy moments. Matt broke the silence first. "Just once," he said, "I'd like to find that someone got involved in a deal like this for a reason other than money."

"Love? Sex? Patriotism?" George wondered.

"Anything."

"I'm disappointed in you, Max," Richler said. "An additional forty thousand dollars is a very cheap price tag for pain and suffering."

"I'm . . . I'm sorry, Maury. I was thinking of my wife and babies. I didn't mean to hurt your business. I really didn't think I would."

"The business? Max, how about the *people?*"

"What, did I take food from someone's mouth, what?"

And for the second time that day, Matt was amazed at the blithe ignorance of key players in this filthy little conspiracy. They had no idea that this was about *more* than money.

"Newcomers have been made sick from the faulty . . . Klees'zhoparaprophine," George explained, receiving an unconscious nod of approval from Richler.

"Some of them have died," Matt added. "I don't know that they could manage wives and babies in addition to the masquerade . . . but I bet they had people who cared about them."

Corigliano turned ashen. "I swear on my mother's eyes, I had no idea! When you said 'bad' Stabilite before . . . I thought you meant counterfeit."

"We meant bad, Max," Matt said.

"Who was it you didn't want to call in front of us?" Richler asked. "Another one of your distributors?"

Corigliano shook his head morosely. "No, I coulda finessed that. I have to—*had*—to call the Serovese Corporation." With a humorless smile, he added, "That's Serovese with an *S* not a *C* and an *E* not an *I*. Don't ask me why, but that's their little motto."

"Not particularly revealing, is it?" observed George.

"What was so urgent you couldn't make the call later?" Matt asked.

"I was supposed to confirm that the old outlets for . . . bad Stabilite . . . are out . . . that the new ones are in place."

"Why the sudden changes of venue?"

"Not sudden. Been in the works for a while. I asked 'em—said they wanted to keep the product floating, difficult to track."

Matt started breathing a little easier, and he saw George's posture relax a bit too. They were sharing the same thought. That maybe—*maybe*—the investigation hadn't been compromised after all; that maybe the Serovese Corporation's strategy was a coincidence of timing.

"Who is your contact at this Serovese Corporation?" George prodded.

"I dunno. Different male voices give me my assignments. They call me at home. Designated times. Machine takes my messages when I report in."

Matt frowned. "Again with the 'I don't know names' routine. I'm sensing a depressing pattern here, George."

George nodded. "Apparently the corporate philosophy starts at the top and works downward." He turned to Max. "How were you first approached?"

"A thousand dollars anonymously appeared in the front seat of my car one day. In an envelope. With a note. If I was interested in more, I should be near a certain phone at a certain time . . ."

"And, of course, you were."

"I meant to blow them off, but . . . once the money was in my hands, it was as good as spent . . ."

"Do you still have the note? Or the original envelope?"

"Didn't want to chance it being discovered by my wife or kids so, uhh, no. I got rid of 'em."

". . . Naturally . . ."

"So you don't know names," Matt reiterated, "and you receive your instructions by phone. How do you get your supply of the drug?"

"There's a—I guess you'd call it a processing plant in Inglewood. I show up at the door, I give a password, they make with a countersign, it's all very 'I Spy.' Then someone I never see gives me the supplies. And I hand off the take from the previous sales."

"Holding back your prearranged fee, of course."

Corigliano nodded.

"Tell me something," Matt said. "'Twixt thee and me. Ever skim off a little extra?"

"Thought about it, to tell you the truth. Then decided it wasn't worth that kind of trouble. Not with these guys. You gotta remember, breaking into my car was their idea of a *friendly overture.*"

"Honor among thieves," observed George, getting an old saying right for a change.

"Uh huh," agreed Matt ironically, and turned his attention back to the pathetic detail man. "Now, the location of this 'processing plant' . . . Where in Inglewood we talking?"

"Around the intersection of Centinela and West Florence."

"That near the Inglewood Park Cemetery?"

"Yeah."

"Apt," said George.

"Why," asked Richler, "did they pick you to deliver for them?"

"I was already in so deep. I'd—" He had clearly hoped to avoid this. "I was the one gave 'em the formula in the first place. . . . They, uhh . . . said they wanted to get a head start on their profits and on serving the public with a reliable generic brand. They *did* say reliable."

"Reliable," Richler repeated. Then he asked slowly, "Do you know why Klees'zhoparaprophine has such a stiff customer price tag?"

Corigliano didn't answer. He couldn't.

"Because what we charge is only slightly more than it costs to make," Richler continued, answering his own question. "There *is* no generic price tag. If there were one, it'd be what we're charging. The drug is so morally ambiguous that my policy has been not to take any more of a profit than absolutely necessary to pay the bills and recoup the cost of supplies. Do you understand what I'm telling you, Max? This Serovese Corporation is using substitute ingredients. They're not even copying, they're *approximating.* That's the only way they can sell cheaper. You can't *do* that with this drug."

"What did you mean," George queried Max, "when you said the Serovese Corporation wanted to get a head start on their profits?"

"The Feds govern the life of a patent on any new medicine." Corigliano sighed. "Patent can't be held for more than seven years. After that, you have to make your research public."

"Although we might hold ours for twelve," Richler added. "If you can prove that a drug caters to a limited clientele and can only see a below-average financial return, you get an extended patent under what's called the Orphan Drug Act."

"Seven to twelve years of this garbage on the marketplace," Matt marveled.

"Does this mean the Serovese Corporation is itself a legitimate manufacturer of generic drugs?" George wondered.

"Oh, please," said Richler.

"Sounds like some kind of holding company to me," Matt

mused. "With that name, Serovese . . . maybe even a Mafia holding company. Am I warm, Max?"

Corigliano shrugged miserably.

"Let's find out," said George. "Mr. Corigliano, is it too late to call in your report without alerting them that something's amiss?"

Max checked his watch. "Tough to know with an answering machine. And I've never been late before. But then again, the delay's only ten, fifteen minutes."

"Call them, then. Don't give them any indication that you've been exposed. My partner and I will listen on an extension."

"Only if it means I can cut some kind of a deal," Max Corigliano insisted. It was his last card, and he intended to play it.

Matt shook his head and spoke under his breath, but audibly enough. "It's always money. And they always try to bargain."

Richler spoke in the soft, terrifying tones of a powerful man who is powerfully angry.

"Here's the deal, Max. You cooperate and I won't press charges; you're in enough trouble with state and federal law as it is. I'll even do what I can, within reason, to see that your family keeps body and soul together, until they can function without you." A beat. "You *don't* cooperate, and what I put you through will make the Wrath of God seem like a paid vacation. Are we clear?"

Max placed the call with almost comic alacrity. As he'd described, there was nothing on the other end of the line but an answering machine, and at that, one whose outgoing message was so noncommittal it didn't even identify itself. The call provided Matt and George with no new information, but at least it might have bought them some time. And they had the phone number.

When he hung up, Corigliano asked Sikes, "What now?"

And Sikes, trying not to enjoy his revenge too much, said,

"I think we better read you your rights. Or whatever it is we do for a living."

They led Max Corigliano, handcuffed, to their cruiser. Routinely putting a hand to the detail man's head, George guided him into the backseat and closed the door.

Quietly, so as not to be heard by their prisoner through the windows, Matt said, "Nice bluff in there. 'We have you on videotape.' Very nice."

"Not a lie, Matthew. We just don't know how useful the tape will be. On the other hand, 'The fingerprints on last month's package' . . ."

"Yeah, that was a lie."

"Hardly necessary. Gelding the filly, if you ask me."

"Gilding the lily. Couldn't let you have all the fun."

After a moment, George said, "It's been an educational day, hasn't it?"

Matt felt fine little droplets of water on his skin. He looked up. Drizzle landed in his eyes, and he squinted against the darkening sky. It had started to rain.

"It's not over," he said.

CHAPTER 17

FRIENDS DON'T STAY angry with friends for very long. And the fact was, Emily would have to have done much worse than she had in order to lose the friendship of Jill Molaskey.

True enough, when Emily approached Jill between classes, the reception she got was a little frosty—to be expected, and Emily had geared herself up for it—but Jill didn't take much convincing to believe that Emily was genuinely contrite. And when Emily told Jill what she had in mind, Jill even volunteered to be a co-conspirator.

"I can't ask you to do that," Emily said.

"You didn't," Jill responded. "I offered. Besides, you're gonna need all the help you can get."

". . . I got everybody that mad, huh?"

"Let me put it this way . . . I like you . . . and *I* wrote the note."

"Good point."

And with that, Jill and Emily set about approaching the other members of the gym club and also the club's supervising teacher, Ms. McIntyre, who was immediately amenable to Emily's idea. (But then, she rather suspected that if her faculty meeting had not caused her to be late the other day, the situation would not have deteriorated so badly in the first place.)

However, the clubmates remained somewhat cynical, which made Jill's participation, as Jill had surmised, essential to overcoming their initial resistance as they were being corralled for a special session of the gym club. Same time: after final period; same place: the reconverted cafeteria.

The girls sat in a semicircle group, Emily among them and yet not quite. She sat at the end of the arc next to Jill, who served as a tacit buffer between her and the others.

Ms. McIntyre took her place in front of them, apologized for her previous day's lateness, and made the announcement:

"We're gathered here today because Emily has something to say to you all, and I think it might be worth hearing. Emily?"

Emily rose as Ms. McIntyre relinquished center stage. Her hearts were pounding with apprehension, and she felt the pressure of peer scrutiny on her back. When she turned to face them, their return gazes covered the limited range from neutral to surly. She took a deep breath and started to speak.

"It's no big secret," she began, "that the Emily Seven was a bust yesterday."

There were a few indistinct mumbles of agreement, somewhere among them a clear-sounding, "You got *that* right . . ."

"So," Emily continued, "I'm here today to present Emily Eight."

The watching faces clouded over slightly—all but Jill, who winked encouragement at Emily.

"As in 'Emily ate her words,' 'Emily ate her attitude,' 'Emily ate her pride' "—the clouds passed; smiles and even some appreciative laughter began to emerge—"and asked her friends to give her one more shot at this."

"What do you say, girls?" Ms. McIntyre asked.

Joannie Delahanty, the redheaded girl who had tripped

over the Emily Seven the day before, raised her hand. "What do *you* think, Ms. McIntyre?"

"I wasn't here," the willowy blond teacher replied. "I don't mind offering my opinion, of course, but I think it's your call." She allowed that to sink in before adding, "I will say this much, though. You've just received a pretty mature proposal. What do you think would be a mature response?"

All faces turned toward Joannie. Being the most seriously offended, she had suddenly become holder of the swing vote.

Joannie thought about it. Then shrugged and said, "Oh, hell, why not?" And immediately slapped a hand to her mouth, belatedly realizing she had used a swearword in front of the teacher. But the immediate laughter from the clubmates and the release of tension made it all forgivable. "Just don't make a habit of it," Ms. McIntyre said, joining in the laughter, and all attention went to Emily again as it subsided.

"Thanks, Joannie," said Emily. And, addressing the assemblage at large, "Now, I didn't really get a chance to rework it. I thought maybe if I started with the basic moves, you could help me modify it, all of you—so that it becomes something we *all* can do."

"Do you mind if she goes through it once more, girls?" Ms. McIntyre asked. "I'd like to see it myself."

Again, general consent . . . and Emily did her thing.

She crossed to the right wall, leaned against one of the huge doors behind which a lunch table was stored and then she took a single hop, bounded up several feet, landed

Thump,

deep bending at the knees, arms up, uncoiling like a spring, arms at the side now, pirouetting full in midair, landing,

Thump,

kick starting a forward tumble,

de,

landing on her hands,

thump,

bending at the elbows, uncoiling again, pushing herself into the air, somersaulting backward until she was again erect and landing,

Ka-flump!

with a flourish, arms outflung, breathing hard.

She stole a look at Ms. McIntyre, whose mouth was open in quiet astonishment.

"Well, my goodness, Emily," was all she could say—at first.

"See, Ms. McIntyre?" said Mei-Mei Harada. "I appreciate Emily's apology, but how are we going to make *that* into something we can do?"

Emily watched Ms. McIntyre's face nervously. It was clear from her expression that the Emily Seven was of a *much* more advanced order than perhaps even *she* could do.

And then the gym teacher's face changed. It was a small moment, of no dramatic import—her mouth closed, she huffed air briefly out of her nose and half-lidded her eyes—but Emily would remember it for the rest of her life. Because she knew in that moment that Ms. McIntyre had quickly analyzed a thorny situation and discovered how to turn a liability into an advantage. And Emily marveled that such things were possible.

"Well, it's not the actual *movement* that sends the message, you know?" Ms. McIntyre said thoughtfully. "It's the exuberance. I mean . . . there's a uniquely Tenctonese zest for life conveyed in it. Even if we can't do those specific steps, the feeling *behind* them is still valid. I bet you can all figure out a way to put *that* across."

It began slowly. With Joannie suggesting that maybe *that* step was a little too involved, but wondering if there was *another,* maybe from some Newcomer folk dance Emily knew, that might go in its place . . . and Emily demonstrated one and Joannie, forgetting herself again, said, "Hell, I can do *that,*" and promptly did . . . and then

Mei-Mei asked if she might *simplify* one of the moves in the Emily Seven to achieve a similar effect with a little less risk, and Emily replied, "Sure, what do you mean?" and Mei-Mei showed her, and now *that* move was incorporated . . . and a rapidly increasing string of *What about this*es and *Let's try that*s followed, and the excitement grew, and the little dance exercise transmuted into a truly collaborative dance routine, one which, in the end, all were performing with gusto and glee.

And as Emily moved with them in choreographic unison, a small part of her mind wandered, for she realized that this thing was no longer hers alone, the glory of this belonged to *all* of them.

And that had never been the fantasy.

But it was still pretty good.

Which was close enough . . .

Meanwhile, at an entirely different place of learning . . .

Buck cut his afternoon classes because he was impatient and could do it without incident. After all, his teachers considered him a good student, and as a Newcomer, Buck was identified as having an intellect superior to his human classmates. Racism in reverse had its advantages.

He arrived at the local Sanctuary of the Kewistans just prior to the warning sounds of thunder in the darkening sky. He had called his Elder-Master the night before, right after the charged and disturbing dinner with his family. He had insisted that now, more than ever, he was ready for his *Tighe Marcus-ta,* and his Elder-Master had replied: "Then come tomorrow. It will be done."

This particular Sanctuary was a reconverted two-storey house in Sherman Oaks, two blocks off Ventura Boulevard. The house was pink and spacious, its interior also done in soft pastels. There were a good number of bedrooms within, and virtually all the walls were lined with shelves upon shelves of books: books of Tenctonese spiritualism and those of a more secular, Earth-bound orientation. When one entered, one spoke only in Tenctonese.

The living room area, just inside the front door, had already been reconverted to a ceremonial circle when he was admitted in. An oval brocaded carpet of deep purple was laid upon the rose-colored rug; incense-producing tapers were spaced about the perimeter of the room, in anticipation of being lit; and in the center of the carpet was a jewel-inlaid goblet plus a small, lidded cast-iron kettle—which sat, incongruously, upon a plugged-in hot plate. An articulated notch in the lid of the pot allowed the handle of a ladle to poke through.

It was disappointing in a way. Like holy writ on a budget.

Buck's Elder-Master, or personal tutor, was named Feshnar. Feshnar was the closest, in Buck's opinion, to what the archetypal image of an Elder-Master—a great teacher who had once walked upon the Homeworld—should be:

He was at least as old and wizened as Buck's Uncle Moodri had been, easily over a hundred and fifty. He was given to epigrammatic wit, existential/philosophical observation and answering questions with questions (the better to make a student examine his/her knowledge and convictions). He wore the traditional vestments of the order, pastel-colored silks under a belted kimono-style robe. And, without pretension or pomposity, he conveyed the signature *aura* of serenity naturally associated with Those Who Are in Touch with the Secrets of the Universe. A comforting presence when the wisdom of the ages is sought.

Which is why Buck found it unsettling when Feshnar said, "I will place you in the care of your *Tighe Marcus-ta* guides, and then I shall leave you to it."

"Leave me to—you mean, you won't be there?"

"No, Buck. It is important that I am not."

"But *why?* I thought I was your best student!"

"That *is* why. For both of us, the principles of *Kewisto* must be inviolate. If you are to be absorbed into our way of thinking, you must not be guided by my influence, to which you are partial. And I must not offer you any unconscious aid. Objectivity is the key. There would be none with me present."

". . . If you say so."

"Tradition says so. But if I were worried about you, I would not have sponsored you to the others. Are *you* worried?"

Soberly, Buck replied, "Not about me, no."

"What then? Your family still?"

"I just wonder what it will do to them, that's all. The change in me."

"If your feelings remain conflicted, feel free to call a halt to the proceedings. There are no 'marks' here, no 'stepping backwards,' no shame in a reconsidered decision. You will simply continue your studies as before."

There was a niggling uncertainty in the back of Buck's mind, but he consciously suppressed it as a natural reflex. *Most* of him wanted to do this very much. And *most* of him, he thought, was what counted.

"I don't wish to reconsider," he asserted gravely.

A tall, lean, and powerfully muscled Elder appeared—towered, really—over Feshnar's shoulder, looking down upon Buck just at the moment he had spoken. This one's name was Von, and he had the advantage, for Buck had never heard *him* speak. Every Elder's approach to *Kewisto* was different, and Von's manifested itself in a studied silence. But his face—when he chose to let it reveal his thoughts, which was sparingly—was expressive enough. As now, when at Buck's words, Von wrinkled his brow meaningfully, his expression one of droll bemusement.

Taking their places behind Von were the other two Elders who would perform the initiation ceremony with him. There was Lewski, an unusually fair-skinned Newcomer with small eyes and a startlingly deep, resonant voice . . . and there was the head of this enclave of Kewistans.

Her name was Ru.

If Feshnar resembled the archetypal Elder-Master, Ru resembled its opposite. She was female, for a start, and even though the Tenctonese culture celebrated male-female equality, female Masters were unusual and therefore much more highly revered. Ru did little to act as if she should be the object of such reverence, however. Her personality, far from mystical, was sprightly, that of an ever-youthful great-aunt. Furthermore, she eschewed the ceremonial garb as too drafty; today she wore a simple open-necked blouse under a vest sweater, and yellow slacks. The wrinkles around her eyes were laugh lines; and when she laughed, which was often, she tended to explode into great, delighted, alto gales of it.

Utterly incongruous in this place, to Buck's way of thinking; and much as he enjoyed and admired her, he couldn't help but feel his *Tighe Marcus-ta* would be diminished in spirituality. But he dared not say so.

Feshnar delivered Buck into her hands—literally, as the first thing she did was put them on his shoulders—and padded upstairs. Separating himself. Buck willed himself not to feel the loss. *Kewisto,* he reminded himself. Don't favor one Kewistan over another.

"Well, my fine, young Buck," Ru said, a twinkle shining in her eyes, very aware of the pun she'd made, "are you ready to find out if life is a fountain?"

This was a reference to the punch line of an irreverent old Earth joke about spirituality—he knew because she'd told it to him some months earlier.

"I'm ready," he replied, wondering if her levity would possibly endanger his psychic journey.

"Oh, goody." She smiled, and then laughed. Arm around his shoulder, she led him to the place he would occupy on the rug, facing the kettle in the center.

"That hot plate looks so weird in this setting," he said.

"I know. I begged my colleagues to let me have an open pit with red-hot coals but they outvoted me. Said it might burn the house down, can you imagine? And I must tell you, it made me *very* cross." She laughed again and bade him sit, which he did, cross-legged. Opposite him sat Lewski and Von, the latter of whom had already lit the ceremonial tapers, which were making the air sweet and fragrant. Ru took her place between them.

Smiling impishly.

Thunder exploded and lightning flashed from outside. And suddenly rain started hitting the windows in furious sheets.

Ru caught Buck's gaze and laughed again, this time guiltily. Buck guessed she must've found his expression far too solemn. Then she said, as if to chide herself, "All right, let's get serious here." Never entirely losing her smile, though, she added, "Before the fun starts, you must vow not to describe the particulars of this ceremony to anyone."

"I do so vow," he averred formally, in the futile hope that his sense of occasion would discourage Ru's informal gaiety.

She gestured to the pot. Lewski, using a cloth to protect his hand from the hot metal, removed its lid. He put down the lid, handed the cloth to Buck, and Ru said, "Go to it, Buck. Ladle yourself some brew."

He took the cloth, hesitated.

"What's wrong, Buck?" Ru asked.

"I'm sorry," he said. "'Ladle yourself some brew?' It sounds so . . ."

Ru smiled with—it seemed to Buck—something like affection. "Pragmatic? Demotic? Unceremonious?"

"Well . . . yes."

"You're about to undertake a life-style that embodies those qualities. I like initiates to remember that before the ceremony gets underway."

"Then . . . why do the ceremony at all?"

"You'll see."

There was no way to prepare for the *Tighe Marcus-ta;* its rituals were never revealed beforehand to those about to go through it. The oath of secrecy assured that each new initiate was at its mercy. Buck felt very much that way now.

Raindrops were landing with such force on the roof of the house, they actually clattered.

He took the cloth, lifted a ladle full of the "brew," and poured it into the goblet before him. The aroma was tangy and a little foul.

Having no protocol to follow, Buck reacted instinctively. He pulled back a bit and said, "What *is* it?"

Lewski and Von exchanged glances at that. Knowing glances. *Insider* glances. Oh, how Buck wished Feshnar were here.

"It's a beverage of herbs," Ru replied. "It's harmless."

"I beg your pardon, madam," intoned Lewski, playfully indignant.

"I take it back. It's *healthful,* the way Lewski makes it." Lewski nodded his satisfaction at the amendment. "But it *does* have a certain mind-sharpening potential. If you're ready to be absorbed, that readiness will absolutely be clarified for you under its influence."

Buck stared at the goblet warily.

Ru said, "Go ahead, ask. It would seem unnatural to us if you *didn't.*"

"All right," said Buck. "What happens if I'm *not* ready?"

"You'll see."

And she laughed again.

When her laughter subsided, Buck asked, "When do I—I mean, at what point do I—"

"Whenever you're up to it. The *Tighe Marcus-ta* doesn't begin until you've drunk the contents of the goblet."

Buck lifted the goblet to his mouth, and the fumes assaulted his nostrils even more strongly. He closed off his nasal passages, hoping to minimize what he expected would be a hideous taste.

He was pleasantly surprised. It was sweet and grainy. He let air through his nose again, enhancing the flavor.

That's when the aftertaste hit him, making his tongue feel as if the grain had been recently fertilized. It was a powerful aftertaste, almost as noxious as the first had been pleasant. Reflexively he pulled the goblet away from his lips.

"All of it," said Ru.

Her gaze upon him seemed impassive now, as did those of Lewski and Von on either side of her. Buck braced his stomach, tightened his chest, and chugged. It wasn't as bad as before.

It was worse.

Trying not to reel from the awfulness of it, he put the goblet down, sucking in air through his mouth to dry out and numb his tongue. And Ru said three of the most unnerving words he'd ever heard:

"Fill it again."

"I'm not sure that I—"

"—For us."

Not hiding his relief, Buck ladled more "brew" into the goblet and passed it over to Ru. She took a few healthy swigs, clearly savoring them. Off Buck's disbelieving expression, she said, "It's an acquired taste."

She passed it in turn to Lewski, who finished the contents without comment or readable reaction and placed the goblet down . . . where it stayed.

"What about Von?"

"The Initiate, the Supervising Master and the Reciter only. The Observer must abstain."

"Why?"

"The designation tells it."

"Is he, like, a witness?" Buck glanced over at Von, but Von's face was revealing nothing now. Buck's eyes flicked back to the female Elder.

"Like," acknowledged Ru.

General silence.

"Now what?" Buck asked.

She lifted a finger, stabbed the air for emphasis as she spoke. "You close your eyes. And you listen." She said it as if it were the most fun-filled activity she knew.

He closed his eyes.

At first he heard only the rain. The thunder.

Then he heard something else—Lewski's voice.

"To understand right from wrong, one must lose one's vested interest in either," he intoned, and Buck recognized the first basic tenet of *Kewisto.* "To understand good from evil, one must seek the context for each, even in the purest extreme, despite that the extreme may seem obvious." The second basic tenet. Was this all there was to the *Tighe Marcus-ta* then? A simple recitation of general principles? "To understand the present, one must view it as history long past." It all seemed anticlimactic and unrevealing. He had been under the impression that the *Tighe Marcus-ta* was a spiritual point of no return with the capacity to ignite great changes. So far it was rudimentary, telling Buck nothing he didn't already know, and it gave no evidence of going beyond that.

Until the fourth tenet.

"To see life, one must step back from life."

Which he knew by rote, of course, but for the first time, he *heard* it differently. It had a different resonance. It no longer seemed philosophical arcana.

(*A man desires to know the meaning of life.* Ru's voice in unbidden memory.)

Now the fourth tenet was a practical instruction.

Now it was something he could *do.*

Why? Why was it suddenly so easy to—

(*So he scrimps and saves for a spiritual journey that will take him to the Himalayas.*)

The brew.

Something about the brew.

The brew and the words. The one amplified your ability to home in on the other, to *concentrate* in an altogether new fashion. Lewski's soothing delivery also figured into the equation, making it absolutely apparent why he was the Reciter. He had the voice for the job.

Buck felt blood coursing through his head, creating a

feeling of intense warmth and liberating *lightness.* He had the strange impression that his thoughts were rising above his body. That his thoughts were *outside* his body, that if they went far *enough* outside his body, they would be outside his *experience* as well. Which was, of course, the goal.

So odd . . . to be drifting and yet to be so *clear.*

Maybe this is how it begins, thought Buck. You separate from yourself first . . . and that allows you to separate from everything else. Could that be the secret?

(*Because he knows that in the Himalayas, there is the marvelous Guru of gurus, the wellspring of all spiritual knowledge, the one being on Earth who can tell him . . . tell him the meaning of life.*)

He became less aware of complete tenets as Lewski recited them, for his own dreamy musings overpowered the input to his ears; thus he faded in and out, sporadically aware of only key words, such as—

". . . family . . ."

And he thought inevitably of Vessna, Emily, Mom, and Dad. Saw them not as *his,* but as an *average* family unit. Not particularly distinctive in the grand scheme. Just trying to get by in an alien culture. It seemed not so terrible anymore that they had adopted the ways of humans; human ways represented a freedom of choice never available on the slave ship. Thinking about it now, it seemed only natural that his family would eschew the old ways he himself sought so fervently to master. Old ways were, after all, unpleasant reminders (unless you went back *before* the slave ship, before *birth,* an enormous leap not only of faith but of rare imagination). And of *course* his father would react strongly against that actress—she represented the next logical step in assimilationism: She was a reminder on top of a reminder. Dad's view was an unspecial reaction. An unspecial reaction from an unspecial man. (Unspecial? Dad? Unspecial? Had to be. The logic insisted, *per*sisted, and would not be denied.)

". . . to understand love from hate . . ."

Love. He had loved a human schoolteacher once, not long ago. Marilyn Houston. She had loved him too. And no sooner had their unwittingly indiscreet relationship begun than it was thwarted; without fanfare, she was suddenly and mysteriously offered a transfer by the powers that be to some school "in the Bay Area." When Buck had subsequently tracked her down, collecting clues like a detective (like his father, she'd said), she told him their continued relationship just wouldn't be a good idea. In fact, she'd be giving up teaching altogether for a while, opting instead to accept an offer from an old grad school professor to be a research assistant in Boston. She promised to write, though. But so far, she hadn't. Buck had resented her bitterly for that, as well as the meddling school board, but now . . . now the resentment dissipated. He now understood that she had been afraid of her emotions—that simple—and had allowed bureaucracy to separate her from temptation. An unspecial reaction from an unspecial woman. (Unspecial? Marilyn? Literate, sensitive Marilyn? Again, *Kewisto,* demystifying so much that used to be so fascinating.)

". . . lust from passion . . . proficiency from artistry . . . worth from worthlessness . . . slavery from freedom . . ."

Images and events from his life swirled before him, each reduced to a concept, a logical construct that made it powerless before his keen and explosive new powers of reasoning.

(*The obsession costs this man everything, his friends, his family, his job—because he pursues it to the exclusion of them all, and when he has to, at their expense.*)

A light of truth was beckoning him. The new revelations were a bit disturbing, rendering unspecial many things he had once thought terribly special indeed, but he knew that if he obeyed the light, followed where it led, nothing would disturb him any further.

"Do you think I might get up and walk a bit?" he heard

himself say, and there couldn't have been any objection, because next thing he knew, he was ambulatory.

(*Two thirds of his life over, he journeys to the Far East, and braves brutally hot weather, shockingly unhygienic living conditions, and years of poverty as he researches the specific whereabouts of his guru. He finally learns of a small cave the man occupies, near the very top of the tallest mountain.*)

As the light beckoned, he wondered about himself. It would be the height of arrogance to think of Buck Francisco as any better than those unspecial people from whom he had separated, and yet he had this *knowledge* that they were not privy to, he *understood* things about them that they might never understand about themselves.

And the light told him: "You must understand Buck. Understand Buck first. Do that and you shall find the balance you seek."

(*So he endeavors to climb the mountain. It's a long, arduous task.*)

The sound of Buck's own breathing intensified in his ears, as well as the double *lub-dubs* of his hearts.

Buck Francisco the individual had started out as the slave-child of adult slaves, part of a collective. At the age of ten, he'd been taken from his parents and trained to be a Watcher—the title being a euphemism for Informer. Like all the other Watchers, he'd known no other life but the Ship, and Overseer propaganda had nearly convinced him that there was nobility attached to being a Watcher. But something within him, something primal, had led him to resist the group mentality the Overseers tried to impose, the suppression of personal identity, resist it so much that he became a rebel almost reflexively. Ironic, then, how his biggest rebellion, the upholding of the old ways, had led him to the Elders of the *Kewisto*—and *back* to a group mentality. And to a *Tighe Marcus-ta,* a willing *absorption* into a group mentality—

—wait, that can't be right—

(*And there's the great Guru of gurus: wizened, frail, wispy hairs trailing from his head, maybe even two centuries old—and if not, he sure looks it—chanting a mantra that may have been going on for hours or days. He looks up upon the entrance of the poor, disheveled supplicant, his concentration broken. And he says, "Yes, my son?"*)

—there was no dignity in the group mentality of slavery. Yet there was dignity to spare amongst the Kewistans. Even if they could not get involved in affecting change but held it as their mandate to remain subservient to worldly events, abdicating responsibility for them—

—just like slaves—

—wait, that can't be right—

(*And the guy says, "Great Guru of gurus, you must tell me . . . what is the meaning of life?"*)

—he was Buck Francisco, he was nobody's damn slave, that's how this whole thing began—

(*And the Guru of gurus says, "Life, my son? Life . . . is a fountain."*)

—don't *tell* me I've come full circle on this. I am not a *slave.* I have *identity.* I am not some *unspecial*—

—but if *I'm* not unspecial, how can I view *others* as unspecial?

(*Well, my dear, our hero is just incensed. "A fountain!" he exclaims. "Life is a fountain? I sacrifice my family, my job, and the better part of my life to come here at great personal risk, and all you have to say is, 'Life is a fountain'???!!!"*)

"Understand Buck," said the light. "Understand Buck first."

Show me where he is.

"I will show you," said the light.

Buck walked right into its path.

(*And the Guru of gurus becomes frightfully nervous.*)

The next thing he knew, he was body-slamming into the ground, under something very large, and he was wet, getting wetter.

His trance was broken on the instant. The light that had

beckoned him zoomed past with the blast of angry air horns and a huge spray of water as a double row of semi truck wheels sliced through a large puddle. In a devastating flash of comprehension, Buck found himself sucked right back into reality and knew what had happened. He had wandered outside—where rain clouds had so darkened the sky, rain-water had so occluded the view, that cars had had to turn on their brights in the thick of the afternoon. And he had drifted into the middle of Ventura Boulevard—very nearly into the path of an oncoming truck. Mesmerized by its headlights.

(*And he puts a shaky hand to his pale face.*)

But at the last possible second, he had been pulled, or knocked, out of the semi's path and onto a patch of wet grass by . . .

Von.

Von the Observer.

Who looked upon him with something that was not quite disdain but very like, as the rain, still slashing down, drenched them both.

(*And he says, "You mean life* isn't *a fountain?"*)

Von gave a curt nod, to himself more than to Buck, his mouth forming a tight, weary frown . . . as if this were all so inevitable. Boringly inevitable. Inevitable, too, that he should have to break his vow of silence.

"Reconsider," he said. Just the one word. And, once he was sure it had sunk in, helped Buck off the ground.

CHAPTER 18

By the time the electric lock had been fixed, they were getting along like sisters. Bickering sisters to be sure, but sisters. As if Fran's behavior had been no more than that of a child testing its limits with a guardian, for now that those limits had been defined, she was adjusting her behavior accordingly. Even when irrationality held her in its grip, she had an instinctive sense of lines that must not be crossed. There was no more need for intervention on the part of the hospital staff. There barely seemed need of the straitjacket.

Steinbach pulled Cathy aside, of course, shook an angry fist, even played the "What if?" game—"What if you'd really been hurt?" and "What if you *hadn't* gotten Fran under control?" and, her favorite, "What if Dr. Casey had been here? He'd have frigging *killed* me!"—but he was really just blowing off steam. Cathy calmly pointed out that none of those things had happened (the best way to win at the "What if?" game), and Steinbach regained his objectivity pretty quickly. In truth, the situation *did* seem under control, so he consented to let Cathy continue.

He very much wanted Fran back in restraints, though, and was not at all happy when Cathy argued against it, demanding that the need of the moment should be the determining factor—wanting, now that Fran was under control, to bring some mutual trust into the situation. The *Leethaag* could still go either way; and the stronger the bond, the better the chances.

Strictly speaking, it was not Cathy's decision to make, but she reminded Steinbach that she *was,* after all, the one who had bonded with Fran—proving herself under stress in the bargain—which made her, ethically speaking, Team Captain.

She actually put it that way. Team Captain. Thank you, Matt Sikes.

"Should never have let you Newcomers near professional sports," grumped the doctor. Then he left them alone.

Fran started losing her mind about ninety minutes later.

They talked about many things and, curiously, none of them was Matt Sikes. It was as if for each of them, the man they had in common had become a private issue. Not to be shared. Guarded, for reasons that neither of them could apply—or confess—to the other.

So now they were talking about auditioning, Cathy marveling at the courage and confidence she imagined it took. "I'd be too nervous," she said.

"Nerves are okay, if you can *use* them," Fran told her, "if you can *incorporate* them into what you're doing. The biggest danger is denying your own feelings. That's death because it sends 'em a mixed signal. If you go with your nerves, you may not give *your* ideal reading, but at least *they* think you're making a conscious, focused *choice.* Sometimes that's all it takes to get the job."

"I don't know. 'Using your nervousness'? Intellectually I can grasp it, but emotionally—"

"—It's a bit of a skill," Fran acknowledged with a nod, making the few hairs that still clung to her pate bob limply in the air. "But do you want me to tell you the *real* trick of auditioning?"

"You'll understand if I'm a little wary of the word 'trick' right now, but . . . Yes, I'd like that. Please."

"Get yourself a secret metaphor. An image to draw strength from. I got mine from doing the PACT classes." By now, Fran had discussed a little of her history with Cathy.

"And what is it?"

"I go in there like I'm going to teach them something. Like it's my job to show them something they didn't know. Like they're my students. That way, I'm in control."

"Oh," said Cathy, putting a hand to her chest, genuinely impressed. "Oh, that is good. Oh, that is *very* good. It just turns the tables, doesn't it?"

Fran nodded. "Anything you can do to empower yourself. I have to take care that I don't bring *attitude* about it into the room. But if I keep the metaphor altruistic and pure, I can almost always get them to see that, my God, there are bugs in my head."

At first Cathy thought it was one of those colloquial American English idioms. Something Fran had picked up along the way, something Cathy needed to have interpreted.

But then Fran asked, "How did they get in there?" and added "Get them out," with such chilling, calm conviction that Cathy realized the actress was serious.

Not three seconds after that, Cathy received an altogether new sympathetic sensation. It was akin to the tingle she had felt on her scalp when Fran was losing hair, but now it was on her brow . . . there first . . . then *very* strongly on both cheekbones and spreading behind the ears. As before, the sensation began as an itch, but it rapidly developed into something more naggingly intense, something *in* there *deep,* too deep for scratching or rubbing to offer any desirable relief.

It felt like the pinpricky sensation on a leg that has "fallen asleep" to which circulation suddenly returns. And, sure, you could liken the pinpricks to insects' feet because they were

pointed.

Moving.

In patches.

Dancing.

Scuttling.

But Fran wasn't *likening* the sensation to bugs, she was *believing* in the bugs. Cathy knew why, and she knew what it meant.

This is the bad part, she thought.

As if the rest had been pleasant.

But, relative to the rest, she was right.

Fran's hands were rising to her face. Cathy gently reached forward and grabbed her wrists.

"I have to get them out," said Fran. "The bugs."

"I know," replied Cathy. "That's not the way."

"Well, what *is* the way?"

"It's my job to do, not yours. Trust me?"

"Yes."

"Stick your arms out."

Fran did, wincing spasmodically every other second.

Her face was starting to revert, to reassert its Tenctonese structure. All the altered bones in Fran's head were beginning to soften, to become malleable, almost fluid, to facilitate the change. The musculature was simultaneously adapting and pulling the softened bones back into shape. Things just as extreme would be happening to the affected areas of her skin. Fran's hands could not be permitted to rub, scratch, or put pressure on her face and skull. Any such contact ran the risk of subverting the regeneration process, causing deformity, nerve damage, brain damage—or worse.

Cathy lifted the straitjacket. Held it in front of Fran expectantly.

Fran regarded the garment, fighting the impulse to touch her face.

"How will that help?"

"No time to explain. Come on."

Like a child, Fran allowed Cathy to guide her arms through the sleeves. And Cathy worked quickly, not even pausing to rub her own face, which, though perfectly immune from the process, still registered the insidious sensation. In order to protect Fran from herself, Cathy had to forgo her own comfort, work at breakneck pace.

When the jacket was firmly on, Cathy got behind Fran, pulled the sleeves tight, and belted them in. Then she reached around and embraced the actress, holding her close. Hoping this would work. There were no guarantees. Withdrawal was still dangerous and Fran could still die.

"Ah!" Fran breathed, in pain. "Ah! Ah-*ah!* You said you'd get them *out! Ow!*"

"I know."

"You lied!"

"I know."

"Why?"

"Because I love you!"

The shouted reply exploded out of Cathy without conscious thought, and amazed her, for somewhere along the line it had become true. She had connected to the fire in Fran's soul, to the dark-bright *passion* that no cosmetic alteration could mitigate, and the thought of such spirit being snuffed out was now more than she could bear.

Cathy didn't know if Fran heard her reply, because on the heels of it, *right* on the heels of it, Fran screamed. It was a sound of exquisite hideousness, of a sentient being in senseless torment, the like of which Cathy had not heard since the days of Overseer atrocities on the slave ship. Only worse, because the sound was not behind closed doors or echoing forebodingly down metal passageways. Cathy was right on top of it.

And now she could *see* the torment as well. Fran's cheekbones were pulsing, little mounds of biological matter seemed to be *moving* under the skin (just like clumps of insects), *scuttling* about, searching for a place to settle.

"Make them stop! They're eating me inside! I can hear them!"

And of course it *would* feel like that, the dissolution of solidity; it might even *sound* like that, like *chittering*—

—and Fran's right ear was dangling. The skull had reclaimed that amount of cartilage it needed for the barely discernible swell of a Newcomer ear and simply discarded the rest . . . closing off the blood vessels to the appendage . . . tightening the skin around its perimeter until the skin around the skull had pulled *free* of the skin around the ear (oh, gods, maybe *that's* what Fran had heard, the sound of skin *ripping* . . .).

Under where the "human" ear had been—something glistened. Cathy had to look away.

Fran screamed again, and Cathy was hit with a fresh wave of shadow pain. She tensed, gritting her teeth, again forgoing her own relief, holding onto Fran as the actress's head thrashed back and forth, seeking to subdue the painful sensations by beating them away upon the nearest solid surface. But only Cathy's breasts were available, and they proved the perfect cushion.

The dead ear was hanging by a long thread of dead skin, and it kept hitting Fran's chin as her head shook back and forth. Fran, dimly aware of the sensation, opened her eyes—

—and *there it was.*

Her own ear.

Hanging below her jaw.

"Put it baaaack!" she shrieked. *"Put it baaaaack!!"*

And now Cathy experienced a *different* kind of phantom sensation, one she hadn't expected. It fell on her like a wall of desolation.

She saw the bugs. Under her own skin. Eating their way out of her own face. Saw them. Believed in them. Crawling around the strands of her musculature. Their furtive antennae, their masticating mandibles, sickly brown chitinous bodies, eye stalks and—

—and then the hallucination was over. Fran was still in the throes of it, but the vision had passed for Cathy. For how long, though? *I didn't know about this part,* Cathy thought. *I knew about sharing the pain; not the delusions . . .*

If her mind was not to be her own any longer . . . if there was to be more of *this* . . . she didn't know if she could maintain her sanity.

She noticed then that while in the grip of the vision, she had loosened her grip on Fran. That scared her. Scared her more than the bugs.

Because with less luck, Fran might have worked herself out of Cathy's grip, done herself irreparable damage. It might still happen.

What to do? Please, please, what to do?

Cathy concentrated, forcing herself to push away panic. *Think simply,* she thought. *Take stock and think simply.* And a simple idea came.

She altered her grip on Fran, worked her arms *underneath* the tightly belted sleeves, the straitjacket holding *both* pairs of arms in place now.

How firmly in the long run she didn't know.

She only hoped that—

Another wave of pain.

The bugs crawled into her mind.

Fran was screaming.

Cathy screamed right along.

And on that note, the *Leethaag* became a living nightmare. . . .

CHAPTER 19

A VERY PRETTY place to have your office, the Silliman Building. Located in West Hollywood right on Santa Monica Boulevard, it didn't look like an office building at all. Four storeys high, it had a tan adobe facade. A full flight of stone steps approached its main entrance on each side, and the front doors were made of clear, thick glass encased in golden, art deco style frames.

A semicircular driveway curved past its small, stone-bordered lawn, in the center of which was a fountain that had been reconverted to a palm frond-based floral display.

Yeah, real pretty, reflected Detective Beatrice Zepeda. Even in this awful, pouring rain. You wouldn't think of it as home base for the scum of the earth, but that was probably why scum rented space there in the first place.

The fronds were collecting water and spilling it onto the lushly green lawn in fountainlike arcs as one unmarked police car—Zep's—and two black-and-whites pulled up in front of the stairway. Ducking against the weather, Zep and her partner pelted up the stairs on one side while a pair of uniforms came up the other. The pair from the third car emerged from their vehicle in ponchos and split up to keep an eye on the building's exits.

Upon entering the building, Zepeda reflexively tossed her head back and forth, shaking water from her impressive mane of long raven hair. Of all the female cops in the precinct, she was arguably the hottest-looking: slender and sleek, olive-skinned, with dark, deep, shiny eyes. On the other hand, no one could say she didn't look like she belonged in her profession. There was a hard beauty to her Hispanic features: too many lines crinkled around the eyes for one so young; elastically expressive lips formed a mouth that was unusually large, covering teeth that were unusually big, in a jaw set unusually forward; so that at odd moments, her cheeks could appear unexpectedly hollow, her face unexpectedly bony—and undeniably cop-tough.

She scanned the directory on a nearby wall for the Serovese Corporation. She saw the names of several literary agencies, a graphics design place, specialty newspaper offices, an accounting firm . . . but not what she was looking for.

"Now what?" said her partner, Laura Stanczyk. She was a small girl, but the size was deceptive. She would bench press a three-hundred pound thug if she had to.

"Got to be here," Zep said. "The reverse directory says so."

The reverse directory was a phone reference whose use was theoretically limited to law enforcement agencies. Rather than look up a name to get an address and a phone number, you looked up a phone number to get a name and an address. Less than an hour earlier, Matt Sikes and George Francisco had requested a reverse directory search—the number Max Corigliano had given them for the Serovese Corporation's answering machine—and the result of the search had revealed three things. One: that the number was indeed held by a Serovese Corporation. Two: that the number was unpublished and unlisted in any public directory (leading all and sundry to wonder just what kind of corporation chose to have an unlisted number). Three: that the Serovese Corporation was located in the Silliman Building.

"May I help you?" said an officious, self-important voice behind Zep and Stanczyk. They turned to find a uniformed doorman. Young fellow, real pretty, an effete Hollywood hopeful with "mean queen" written all over him. "Visitors *are* supposed to be announced. As I'm *sure* you've read." With his eyes, he indicated a nearby posted advisory to that effect.

No time for this, thought Zep. She flipped her badge and, for the hell of it, pulled her gun.

"Yeah, you can help," she said tersely. "You can give me the room number of the Serovese Corporation and you can bag the attitude. I'm really not in the mood."

The response was immediate and satisfying: The young fellow fuhmfured quite impressively. "I . . . uhhh . . . that is, the, uhh, Serovese Corporation has a strict no visitors policy. That's, you know, why they're not on the direc—"

Zep leaned in closer.

"Am I to understand that you wish to be considered an *accessory* to these guys? Speak up so my partner can corroborate me in court. I am just *dying* to run somebody in today."

Laura smiled prettily at him.

"Four-oh-seven," said the doorman, and that was that.

They left one of the uniformed cops with the doorman to see to it no warnings were called up to room 407. The second uniformed officer took the stairs up as Laura and Zep took the elevator.

The three converged on room 407 together. The uniformed officer and Laura took positions on one side of the door. Zep took the side nearest the knob.

Guns drawn, pointed up. Ready.

All further communication would occur in silence now. Nods. Mouthed monosyllabic words. Hand signals.

Zep reached for the knob with her free hand. Turned it, testing it. In agonizing slo-mo. Not wanting to make a noise.

Surprise.

It wasn't locked. She could feel the metal tongue sliding into its socket.

Easy entry.

Too easy?

She made eye contact with Laura, with the uniformed officer. Imperceptible nods. *Yeah,* the look said. *We're gonna do this.*

One . . . two . . .

On *three!* she threw the door open and burst in, gun drawn two-handed, Laura right beside her, the uniformed officer at the rear.

"FREEZE!" shouted Zep.

"POLICE!" Laura augmented.

The room was nearly bare. It was just that, a single room, possibly the smallest office in the building. It contained six things.

A desk.

A swivel chair.

A phone.

An answering machine.

A Barbara Cartland romance novel.

And a blinking, gum-chewing secretary.

"You ladies looking for somebody?" she said. She spoke in a nasal voice, making her sound for all the world like Miss Adelaide in *Guys and Dolls.* Her hands were on the desk, steadying the book she'd been reading when Zep and Laura had burst in. The notion that she had any concealed weapons at the ready—or that she was in any position to grab one if she had—became increasingly farfetched with every passing second.

Starting to feel profoundly silly, Zep lowered her gun. "We're looking for the Serovese Corporation."

The secretary kept working her gum and smiled hugely.

"Honey," she announced, "I *am* the Serovese Corporation!"

She wasn't, of course. She was simply its sole visible employee. She was Maureen Goldfaden, a woman who had answered an ad. Her job interview had been conducted by phone, and when she showed up at the office nearly a year ago—the key having been left with the doorman—she'd found her first week's salary and an innocuous list of instructions.

Her duties mostly included maintaining the neatness of the office and seeing to it that the answering machine never ran out of tape on its incoming reel. When a cassette looked to be running out, she was to replace it with a fresh one. She would put the old cassette in an envelope and leave it at a "drop" in the local public library—behind the books on the second shelf of western novels. This she did every Tuesday at 4:30.

The answering machine had been jury-rigged so that she could not hear incoming messages, although she always knew, by the sounds the machine made, when her bosses were accessing messages by remote (which they had not yet done today). She was given strict instructions *never* to listen to the tapes herself. She was told that they were somehow encoded by the answering machine, and if any but authorized ears listened, the Serovese Corporation would know, and her job would be terminated.

She suspected this was a bluff; the answering machine looked like a bargain-basement Panasonic to her; but she had chosen to behave as if she believed the warning because the paycheck was extraordinary, and why mess with good fortune?

She'd fully expected that the good fortune would run out someday. The arrangement was too fishy, the bosses too anonymous, the security measures too paranoid. But she'd also known that she was legally untouchable. Her safety net was the letter of her routine, which contained not even the implication of illegality. As long as she adhered to it, she imagined she'd stay out of trouble—and she was right.

In regard to her job at the so-called Serovese Corporation —hey, it had been a nice ride while it lasted. If it was over, it was over. She thought she might take a week off, maybe go to Hawaii with her boyfriend before hitting the job market again. What the hell, she could afford it on what she'd socked away.

Zep and Laura took her number and address, advised her that plans for Hawaii might be slightly premature, and let her go.

When they reported in, they wound up having a twelve-minute police radio confab with Grazer, Sikes, Francisco, and Billy Youmans, a lanky lieutenant who headed up the SWAT team. Together they formed a plan of action.

Shortly thereafter, a trace was put on the Serovese Corporation's phone line to locate the sources of any incoming calls. Maureen had been correct about the answering machine: It *was* a bargain-basement Panasonic, and its speaker had been rendered useless. But it had a jack for an external sound system. No need to wait for elaborate electronic hardware: A patch cord and a cheap speaker from the local Radio Shack solved the problem of monitoring any incoming calls.

If new messages came in . . . they would know.

If the Serovese Corporation beeped in for its messages . . . they would know.

If anybody tried to warn the Serovese Corporation—at *this* number anyway—about the bust about to go down in Inglewood . . . they would know.

The phone line was secure.

Phase One of the operation was complete.

Outside, the rain was less fierce, slowly ebbing back to a drizzle.

* * *

Phase Two went into effect at 4:46 under a clearing sky, when Matthew Sikes walked up two worn iron steps onto an iron landing, stood before the metal door of a former warehouse in Inglewood, and activated the door buzzer.

From the speaker over the button, he heard an edgy, *"What is it?"*

"I'm here to do the memory upgrade on your computers."

For a long time only an electronic hum issued from the speaker.

Save for that, the building appeared dead. It was three storeys tall; it sat on land that was overgrown with weeds; and its many tall windows were either boarded up or painted black from the inside.

At length, there was a response. *"That's Corigliano's code. What're* you *doing with it?"*

"Wrong answer," said Matt, and started to walk away.

"Wait a minute."

Matt turned back to face the door.

More electronic hum. Then:

"We weren't expecting you until tomorrow. Thanks for being so prompt."

The surly tone of voice belied the words, but it was the correct countersign.

"You got a question now?" Matt challenged.

"Same one. This isn't even Corigliano's time. Who the fuck are you?"

"Name's Matt Sikes. I work with him at Richler; you can call him, run a check on me, or I can just show you ID. I've been hip to his operation for a while. I gave him a choice—cut me in for a little taste or face the music."

"So now you want a route of your own, is that it?"

"Not even close. There's possible trouble. The cops may be onto him. He doesn't know for sure but he thinks they're tailing him. He sent me in his place to warn you."

"And you actually came?"

"Is it so inconceivable that I'd want to protect my investment—or are you actually as dumb as you sound?"

"All right, you've warned us. Begone."

"Don't you want your money?"

Again, electronic hum.

Lots of it.

Then: *"Wait there."*

The rain had ceased, but it was the rain that saved his life.

Matt heard the door unlocking and reflexively took a step back. His foot landed toe first on a part of the iron landing that had been worn smooth by six or seven decades of shoe traffic and had subsequently become a shallow recess, where today, as on all inclement days, a puddle of rainwater had collected. Slippery when wet.

His foot shot out behind him, he overbalanced, and nearly fell backward onto the hard steps. He grabbed for the metal banister, whose peeling, lead-based paint cut into his skin, and found himself swinging against it like a gate.

In this manner, he missed the path of the shotgun shells.

For when the door flew open, a Newcomer with a sawed-off rifle stood there and fired at where Matt should have been. Seeing his error, the Newcomer pivoted to adjust, but by now George had popped up from behind the unmarked police cruiser parked at the curb, his own gun at the ready, and fired into the shotgunner, who staggered back floppily and dropped like a suddenly stringless marionette.

Leaving the front door wide open.

Which was the first thing they needed.

George barked a signal into a walkie-talkie. Meanwhile, Matt, steady and gun-ready, peered around the door into the illicit drug factory. He ducked down as bullets whined over his head, but he'd seen what he needed to see.

He pressed himself flat against the wall next to the door, shouting as he did, "Ten human males, three of 'em armed, four long tables full of equipment, center of the room!" All of which George repeated into the walkie-talkie as five cop cars and a SWAT truck came tearing around both sides of the block to surround the building.

Matt fired a few shots through the doorway. Upward

warning shots. To keep anybody from trying to close the front door. Which might be hard to do in any event. The Newcomer's body was blocking it.

The uniforms took defensive positions behind their vehicles as the SWAT guys mounted the offensive, firing assault rifles upward into the large first-floor windows, whose blackened glass shattered and fell away to expose the first-floor operation, just as Matt had described it. One man attempted to fire back; a SWAT marksman *ping*ed him before he could steady his aim.

Lieutenant Billy Youmans, SWAT team leader, reed thin, red-haired and wire tough, spoke into an amplified bullhorn.

"THIS IS THE POLICE!" his voice boomed. "YOU ARE UNDER ARREST! LIE FACE DOWN ON THE FLOOR WITH YOUR HANDS BEHIND YOUR HEADS! AVOID THE LINE OF FIRE! DO NOT ATTEMPT TO RESIST OR YOU WILL BE SHOT! I REPEAT. THIS IS THE POLICE! YOU ARE ALL . . ."

The litany continued as the first floor was secured and cops, Matthew and George among them, began swarming in, rounding up prisoners. George chose a random prisoner and threw him up against the nearest wall.

The fellow cowered. "Don't hurt me, please! I'm just a chemist here!"

"What's the layout upstairs?" George demanded.

"Same on floor two, supplies and storage on floor three! I'm cooperating, see?"

"Continue to do so. How many more weapons? How many more men?"

"Weapons I'm not sure. Seven other men, all human. Five right above, two in supplies."

George passed the chemist over to a uniformed cop for cuffing and again spoke into his walkie-talkie, relaying the information.

On the floor above, three criminal guns were trained on the elevator and the stairway access was locked. The five men thought they had a chance. At least to wait out the cops and think.

If the windows hadn't been blackened, they might've thought otherwise.

Two SWAT guys, who had rappelled off the roof, exploded through the panes, bullets from their assault rifles first and boots after, the former to shatter the glass, the latter to kick it inward. They landed on their feet, battle ready. One of the bad guys overcame his surprise quickly and spun to fire. The SWAT man on the left had an unusual opportunity and took him down without killing him, merely blowing his gun hand off. The SWAT man on the right grunted dryly at his partner. "Showboat," he accused.

Matt and George were already pounding up the stairs toward floor three. Storage and supplies. Taking the elevator up had been out of the question; it was a slow, manually operated mesh cage; with gunmen possibly awaiting their arrival, they might just as well book passage on a moving coffin. The stairwell had been the only option. But of course, the heavy-duty, metal stairway-access door to the third floor was locked.

And there was acrid chemical smoke drifting out from under it.

"Shit!" exclaimed Matt. "They're destroying evidence in there."

From behind them a voice said, "Not for long."

The voice belonged to Eric Pettiford, a young, black SWAT guy who sported dreadlocks. And a bazooka.

Matt and George backed down half a flight as Pettiford aimed at the door and fired, blowing it all the hell off its hinges and out of the frame.

The two supply men inside were so unnerved by what had happened to the door that they immediately dropped what they were doing and reached for the overhead fluorescents, as Eric and Matt barreled in and secured them.

"Where's a fire extinguisher?" roared George, right behind them, because at the center of the room, in a free-standing washtub, a pyramid of boxes and chemicals was in flames. The question proved to be rhetorical, for as soon as he spoke, he spotted the canister, red and waiting on the wall. He took it down, aimed its nozzle, and let the white foam fly.

It killed the flames almost upon contact, leaving molten chemical sludge underneath as the foam dissolved into a gucky puddle that left a greasy film over everything.

Gun trained on the supply men, who were now supine and awaiting cuffs, Matt glanced over his shoulder at the mess.

An unpleasant thought came to him then, unbidden.

What have I done, really done, to poor Fancy and countless others like her? This stuff was poison, but it was their personal poison, and they built lives and careers around it. Who am I to say the damage it would have caused them in the end isn't worth what they felt they were gaining along the way? The Newcomers depending on bad Stabilite weren't junkies looking for a high . . . they were desperate people looking for respectability.

What they did, they chose to do.

I've just taken Choice from them.

Not alone, but I started the ball rolling and I'm here now at the finish.

Whatever happens to them now . . . for good or ill . . . I caused *it to happen. I was the catalyst who—*

—Matt cut the thought short. To pursue it was to pursue too many sleepless nights. The truth was: there were no clean answers. He had done what he had done. It had seemed a good and noble idea at the time. He would have to be at peace with that.

And he was.

But not before he remembered his last encounter with Fancy Delancey, Newcomer . . .

He stands in the hall, across from the door to the squad briefing room, which is, at this moment, in temporary use as a classroom. Another PACT class for another group of cynical cops is wrapping up inside.

He is restless, uneasy. He fully appreciates the covenant he made with his soul about the rightness of doing what he is about to do, but he hadn't planned on the sensations it would evoke, the resonances from high school and grade school.

Student sensations. That's what they are. Sensations he associates with being at someone else's mercy. With not having power.

With not being a grown-up.

It's a feeling he struggles with all the time—privately, in metaphor—but here the connection is just too terribly literal. He *is,* in fact, outside the classroom, waiting for the teacher, totally without control over the situation.

Unless he just leaves. Right now.

Yes. Leave. This is stupid. There is no reason *to put yourself through this, to willingly place yourself in a position of—*

And the door opens. And the cops are filing out, some of them with familiar, angry dispositions. No doubt someone in there has just "taught them a lesson" about Newcomer psychology—and maybe their own. Business as usual. Paul Winograd, the director, exits next, flanked by his PACT workers. Among them is Fancy Delancey. Matt thinks, *Maybe if I avoid eye contact—*

But he wills himself to *make* eye contact, despite his protesting ego, even feels his hand lifting in a half-assed wave. She sees it, and she splits apart from the group to approach him.

They just eyeball each other for a while. The last meeting is obviously as vivid for her as for him, and emotions are still very raw.

In a stunning moment of insight, Matt understands that he isn't just here to ease his conscience. She gives the appearance of appraising him coolly, but he can see in her eyes that she has her *own* apprehensions. She's been afraid to bump into him again, would have avoided this if she could. The wounds he inflicted have not yet healed; he hurt her in a place no one should ever be hurt—her self-worth. This is a very large idea for Matt, too large to let out of his head. He can't begin to articulate it properly.

But she is braver than he is, breaking the silence first.

"I heard," she says. (Referring to the jumper Matt talked off the ledge. It's currently being bandied about in police PR circles as "a major breakthrough in Police-Newcomer interfacing." The story has been making the rounds quickly, and Matt is currently Flavor of the Month.) "Good for you," she adds.

"Yeah, well, you know," he says uneasily, not remotely what he'd rehearsed. He grits his teeth. Fuggit. And—*just like a shy schoolboy*—he takes the thin, long, beribboned box from behind his back, shoves it into her hands, and takes off at a run.

He doesn't wait to see if she opens it and discovers the exquisite long-stemmed rose within. He doesn't pause to consider the expression on her face when she reads the small card, whose inscription is:

I KNOW YOU'LL MAKE IT.
THANKS.

—MATT

He only hopes—in vain, as far as he is concerned—that she'll hold on to it for more than ten minutes before tossing it in the garbage. . . .

The garbage—which was to say, the evidence—was piled high. There was lots of it. This wasn't just a Stabilite operation. Other drugs had been processed here too: heroin, crack, cocaine, and jack, a Newcomer addictive.

Matt Sikes was on the police radio, standing outside his car. He'd reported in to Grazer that the bust had been a success—two casualties, one injury, none of them on Our

Team; and the biggest roundup of illicit merchandise L.A. had seen since . . . well, since Grazer himself had bucked the system over his sister's kid.

"Congratulations, Sikes. To both of you."

"Thanks, Bry."

When it really got down to basic cop stuff, sometimes—*sometimes*—Grazer could be straight ahead and sincere. And in those rare moments, Matt actually liked him.

"Think you can stand a little heartbreak?"

Matt's blood turned to ice water for a moment. "What? Is it Fancy? Cathy? Is something—"

"No, nothing like that. Hell, I'd forgotten all about them."

Matt sighed, relieved, remembering that, on the other hand, you could rely on Grazer to be an insensitive asshole no matter *what* the circumstance.

"I haven't, but that's another discussion. What's up?"

"We just computer interfaced with FBI and Interpol records, also did brief confabs with a couple of their organized crime experts. Whatever the Serovese Corporation is, it sure ain't Mafia. Nobody's heard of it . . . or anything like it."

Matt swore. There was nothing else to say.

"Yeah. See ya on campus, Cap'n."

And he clicked off, looking over at his partner a few yards away. George had asked all the prisoners a battery of basic questions, and the last scuzzball was being loaded into the paddy wagon. At the same time, the two corpses were being zipped into body bags and loaded into a meat wagon.

Matt closed the distance between them. And told George what he'd learned, or rather, hadn't learned, about the enigmatic Serovese Corporation from Grazer.

"My luck has been no better, Matthew," George reported. "The men all knew they were working for a Serovese Corporation, but their only contact was the person who hired them."

"Who was . . . ?"

"The Newcomer who tried to gun you down."

"And he's dead."

"And he's dead."

Matt swore again. "I get the feeling we won a battle, not a war. Hate to say it, George, but these garbanzos are good. I bet you no matter what we follow through—phone bills, rent bills, checks, leases on property, any of it—we get a paper trail leading nowhere."

"That kind of pessimism is not like you, Matthew."

"I know. I don't like it either. But we haven't heard the end of the Serovese Corporation. I can smell it." He exhaled heavily through his teeth. " 'Serovese,' " he recited, " 'with an *S* not a *C* and an *E* not an *I*' . . . what the *hell* kind of motto is that? It's like a private joke or something."

And George's face fell.

"What, George?"

"Oh, no."

"George, *what?*"

"The brazen *arrogance* of it, Matthew."

"Will you *talk* to me, please?"

But George had already started trotting out of earshot the moment he saw the meat wagon pulling away from the curb. Matt watched, bewildered, as the trot became a full-bore desperate run and George began shouting "STOP!" at the top of his lungs. Before the meat wagon reached the corner, George had caught up with the open driver's window; and as Matt raced to find out what was happening in his partner's spotted head, he was startled to see George leap onto the car like a lunatic, reach in to commandeer the steering wheel, and turn it toward the curb.

Matt finally reached the wagon, which by now had slowed and stopped. He was too out of breath to ask George if he'd lost his friggin' marbles, but that was okay, the assistant coroner was asking it *for* him. George, however, was heedless, just insisting that the back of the wagon be opened, he *had* to inspect one of the bodies.

The assistant coroner unlocked the doors, and George jumped into the back of the meat wagon, unzipped the wrong bag, muttered an imprecation in Tenctonese, zipped it closed, and proceeded to the other, exposing the dead Newcomer.

Matt watched as George's hand plunged into the bag, grabbing something.

George expressionlessly studied whatever he had found for a long time. Then he lifted it into the light where Matt could see.

The arm.

"I don't—" Matt began.

"His wrist," George directed quietly.

Then Matt saw the telltale marking.

"'Serovese' isn't an ethnic name, Matthew," said his partner. "It's an anagram. For Overseers."

CHAPTER 20

CATHY AWOKE IN the early evening, sitting against the rubber wall. Her arms were still belted around Fran, who seemed to have nestled in against her chest, between her legs. Fran's head was thrown back, mouth open, the smooth skin of her bald, spotted head brushing Cathy's left cheek.

For a disorienting moment, Cathy wondered if Fran was dead—but then felt, with the hands she held around the actress's abdomen, the rise and fall of Fran's breathing. Asleep. Soundly asleep.

Cathy had an urge to relieve herself—hardly surprising—but there was something very peaceful about Fran right now, and Cathy was loath to disturb it. The urge was not terribly powerful. It would hold a while.

Cathy rocked Fran in her arms ever so gently. Barely realizing she was doing so, she softly began singing a familiar Tenctonese lullaby. It translated like this:

> Anything you want to be, you get to be.
> Try to do it hard enough, it's done.
> Spirit matters more than size. Let the ocean roar.
> Noble hearts are louder still, my little one.

Cathy began the second verse, not seeing Fran's eyes flutter open.

> Anything you need to be, you're sure to be.
> Conquer fear, and life is yours to run.
> Shadows are, though tall as trees,
>   harmless when they fall.
> Seek the light behind the hill, my little one.

She was in the middle of the bridge when she noticed that Fran had begun humming along every now and then in harmony.

> These are small words—simple as a flower;
> Small words—still we pass them on;
> Small words—in your darkest hour
> They'll be there, whatever else is gone . . .

"Hey," Fran said. Croaked, really, her voice still thick with sleep. "You have a pretty voice, civilian."

Cathy smiled. "Hey," she replied. "Thanks."

"Ever thought of the acting game?"

"Not me."

"Too bad. You'd clean up."

Cathy bent her head forward to get a better view of Fran's expression. The irony had been intentional, of course, but it was not bitter. Fran was composed. Centered for the first time since Cathy had met her.

"So?" asked Fran, returning the gaze as best she could, given the awkward angle. "What do you think about the new me? The *old* me?" She exhaled. It came out a resigned sigh. "How do I look?"

Cathy eased her hands out from under Fran's restrained arms, shifted her angle a bit. Touched Fran's head, her cheeks, inspecting. The bones had hardened properly, spots were starting to emerge on her skin in an exotic pattern, and the features were those of a Tenctonese woman. Around the ears the skin was pink, blotchy, tender, like a baby's. And if the inspection started to resemble something of a caress, it seemed entirely proper.

"Beautiful," Cathy told her.

"Like you, you mean."

"No. I mean beautiful . . . How do you feel?"

"Wasted."

With a touch, Cathy indicated that Fran should lean forward. The actress did, and Cathy undid the straps of the straitjacket. Falteringly, Fran tugged the garment off herself. As she did, she caught sight of something on the floor nearby. The two "human" ears her body had rejected. With a slight shudder, she tossed the straitjacket atop them, shielding them from view.

"Damn," she whispered.

"I know, I'm sorry," Cathy said.

After a moment, Fran began touching her own face, skull. "I can't say it doesn't feel like home," she said unexpectedly. A moment passed before she added, "I just wish I'd had some say in the matter, that's all."

"And if you had . . . would you go back?"

"Moot point. Not possible. Why dwell?"

"I'm a biochemist, remember? What if I could make it possible?"

Cathy had spoken impulsively, not meaning the offer. But wanting Fran to feel as if she had control. Trusting an instinct. Acting—not as well as Fran perhaps, but with luck, well enough not to get caught at it.

Fran tensed and Cathy could see the question starting to form: *Are you serious?* But it was never articulated. To come right out and ask it would be to undermine the premise behind it: that choice was still possible. Fran needed to *believe* that choice was still possible, even if such belief required doing a little acting herself. For the audience of one within her own soul. And thus, Fran, ever the actress, considered the false proposition with conviction.

And at length she answered, "No. I learned what I needed

to learn. Proved what I needed to prove. No more revelations back there."

Interesting response, thought Cathy, remembering that Fran was more than just an actress. After a fashion, she had also been a teacher. Matt's teacher, come to think of it. Maybe that's why he had asked Cathy to be here. Maybe Fran had taught him something. She wondered what it was.

"Want to look in a mirror?" Cathy asked. "See what lies ahead?"

"Not yet. Won't see anything new, after all."

"Oh, you might."

And then, so gradually it was almost imperceptible, Fran dissolved into tears. Finally. She tried to hold herself together but couldn't—and at this point, of course, there was no reason that she should. Next thing Cathy knew, Fran was reaching for her and curled up in her arms again. Cathy shushing and cooing and rocking and holding tight.

The initial bout of intense sobbing abated after a few minutes.

"I love you, too," Fran said in a half whisper.

"I know."

And, because it seemed somehow *right* to do so, Cathy finished singing the lullaby:

> All you want and need to be, you'll *have* to be,
> Just to keep alive the dream you've spun.
> Giant is the challenge, true,
> Mighty as the sun . . .
> But, then, so are you, my little one.
> Hear the small words, my little one.

And on those notes, the *Leethaag* concluded.

George was late coming home, and Susan hadn't felt much like preparing a meal. But everybody's day had been pretty full, one way or another, and the general consensus of the family Francisco was that they had to get out of the house and *do* something—to escape or to celebrate or simply to break up the pattern—so the entire clan, baby included, bundled into George's car for dinner at a nice restaurant.

On the way, Emily spoke of her achievement in school. The story quickly diverted George's attention from the Serovese Corporation, and when it was over, he couldn't have been more proud or happy. And said so.

Then Susan talked about what had happened to *her* at work. The family rallied to her side. She should never doubt that she had done the right thing. Touched though she was, she couldn't completely drop the role of conscientious mom. She reminded the kids that with less income coming in, everybody would have to go easy on extracurricular expenses—at least until she could find another job, which would not be easy in the current marketplace. "This meal may be the last real blowout we have for a while," she warned, and the warning was soberly heeded.

Talk of Susan's job led naturally enough to talk of George's. Under normal circumstances he might have been candid, but the occasion of this rare dinner out had become modestly festive. If he talked about the Inglewood bust—about the fact that he'd gunned down an Overseer while defending Matthew—it would only upset them that he had been in such physical danger. If he talked about the Serovese Corporation or the little scientist in the wheelchair (and his ambivalent feelings about both), he'd only upset himself. And he was not privy to Fran Delaney's condition. So he said simply that the investigation was still ongoing—which was not, strictly speaking, untrue—saving the details for a more appropriate time.

They arrived at the restaurant and were led to a table where a high chair was brought for Vessna. Buck adjusted his baby sister in it as Emily and Susan went off to the ladies' room. As soon as he was alone with his father, the shame he'd been holding in over his fiasco amongst the Kewistan Elders became too much to bear by himself—and he broke his vow of secrecy as delicately as he could, thumbnailing the outline of "the ritual" and its aftermath . . . speaking quickly so as to resolve the conversation before the females returned.

When he finished talking, he expected any number of responses from his father, most of them variations of disapproval, and certainly an admonition for attempting such an undertaking behind the family's back. None of the expectations prepared him for the response he got.

"The *Tighe Marcus-ta,"* George mused. "Yes, I know it well."

"I never mentioned the name of it!"

"You didn't have to, son. It's quite famous. In its secretive fashion."

"Famous—?"

"Notorious, really. No one ever makes it through the first time."

"They . . . they don't?"

"No one's ever *ready* the first time. One must *experience* it before one can properly assess its demands and one's desire to meet them."

"I had the desire!"

"Had?"

"Well, Dad, I mean . . ." Buck went silent, unsure of *what* he meant.

"Buck. The *Tighe Marcus-ta* demands that you redefine yourself. You are barely eighteen years old. I know how this may sound to you, but you can't *re*define yourself until you have *defined* yourself. That kind of change is not an abstraction. It's practical and purposeful. And you can't make it without life experience. Your first *Tighe Marcus-ta* tends to indicate just how much more life experience you need."

"What about Feshnar, my Elder-Master? He said I was ready! And Ru—were they playing some *trick* on me?"

"No. The paradox of the first *Tighe Marcus-ta* is that the Kewistans are genuinely hopeful. For them, *disappointment* is part of the ritual. But it reinforces the wisdom of seeking maturity in stages." Then his father's expression changed. "Did you say Ru?"

"You know her?"

"Her husband. On the slave ship. He didn't survive." George was silent for a moment. Then he smiled. "He was quite fond of her. Said she liked to shake things up—a real iconoclast. Is she like that still?"

"She was *married?* But she's a Kewistan *Master.*"

"Yes," George nodded. "Now."

With that, the Francisco patriarch rested his case. And, astonishingly, some of it even made sense to Buck, who then asked, "Dad . . . ? How do you know so much about the *Tighe Marcus-ta?*"

George lifted his eyes from the basket of rolls at the center of the table and met his son's gaze, a very *intriguing* grin on his face.

And then the girls were back, chatting and laughing. The meal went forward in high spirits; George tipped the waitress too well under the circumstances; and on the ride home they unabashedly sang songs along with a Newcomer station on the radio.

Once back in the house, Emily went to the kitchen to deposit a "doggie bag" of leftovers from the restaurant in the fridge. Stepping in, she took note of the answering machine by the kitchen phone. Its little red light was flashing. Then it went dark. Then it flashed eleven times. Repeated the pattern. Eleven messages.

"Mo-om?" she called.

Susan entered the kitchen, Vessna in her arms.

"Yes, *odrey.* What is it?"

"You didn't check the messages today, did you?" It wasn't exactly a question, the way she said it. More of an accusation.

"I couldn't bring myself to, Emily. More grief from the office; I just didn't want to put myself through it."

"Eleven messages, Mom! Some of *us* have a life too, you know!"

Susan smiled indulgently. "You're right, I'm sorry. Tell you what. You listen to the messages for me, okay? Let me know. And the ones from work? I don't want to hear about them. At least not tonight. I feel too good right now."

Mollified, Emily's petulance vanished. "'Kay, Mom."

Everybody else retreated to their personal corners over the next few minutes. Buck to the RV, George and Susan to their bedroom where they helped Vessna retreat to her crib. They were just beginning to get undressed when Emily knocked on the bedroom door.

When she received the okay to enter, she didn't quite. Just peeked her head shyly around the edge of the door.

"Mom? I think you really ought to listen to the machine," she said.

There wasn't much conversation when Matt showed up at the hospital that evening. But unlike the previous night's brief exchange, this one was not strained.

Cathy saw him waiting for her, and she was very easily in his arms after that, neither one of them sure who had made the first move.

"Called in, as ordered," he said. "Got your message."

"Mmmmmm," she replied, tightening her grip.

"How's Fancy?"

"She's fine. You can see her tomorrow."

"And you?"

She lifted her head from his strong shoulder, smiled into his face with a tired impishness.

"No problem," she replied. Then she touched her forehead to his and said, "Take me home."

Her wish was his command.

DAY FOUR

CHAPTER 21

ALL THINGS CONSIDERED, her morning could have been worse. She woke up in a comfortable enough bed in a semiprivate hospital room, no restraints and no lock on the door. Her roommate was a dear human lady of seventy-eight years named Lee, who made just the right amount of conversation and was sensitive enough to allow her some privacy with her own thoughts.

When she got up to use the john, she checked the chart at the foot of her bed. It had her registered as Fran Delaney. Hmmm.

She checked herself over in the bathroom mirror. Fran Delaney wasn't there. Some Newcomer was there instead. Very familiar and yet—because it had been so long—very different, too. But there was more to the difference than just the passage of time, and she knew it.

So there she was. Fancy Delancey. And that didn't sound right either. She didn't mind taking a few metaphorical steps backward if she had to, but she wasn't sure she wanted to step back quite that far. At least Fran Delaney had been a name of her own choosing, not the joke of some faceless bureaucracy.

Zho'pah had been the name she was born with. She'd even used it in a couple of crisis improvisations, way back in another life, when she was putting the cops through their paces. It had rather a snap to it.

She walked back to bed, pausing to look at the chart again.

Zho'pah.

Fancy Delancey.

Fran Delaney.

She found herself favoring the last one still. It would be neatly symbolic if she went back to one of the other two—the reassertion of her Tenctonese identity—but she kept returning to the same thought: Fran Delaney had been *hers.* It would be nice to come out of this experience with something that was *hers.* She just wasn't sure it applied anymore.

Ah, well. She'd reinvented herself before. She'd do it again if she had to. This time from *within.*

A little while later a nice, boyish intern with curly blond hair came in to check up on her. Steinbach, his name was. She asked him his first name. He blushed and told her it was Thaddeus. Thad. She told him it was a *hell* of a name, a grand name. He was as sweet as pie, treated her with enormous respect, and told her they'd release her tonight or possibly tomorrow morning. He just wanted to keep her under observation for a while longer.

He then got very serious and spoke to her about what she'd been through, the medical implications mostly, leaving the social-moral issues for her to sort out. Some of it she knew or had guessed. Some of it was news. Some of it was obvious—preaching to the converted. But she endured it graciously because he clearly cared so much, remembering what it had been like to care about strangers. Maybe it was worth getting back to.

Thad concluded by mentioning a drug abuse support group he and a psychologist ran once a week. He *strongly* advised that she participate in it. Or something like it. She was not, of course, a drug *addict* in the strict sense. But readjusting to society—and to her own culture—would require a support system. All the more because she was sophisticated enough to rationalize the need away. She assured the young intern she'd give it a think. And she would. He took her at her word and left, promising to return in a few hours.

She ate well—about as well as anybody eats in a hospital—and it wasn't until visiting hours that the day had its first potential bump.

Iris McGreevey and Dallas Pemberton came into the room. The producer and the director. They hired you, they could fire you.

Here it comes, she thought. The blow-off. The bailout. An obligatory *How are you?* and then a raking over the coals. And the shame of it was . . . she'd brought it upon herself.

She was so firm in her conviction that matters would proceed in such a fashion that what they said at first made no sense to her. Not because they were speaking insensibly but because it didn't compute. It didn't fit. She asked them to repeat it.

"I said I need to know what you'll need in the way of brushup rehearsals," Dallas said. "And when you'll be ready to return to the show."

"We're losing money," Iris added. "We need you back badly."

"I . . . I don't think you understand," Fran protested. "I can't be what I was before."

"Illness does not diminish goodness," Iris insisted. "You can still be good."

"Yes, Iris, but—"

Dallas took her hand then. "We *understand,*" he said meaningfully. "We *get* it. We wouldn't have it any other way."

It hit her then. As she was right now. They wanted her to continue in the role *as she was right now.*

"It occurs to me . . ." Iris began, and faltered. She had no real gift for humility. "It occurs to me that I can't call my theatre The Healthy Workplace and not give your people a healthy place to work . . . So I think I'll be revising our casting policy and there you are," she concluded quickly.

"Furthermore," Dallas added, "some of the institutional theatres from New York sent scouts last week. While you were out, there's been some . . . how you say, *interest.*"

"In . . . in what?"

"Depends on who you talk to. The Public Theatre made an offer to transfer the production intact. The Roundabout would like me to remount it with you in the lead and a higher profile supporting cast. Both of them are interested in you for other shows in their season next year."

Fran started to say something obvious, but Iris lifted a hand to stop her.

"Before you point out the same tiresome fact about your former physical appearance," she said huffily, "let *me* point out that I took the liberty of delicately explaining your . . . situation. In confidence. Their interest only increased."

"It's a double-edged sword," Dallas cautioned. "By default, you'd be going public with your story, even if you didn't want to . . . but that would also give you the opportunity to speak on behalf of all the . . . well, you know. Public awareness. Performing a valuable service and all that."

Tears came to Fran's eyes. She tried to stifle them. Couldn't.

"I can't thank you both enough. I'm just so grateful and—" She slapped the blanket over her thighs, sudden anger mixed in with her joy.

"What's the matter?" asked Dallas.

"Damn it," Fran said. "If their interest 'increased' . . . if I go public as you say . . . I'll just be a curiosity in New York. Like a fad. And once the novelty wears off—"

"—*That,*" Dallas said, "will be up to you, I think. I won't make any phony showbiz pronouncements—we're both too smart for that—but in my opinion, Newcomers are going to be around for a long time. And if you keep plying your trade with care, craftsmanship, and heart, there's no reason why *you* shouldn't be as well."

Now the tears flowed freely. She hugged them both—made Iris's hug *especially* tight, because it made the old babe so uncomfortable—and bade them goodbye. Her vision was out of focus from the tears, and it wasn't until she wiped them away that she saw another visitor standing in the doorway.

Wearing a real shit-eating grin on his face, too.

"Hey, Fancy," he said.

It was one of the nicest smiles she'd ever seen.

"Matt," she said softly. "Matt Sikes."

He gestured with a sheepish shrug toward the outside, toward the exit of Dallas and Iris. When he spoke, she noticed he was a bit out of breath.

"I, uhh, overheard some of what was going on," he said, "so I ran down to the gift shop to get you something."

He approached her, and now she noticed the thin, long, beribboned box he held. He placed it on her lap.

"I hope you like it," he said, and stood back.

She just touched the box at first, savored the feel of its ribbon under her fingertips. Then she carefully lifted the lid.

Inside it was an exquisite long-stemmed rose.

And a small card.

She opened it.

It read:

I TOLD YOU SO.
—MATT

And this time he stayed to see her reaction.

FIVE YEARS FROM TODAY;

SIX WEEKS BEYOND DAY FOUR . . .

EPILOGUE

ANOTHER CASE ALTOGETHER.

Detectives Matthew Sikes and George Francisco had a convenience store staked out in anticipation of an attempted robbery by a street gang. There was some reason to believe that the gang was being bankrolled and encouraged by the elusive Serovese Corporation, but neither of the two detectives held out much hope of proving it.

Matthew's prediction had been right. In what was now being referred to as "the Stabilite Case," all avenues of investigation into the Serovese Corporation had followed intricate paper trails leading nowhere. As for this street gang currently under investigation? The Serovese Corporation, if involved, wasn't about to entrust incriminating information to a bunch of punks. Doubtless the teen hoods were considered small fry by their "benefactors," to be used only as pawns in a much larger game.

Then again, that "small fry" attitude had been known to make master criminals cocky, careless. You just never knew. The Serovese Corporation couldn't be infallible *all* the time.

So with what little hope they had, the two detectives sat in their unmarked cruiser and played anagrams. Matt wasn't nearly as fast as George, and sometimes he had to use a pen and pad, but he had a knack for finding uncommonly nasty ones.

He pointed to a new billboard.

"What can you make out of *that* one?"

"That one I tend to leave alone, Matthew. That one I prefer to savor . . . in its pure form."

Matt didn't quite see what the big deal was, but he understood the reasoning behind his partner's feelings. "Your call," he said politely, and moved on.

The billboard advertised a new product. A breath freshener that came in three formats: mint, spray, and wash. Also in two distinct varieties: one for Newcomers, one for humans.

The presentation of the product was fairly matter-of-fact: The various formats of the product were displayed neatly under a large version of the logo, a positive-negative silhouette design. Looked at one way, it resembled an unevenly shaped goblet. Looked at another, it resembled two faces—one human, one Tenctonese—in intimate proximity.

The billboard, of course, represented the campaign and logo design of Susan Francisco, in whose accomplishment George took uncommon pride. She had not, after all, been fired; and her comments to her employers had not, after all, fallen on deaf ears, jaded human ears though they may have been.

Susan regularly expressed to George her mixed feelings about the firm that paid her salary these days. She wasn't so sure anymore that she wanted to keep working there. But stay or leave—George was quick to remind her—for the moment she could do either on her own terms. She liked being reminded of that, and he liked the spring in her step the reminder produced.

As much as he liked the billboard.

And her logo, underneath which was the slogan containing the product's new name.

"A Little **SCENTS-ITIVITY®** Goes a Long Way . . ." it read.

Not especially clever.

Not particularly flashy.

Plainness itself, really.

But you sure couldn't argue with the sentiment.

ABOUT THE AUTHOR

DAVID SPENCER was lyricist to composer Alan Menken, and co-librettist with Alan Brennert, for the recent SF musical *Weird Romance* (original cast album on Columbia Records, published version by Samuel French). He has also written the English adaptation and new lyrics for *La Bohème* at the Public Theatre; book and lyrics for *The Apprenticeship of Duddy Kravitz,* based on the novel by Mordecai Richler (music by Alan Menken); the music and lyrics for *Pulp,* a one-act musical (book by Bruce Peyton) that has been produced in various regional venues as the most acclaimed segment of the anthology evening *Stories; Playthings,* a one-act play produced at Theatre Three in Los Angeles; the music and lyrics for two new musicals, currently in progress; as well as scripts and stories for episodic television.

Mr. Spencer is on the faculty of the BMI-Lehman Engel Musical Theatre Workshop and a member of the Dramatists Guild.

Alien Nation: Passing Fancy is his first novel.